THE PATENT CLERK'S VIOLIN

Screw
Pegs
Head of Violin
Nut
Neck of the Violin
Finger Board
Sound Hole
Bridge
Tail Piece
Tail Pin

THE PATENT CLERK'S VIOLIN

David Ackley

Rain and Breeze Books

MOSCOW, ID

Book Layout © 2014 BookDesignTemplates.com
Cover photo: istockphoto.com/cjp
Frontisepiece: istockphoto.com/antiqueimgnet

The Patent Clerk's Violin/ David Ackley. -- 1st ed.
Library of Congress Control Number: 2019904956
ISBN 978-1-950631-00-1 (Paperback)
ISBN 978-1-950631-01-8 (Ebook)

This book is lovingly dedicated to Lynn, Brianna, and
Raineka

*If I were not a physicist, I would probably be a
musician. I often think in music. I live my daydreams
in music. I see my life in terms of music.*

Albert Einstein

CHAPTER 1.

Bern, 1904.

He felt like he must be covered in sawdust. Sure enough, looking down he found bits of wood mottling his grey sweater,
and an ashy puff rose from his hair when he ruffled it. Removing his apron and gently shaking it out, he coughed as
particles flew up to his face. The hacking roused Flecken who
lazily jumped down from his perch near the stove, stretched,
and sauntered over towards the workshop entrance. Opening the window-paned door, Carl began to pick out the shavings from his sleeves as he trudged up the steps to street level.
Flecken raced him to the top, paused at a passing shopper,
and disappeared. Carl soon gave up on prizing bits from his
sweater and, pulling the rough wool over his head, shook it
out as best he could at the top of the stairs. A small cloud of
dust and slivers flew up the street in the strong breeze. As
usual, Flecken was by now nowhere to be seen and off on his
nightly prowls. Carl's work apron had protected the front of
his clothing, but the fibered sleeves were always like a magnet
for the chips, and many bits still clung to them. He closed and
locked the shutters to the shop entrance and then climbed
the stairs to his empty apartment one level up. Once inside,
he filled a basin with cold water and cupped handfuls of it
over his head and face, the water running off of him turning
brown, and then he dried off with a towel.

Feeling human again, he looked down at his hands. The sawdust drew out the natural oils and they were beginning to crack from the dry autumn weather. He searched for his tub of salve and rubbed some briskly into his palms and fingers, feeling immediate relief. The greasy balm caused his after-work glass of wine to slide in his grip, but he was easily able to hang on. Not like the coffee mug this morning.

He rarely made mistakes in the shop, but today was an almost laughable exception. This morning, he'd nearly finished forming a large piece of maple into the curved shape of a violin body for an instrument he'd been hired to repair when he'd paused to take a sip of coffee. Missing the handle with his fingers, the mug had begun to tip and his rescue attempt had made matters worse – he'd actually pushed the cup over, spreading the entire contents across the maple and a portion of his workbench as well. The time it took to find rags and soak up the mess allowed the dark brew to penetrate fairly deeply into the once pristine white wood. Luckily nothing else on the workbench was seriously affected, but the mishap meant he'd need to set the slab he'd carved aside to dry before he knew if it could be salvaged. He'd then spent the entire afternoon in the laborious process of shaping a new violin back in the event that the previous one was irretrievably stained.

He made a simple one-pot dinner of cabbage and a chunk of meat and after cleaning up had another glass of burgundy in the small sitting room. "Brilliant, Carl, absolutely brilliant," he mumbled to himself as he thought back to the spilled coffee. And "Ah, well, not every day is the best," as he sank philosophically back in his chair. Soon, however, he found himself brooding about losing half a day's income due to his own clumsiness.

He suddenly thought of the perfect remedy. Moving to the bedroom, he reached under the bed and pulled his father's violin case out from underneath. Opening the case, he tenderly removed the instrument from within and, as always, admired the craftmanship his father had put into it. He usually played his own more battered violin and reserved his father's for more focused or intimate sessions. Back in the sitting room, he found the sheet music for a Haydn concerto among stacks of musical scores and seating himself on a straight-backed chair began slowly and gently to play the piece. He soon warmed to the tempo and became absorbed in the music and the wonderful tones the instrument created. In his mind, he was suddenly a young boy circling his father in a tentative dance – unable to approach him, but unable to distance himself either.

◄ ■ ►

"Now, what's keeping Paul?" thought Carl feeling awkward just standing there holding his fishing pole on a city street so far from the river. They'd arranged to meet in the Munster gardens that Sunday morning, but the appointment had been made in a passing comment, so it could be that his young friend had forgotten.

From his high vantage point on the bluff overlooking the river, he could see that the water was clear and could even make out the rocky bottom. The transparency was a nice relief from the spring and early summer cloudiness when the river ran a milky blue from glacially fed runoff. Hopefully his day off work would be a good day for fishing since he'd heard that the grayling were biting and seemingly abundant. One could never tell with fishing, however. He was now anxious to get to the river and give it a try.

Knowing that Paul would eventually find him, Carl purchased some sweet buns from a nearby bakery and bit into one as he descended the steep bricked path that angled sharply down below the imposing Munster cathedral on the right. He watched for slippery sections as he made his way towards the banks of the Aare. The sun was just warming the early-autumn morning and quickly dissipated the thin fog that now hung only along the portions of the river remaining in shadow. At the bottom of the path, he walked along Aarstrasse paralleling the river. The cluster of white three-story buildings to his right soon gave way to a broad park which spread out below the commanding Parliament building on the edge of the steep hill that comprised the heart of Bern.

Carl stopped for a moment. Although now protected from flooding by a low rock wall, this was the spot on the river where his father would bring him fishing as a child nearly thirty years before. Standing in a green felt cap, tattered leather coat, and with bushy white sideburns, holding an ever-present brier pipe, his father would meet with friends around a small bonfire at this riverbend nearly every weekend in the fall. Chatting over a bucket of beer and never bringing bait, his dad had left the fishing up to him. Carl had learned angling from his friends.

Walking into the park and the widely spaced trees, he was careful that his long pole didn't snag in any overhanging branches as he made his way a little further upstream. The upcoming section of river was wider and slower than the quick and churning current it became further downstream as it carved the large curves defining the sharp-cut rock boundaries of the old city. Here one could fish more easily, and the grayling tended to lurk in these more languid sections. Choosing a likely spot, he leaned his one-piece pole against a tree limb. He then freed the sharp barb of his hook from the cork in the butt of the pole, needled a white grub, and a little piece of bread for good measure, onto the fishhook, and swung the long line out into the current. The small attached bobber made a light ring of ripples as it hit the surface, and the bait further beyond sank quickly into the main stream. The surface of the Aare was filled with etchings where the water rose and fell as it flowed over the varied substrate below, creating a reflective matrix of the bottom contours. Now in the advent of autumn, golden leaves were becoming a fixture in the moving water, as well.

The first cast showed no change in the bobber, but he'd seen light activity and flashes of the sides of fish near the surface as he'd walked upstream. Realizing he'd passed the best spot, he retrieved the line and headed back downstream to another clearing in the trees. Noticing the small whirls where the fish were hitting the surface, it dawned on him that the grayling were eating the early midges that had begun to show, so he selected a new midge-like fly from his packet of bait and tied it on the end of the line. He didn't really need the bobber, hoping that the fly would float by itself, but kept it attached for security. He swung the line out and began to follow the current as far as the trees on the bank would allow. Twenty meters downstream there was a small splash, the bobber sank, and the line and pole were suddenly in direct contact with a fish. The pole dipped and slacked and, when it dipped again into a full arc, he could feel the back-and-forth flicking of the grayling. Giving the fish some time to fight and then to tire, he soon lifted the pole tip and swung the wriggling fish out of the water.

He was sliding the grayling into his creel, admiring the purplish hue along its back and the fish's extraordinary sail-like dorsal fin, when someone gave a welcoming shout.

"Hello, Carl!" called his younger friend, Paul, "Sorry I'm late - looks like the fishing's good." Paul came up and joined Carl on the bank, appearing eager for a morning on the river.

"Hi, Paul," responded Carl. "I just started, but I already hooked up a nice grayling on my second pass."

He opened the wicker creel to show his catch, and Paul, peering in, gave an approving nod. "Nice looking fish," said Paul. "I hope they keep biting; my mom's expecting some for dinner tonight."

"I expect she'll have some, too," replied Carl. "How are your parents doing anyway? Your mom's such a soldier with all she's gone through – is she feeling well?"

"Oh, she's fine and just as energetic as ever. It's still amazing to me that a woman confined to a wheelchair can have as commanding a presence as a full standing, healthy bear wrestler," chuckled Paul. "Even Dad quakes when she gets in a mood."

"She's one of a kind," agreed Carl with a smile. "Give Ida my best, won't you?" Paul joined Carl in his walk up to the beginning of the fishing circuit as Carl continued, "I haven't seen you much lately until this last Monday, but I did hear you play in a concert earlier this summer. You have such a fantastic touch with the violin, and I'm constantly amazed at how you've progressed since you were little. In fact, I'd say that you're now a true professional."

Paul gave a non-committal shrug. "I've just this month committed to playing in the symphony orchestra for the entire year and I'm always busy with little trios and quartets, too. But you know what? Now, I know you may think this is odd, but performing in concerts is slowly losing its appeal for me. I feel lately like I'm being pulled in a different direction that's actually much more satisfying." Carl wanted to ask about this new direction, but Paul continued, "Say, I'm going to be giving a performance at the Munster cathedral in three weeks; it's open to the public, so you and Maria should try and attend – unless she's still in Zurich?"

"Yes, she's still there," Carl said with a sigh, "and I'm not sure if she'll be in town on the concert date, but I'll make sure to come even if she can't. It's things like this that make it tough on us for her to be out of town – I know she'd love to hear you if she could."

"Well, I'm sorry if she can't make it," said Paul. "Oh! And don't forget about the upcoming symphony event, too. Come to think of it, my violin could really use some adjustments before the concert season gets fully underway; any chance you could fit it in for a tune-up?"

In the back of his mind Carl was mulling the implications that Paul, an outstanding talent on the violin, was moving away from performing, but he quelled his impulse to ask about it and said, "Sure, things are getting busy for me, but I can easily find the time to look it over and make adjustments if they're needed. Stop by the shop anytime – and I'll look forward to hearing you in the concert, as well."

They talked some more about Paul and his family as they got down to fishing in earnest, and Carl explained that the grayling were turning to midges so he might want to adapt his tackle accordingly. By the end of the morning, Carl had eight grayling and Paul had one. Against protests, Carl gave Paul five of his fish along with best wishes to his father and mother and then climbed back up into the city towards home while Paul followed the road along the river.

◄■►

Carl had spent long hours on the repair of a viola the next day and had afterwards sought some distance from the shop. He sat on a stone bench in a small square once again overlooking the river far below and focused on the shapes and colors around him. His eye delighted in the small glint from a window, the black trapezoid of a room interior, the golden textured sandstone, the luminous blue of the sky that was tinged with the beginnings of the yellow and orange of a setting sun.

The vibrant colors seemed to him that they could almost have flavors, and the shapes of the shadows were transfixing.

In his heart of hearts, Carl wanted to be an artist. He felt like he could detect the essence of a scene, the parts that would make a drawing come to life, but transferring those images to paper seemed to be, unfortunately, beyond his grasp. Luckily, he was mostly in love with the attempt, and would sometimes sit in the early evening above the river and try and will his pencil and sketch pad to perform the magic he envisioned in his head. Instead, the pages would end up blank or covered with lines and squiggles that seemed like a fine start only to end up in the trash bin. In his mind were beautiful compositions, but in his hands were only a pencil and pad. Most of the time if he brought the drawing materials, they just sat with him as comfortable companions. But if he had the sketchbook open while he started thinking of other things, the pages would soon fill with doodles – intricate abstract shapes that he drew almost unconsciously while his mind was elsewhere.

Bells clanged in the clock tower a few blocks away, and he imagined the tourists gathered around the base of the tall turret, craning to watch the small bear figures parade in their circle and the clockwork jester pull the chimes that hung next to them. At the proper time, the golden figure with the hammer would strike the hour on the big bell at the top of the tower, which was what he heard now.

Here where he was sitting, what he saw as a mouse with tail raised skittered past his feet and headed out across the square. The wind and the edge of a flagstone flipped it and revealed an oak leaf that tumbled and continued on its path.

His eyes again focused on the scene before him, but his sketching hand immediately missed the perspective. Sighing, he let the pencil rest. Not for the first time, he thought of the lost opportunities that, unseen and unheralded, might be occurring all around him. He had no doubt that someone, somewhere, had in his or her own head music worthy of a symphony hall, a story that could brush elbows with Dante's *Inferno*, the vision to paint a treasured masterpiece, or ideas that would leapfrog man's understanding about the world around them. However, this creativity was in the heads of those, like him, with the inability to take the next step, or in the minds of those who were fully capable, but without the means to bring the thought to fruition – a musician without access to an instrument or paper, or the inventor with a flash of genius who has the thought interrupted by his child or never pursues the avenues to make the thought a reality. He was sure that if time and resources were available to those with the insight and ability, the world would be an even more miraculous and beautiful place to inhabit. He was an optimist.

Then again, he reflected, he was also a realist and knew that the day-to-day necessities and burdens required for simple existence wouldn't allow most people the chance to ever embrace a fully creative life. It seemed that there were only those uncommon few who could remain focused on their passion and avoid the distractions that inevitably arose. It took the rare combination of purpose, time, and ability for true genius to flourish, and there were little enough of any of those in supply in any one lifetime.

"Well," he said to himself, "I can also be a pessimist," as the natural extension of his thoughts tripped over his father as an example. There were those who purposely cut the cords of creativity. His father had stood out for a time among his generation's luthiers, and had also managed at one point to be a competent composer. But flashes of brilliance proved to be no match for natural inclinations, and like many others, his father had followed a path that slowly snuffed the spark. The attraction of the tavern had been greater than that of creativity and Josef had quickly turned from craftsmanship to a focus on instrument repair that required less motivation as his source of income. Carl sighed. *He may have also dimmed the light of others in the process,* he thought glumly.

He closed the sketch pad slowly on more doodles as the sun was setting and strode between the grand and heavy sandstone and granite buildings, uniformly four stories high, and along the brick-lined street to his shop and home. The lighting slowly turned from a yellow that exaggerated the coloring of the buildings to an orange that complimented them and brought out the reds in the street bricks. Although the colors were warm, the sun was losing its strength to keep them that way.

He had the apartment to himself these days and let himself in as the final rays of the sun were striking the top of his building. His wife was a professor of German literature and, unable to find a position in Bern, had accepted one at the University of Zurich, teaching what would become a minor to all of the budding scientists and economists at the university. Maria and he were able to visit each other frequently enough, and she would come home for extended stays during some of the summer months. They'd married rather later than was common and had each become comfortable living by themselves as well as together, so the arrangement, though difficult both for their marriage and financially, worked out satisfactorily for the two of them.

After a small dinner of left-overs, Carl let himself into his violin repair shop below street level to finish up a few of the projects he had underway. This was becoming less characteristic of him, as he had decreasing stamina and waning interest in working more than what was already a full day. More often than not, he would sit down with a book, take an evening stroll, or visit one of the neighborhood taverns instead. He currently had a large pile of violins in their cases to work through – two of the local primary schools and one of the higher-grade schools found that they had violins in need of attention as the academic year was underway and performances would soon be starting up in earnest. A few of the violins demanded serious attention, and he spent some time that evening on a some of the easier ones that only required new strings and some finer adjustments to make them playable.

CHAPTER 2.

The next day unexpectedly brought the first real taste of the coming winter. The temperature had dropped, and a cold intermittent rain lashed the windows of the apartment. In the street that had only a day earlier been nicely baking in the sun, the bricks now looked cold and glistened from the reflections of lamps that had been lit so that the Rossellis across the street could see their way through the morning routine of opening their small grocery. Carl had loved winter in his youth, but now facing it each year seemed harder than the last. He sighed as he shouldered on a heavy coat that hadn't been used for months and went out for a bun and a morning paper. Flecken was sitting on the street huddled next to the shutters waiting for Carl to open the shop. "Sorry, buddy," he said as he passed, "I'll be back after a bit." He found the air wasn't as cold as he'd expected, and he hoped wistfully that perhaps there was some summer left yet.

He had two errands to run this morning and after the hot-cross bun and a cup of coffee, he left Kramgasse to a lifting sky, and ducked down a series of side streets to Brunngasse and Old Carl's shop. When he entered, Old Carl was in his back office, so Carl stood for a time and watched Gustav, one of the more seasoned apprentices, begin the initial stages of carving a violin top. Gustav held a small plane with a convex curve to the blade that was used to carve the slightly concave contours that created a violin shape from a blank of spruce. The blank was thicker along the midline running from head to tail and thinner at the outer edges. Gustav's job was to form a slight dome that swept down only to rise again just at the edges where the sides would be attached.

Shafts of sunlight streamed in intermittently through the high window, and when the light was shining in fully, Carl could see the shapes of Gustav's fingers through the long and thin curled shavings. Gustav seemed to be in a trance, lost in the action of the plane and how it felt going through the spruce with each pass. He wasn't using his eyes as much as his hands to guide the plane. There was a pleasant, soft swishing sound as the plane moved through the wood, and Carl could tell Gustav was using a nicely sharpened blade with just the right amount of cutting surface exposed. He knew from experience about the fine sawdust that would be produced from a blade that was not exposed enough, and the rough tugs or catches that could happen with too much blade protruding. The two men were both lost in the shavings until the office door was flung open, and Old Carl began his morning harangues at his staff.

"Mind what you're doing, Gustav!" he bellowed as he approached. "You've already ruined two tops this week!" he reminded his apprentice. Like an orchestra leader, he turned to Rolf, the junior assistant, and yelled, "Don't just stand there Rolf, clean the place the hell up!" Dieter was next, "Get back in there and rotate the fresh maple stock for drying! We don't need more warped boards on your watch!" With a wink and a growl, he told Carl, "You. Stay the hell out of the way."

Gustav shrugged, Rolf swept, and Carl grinned to himself. Same Old Carl. The younger man went up and shook the older, hard, square hand and could already smell the schnapps bracer on its owner's breath. Old Carl met him with a beaming smile despite the shouting.

"I can't leave them alone for a second," muttered Old Carl, but loudly enough for everyone to hear. "What brings you by? Are you ready to start working for me yet?" Old Carl knew that Carl was doing fine in his own business, but had liked the craftsmanship and diligence that Carl showed under his brief apprenticeship, so he asked him this same question every time Carl paid a visit. Old Carl had been a friend of his father's and for a time had been one of Switzerland's finest luthiers but now directed others in the art.

"Nope. I just stopped by to see if I could pick out a few blanks of spruce for tops if you have any more of the sets from last year," said Carl. "Those were a couple of very fine billets, and I have three or four instruments from the schools that are unfortunately going to need completely new tops."

"Students!" spat Old Carl. "Wouldn't know a Stradivarius if they were given one. What are you doing wasting your time fixing what they wreck? You're a great builder and could be making your own gems."

"Thanks, but you know I'm very happy fixing what's needed so they can learn to play. What do you think about the wood?"

"Yeah," said Old Carl, "I'm running low on that stock, but we have another good year coming up, so I don't mind parting with some of it. I find the color seems to be a little off anyway, even though the customer can't tell from the outside once the finish is applied. Go ahead and talk to Dieter, and he'll let me know what you run off with. Good to see you, Carl ... Gustav, Goddamnit!" Old Carl wheeled off to feel useful.

Carl made his way around the workbenches and into the wood storage room that was Dieter's domain. He stood and observed Dieter at work, waiting for a good time to interrupt him. He was making thin, useable sections out of a quarter of a round of spruce. The wood stood on end and was about 50 centimeters tall. Dieter held a wooden mallet and a wide chisel. Carl watched him place the chisel against the top of the quarter round so that it was as close as he could get to perpendicular from the direction of the growth rings and, using intuition and luck as much as anything, strike down hard with the mallet. A nice flat section of wood split from the quarter round making a natural wedge – thicker at the bark edge, and thin at where the center of the tree had been. As another perfect slice of wood fell to the floor, Carl cleared his throat to announce his presence. Dieter looked up and gave Carl a big smile as the two shook hands.

"It's good to see you, Dieter," said Carl. "Old Carl said that I could raid your stocks again."

"Take your pick," said Dieter making a sweeping gesture at the wall filled with organized stacks of spruce and maple. "I'm always glad to see this go to good use. The old man has enough stored for another entire generation of violin makers at least."

The billets that had already been split into book-matched pairs were stickered in stacks with thin slats between each pair allowing airflow for drying. There were many more than Carl expected in the section he'd chosen from in the past, and so he was now certain that this was a cache of wood he could draw on for a long time. He picked out four nice sets where the coloring was fairly consistent across the surfaces and the grain had a nice close count – about 10 to 15 dark bands per centimeter of wood. With a satisfied nod, he slid them into the large satchel he was carrying over his shoulder.

"That's four more to add on my tab," said Carl. "Tell Old Carl that I'll settle up for the month next week. See you, Dieter, and thanks again." Leaving the storage room, he waved at Old Carl as he headed for the shop exit. Old Carl gave him a back-handed brush of the hand, and Carl stepped outside as the air within was filled with more vitriol.

◄ ■ ►

For his second errand, he headed back toward the street on which he lived, Kramgasse, but when he reached it, he turned in the opposite direction from his apartment. A message had been left for him the day before from someone needing adjustments to their violin, so he'd replied that he'd stop by and see what was needed. The sun was shining enough through the clouds now that he contemplated returning his coat to his apartment first, but decided to just throw it over his arm as he walked the several blocks to the address.

The message had indicated that the apartment was on the third floor, so when he came to the correct street number, he climbed the straight staircase up to the second level and then followed a large spiral staircase up to the third. At the end of a short and narrow entrance hall capped by a high ceiling he knocked, heard some rustling, knocked again, and the door was opened by a man with a small baby cradled in one arm. The harried father had black tousled hair, a thick mustache, and dark expressive eyes. He nodded with a smile, stepping back into the apartment at the same time saying, "Hello, you must be Carl, come on in," then, "Mileva, could you come and get the munchkin? The violin man is here."

As Mileva came from around the corner of the small living room to retrieve the baby, the man said "Carl, I'm Albert, and this lovely woman is my wife, Mileva."

"I'm glad to meet you both," said Carl, shaking hands awkwardly as the baby changed hands between the two parents and he jostled his coat and satchel to his left arm in order to greet them.

"Thank you for coming to our house, Carl," said Mileva and paused briefly while the baby squirmed in her arms, "so that Albert could get some lunch at the same time that you look at the violin." Carl nodded and she continued, "I've made some nice potato dumplings – have you eaten? Oops, it looks like it's feeding time again here, too," as the baby began to cry.

"Oh, yes, I've already had something," Carl lied out of politeness, but the smells in the apartment made his stomach growl.

"Well, you simply must try some anyway," said Mileva as she disappeared into the back room and the kitchen.

Albert had eaten another dumpling off of his own plate while the two were talking and now rubbed his hands together. "I want to thank you for coming as well, Carl. You're probably anxious to see my violin," he said as he moved to retrieve the case off the floor near the table. "I have no idea what happened to Lina, but since I returned from playing at a friend's the other night, she just hasn't sounded the same."

"Lina?" asked Carl.

"Oh, yes, that's her nickname – short for violina," chuckled Albert.

"Did you drop or jar... her?" asked Carl, the usual cause for a violin jumping out of tune.

"Nope, not that I recall. You'll see – to me she looks the same, but sounds, well, just terrible now. It's as if someone stuffed her with wool or something." His dark eyes glittered, and his hands moved as he mimed stuffing something into his instrument.

"Well, let's have a look, it's usually something very simple," said Carl as Albert had turned and was drawing the violin out of its case. Carl noticed that the case was solid and that Albert treated the violin with great care – to the luthier this was usually the sign of an attentive, trust-worthy person.

Mileva was back with a small plate of dumplings and butter. "Here, try these. Albert, you should give Carl some pepper to go on them," as she turned quickly to return to the now squalling child.

Albert nodded to her and passed Carl the instrument. "Now, hold her gently," he said.

Carl smiled at him. "Naturally - it's my job, after all."

Albert smiled back and then turned to the dumplings. "Pepper, pepper, pepper," he murmured pleasantly to himself as he cranked a small mill, withdrew the tiny box at the bottom, and pinched some pepper over Carl's dumplings without asking whether Carl needed the spice.

Carl had plucked at the strings and now took up the proffered bow and ran through the notes of a quick scale. He'd never played this violin before and knew, unless Albert had been playing a fourth-rate instrument all this time, that something was not right with Lina. She had no volume and her tone was absolutely dead. He inspected her more closely. She wasn't a make he was familiar with, and had come out of Italy, he saw based on a quick glance at the label visible through the f-hole. The strings were in good shape, and the bridge didn't seem to be cracked or deformed. He examined the base of the bridge, and it appeared to sit in roughly the position it should, but there were marks of different placements scuffed into the top. He gently detuned and retuned each string, felt that the tuning pegs were solid in their slots, and then shook his head.

"It's not immediately apparent what the problem could be," he told Albert. "Can you describe how she sounded before?"

"Well, for one thing, Lina could sustain a note for more than a few seconds, and she's always had a very sweet tone and temperament about her. I play in both a trio and a quartet with friends – chamber music, mostly – and I know that I'd be unwelcome now, where I wasn't shunned before," he said with a self-deprecating wink.

"We definitely need to make this right, but I think I should take her back to the shop with me and have a closer look at her to find out what's wrong. Would a couple of days be OK with you? I have a huge pile of instruments that I'm working on right now, but I should be able to fit this in with no problem."

"Sure, I usually play several times a week, but I think that this demands a necessary break to make her playable again, don't you? Hopefully not more than a week or two, though?"

"OK, I'll see what I can do and send a message or stop by if I can't find an easy fix for the problem or if something else unexpected comes up in my schedule. If it looks like it'll take too much time, I'll make sure I get you a loaner. Do you know where my shop is?"

Albert nodded as they shook hands, but he maintained a light grip as Carl attempted to let go. Albert was pulling him back to the table. "You must try Mileva's dumplings before you go!" he said with a chuckle.

Carl took a tentative bite and then appreciatively ate all of them on his plate.

"It's the pepper that makes them so good – isn't it?" asked Albert as he finished his own lunch.

Carl nodded and looking around for Mileva said, "You must send my compliments to the chef."

"He likes them!" shouted Albert to the other end of the house with another laugh.

They said their farewells, and Carl stood for a moment at the base of the spiral stairs before heading back to his shop with Lina. *What an interesting man,* he thought. *I wonder what his playing style is like?* Carl had found that that told him even more about a person.

◀ ■ ▶

A well-dressed man with a cane was standing near the entrance to the shop as Carl approached. Flecken had withdrawn to wait a safe distance away. "Herr Veblen?" the man ventured when he noticed the violin case that Carl carried.

"Yes, Herr …?" asked Carl as he extended his hand towards the stranger.

"Weber," answered the man as he shook Carl's hand. "I'm new to the city, but I understand that you make violins, and I was hoping to have one crafted by you."

"I'm sorry," said Carl shaking his head. "There's a very fine builder in town near the train station who has a business named, appropriately, *Instrumentenbau Violin.* I'm the person you see after something unfortunate has happened to the one you already own. I provide maintenance and repairs, but not new instruments."

Carl gave directions to *Instrumentenbau Violin* as he drew open the large shutters and, starting down the steps to his workshop, wished Herr Weber the best of luck. Flecken was suddenly beside him at the bottom of the stairs.

The shop was accessed, as were many below street level, through a pair of hatch doors built into the base of the building at a 45-degree angle, and his apartment was located above it on the second level overlooking the avenue. His business below, along with a growing number of other shops, was a converted storage cellar. The entrances on the main level fronted a raised, covered sidewalk and consisted largely of businesses like Herr Gelder's jewelry store just above his own, but the rent for these was well over what he and Maria could afford. His wife and he had picked out the location when they'd formally decided to take over his father's repair business, and he was very happy with the arrangement, except for the not-so-convenient access into the shop. A friend had made a sign with 'Veblen Violin Repair Cellar' and a wood-burned image of a violin that hung above the shop entrance to make it more visible to passing traffic. He'd thought that a basement location would be too dark and confining, but he found that with the shutter doors open, plenty of light was available through the glass windows on the secondary door at the base of the stairs. The worn stone steps were very inviting if not a little slick when wet, but in no way dank nor dark.

He would have liked to have helped Herr Weber, but Herr Zenger at the *Instrumentenbau Violin* was an excellent luthier. He might have recommended Old Carl, but unfortunately the elder man's business had fallen below its previous high standards, as had his father's in the past. Carl himself had initially trained as a luthier, which had been his father's original career hope for him, too. He'd started as an apprentice under Josef's best friend Old Carl, but his father had died before Carl was able to establish himself as an independent craftsman. Carl had never questioned that violin construction was what he wanted to, and should, do as his life's work and he'd shown promise in his training as a luthier, crafting very playable instruments, although never seemingly able to meet his father's high standards. Upon Josef's death, Carl had abandoned the instrument-making side of luthiery and had taken over what turned out to be a reasonably successful business of instrument repair, restoration, and maintenance. He often wondered whether his father would have regretted leaving him the repair business rather than the lutherie shop Josef had first established as a young man, but Carl was now a committed repairman, regardless.

◄■►

A few nights later, the wind was howling, and the rain was intermittent, lashing in sideways sheets when it fell. Carl wrapped his fluttering coat tighter around his collar and bent forward to make progress against the gusts as he picked his way along the slick cobblestones. It was pitch black away from the light, and when he approached a row of street lamps, each bright flame was haloed by reflections on the wet branches surrounding it. The more the gusts shook the trees, the more solid the perfectly round circle of light around each lamp seemed to become. The lampposts were set back into recessed alcoves formed at intervals in a stone wall, and under almost every lamp huddled a bedraggled figure or a street merchant tucked into the periodic wind breaks. One of the last vendors along the wall had a small fire that somehow managed to stay lit below a shallow pan filled with sand. On the sand were roasting chestnuts. Carl stopped and bought some which the seller stuffed into a cone he'd fashioned from damp newspaper.

Carl hurried across the street into a narrow alley that had neither wind nor rain, and peeled and blissfully ate the chewy, hot, and sweet chestnut meats. This warmed him and the respite from the wind was reviving, so he set off again as if from home. He had no real destination in mind, other than that it had to be a tavern, that it had to have beer, and that it had to be far from his own house.

He occasionally liked to visit a tavern other than *Zum Bären,* his customary social spot, and would try and pick one where few people would know him. The anonymity allowed him to sit back and think, and to watch the people – which was actually one of his favorite pastimes and he found it to be very relaxing. A few blocks along, he saw a tavern sign swinging wildly in the staunch gusts that he recognized from infrequent visits. He entered the establishment and was immediately hit by another storm, this one of warm, almost hot, smoky air, filled with boisterous noise from the rear, and strewn with colorful faces, hats, and cloaks. He was in luck; a single table was unoccupied just under the shuddering front window. As he walked toward the glass, he noticed there was no reflection except in random streaks where the warm moist interior air that was condensed thickly on the cold glass surface sweated in large glistening beads.

He shrugged out of his coat, ordered a stein of beer, and took in his surroundings. A man he didn't recognize nodded in his direction and he dipped his head in reply, but no one else paid him any attention. When the beer came, he took a long draught and then sat back and felt his entire body relax. He'd been tense from the wet, the cold, and the fast pace at which he'd walked to get out of it, but also from work. He was behind schedule in repairing the school violins, and one school in particular was sending a messenger on a daily basis to remind him of upcoming recitals. It felt good to take a break and get away from his home which on days like this was just too close to the shop.

A young couple was seated near him in the corner, and both the young man and woman were trying to not look interested in each other, all the while not being able to take their eyes off one another. Heads would turn to the side, but the eyes never strayed. Another set of eyes were straying much more than they should – an older married couple was comprised of a wife worrying the coaster of her drink and a large and obviously, or wanting to be obvious, prominent businessman who had his eyes trained on every aspect of the busy waitress. Otherwise, there were solitary regulars at a side bar, communal regulars at tables arranged in the middle, and younger patrons crowded, clowning and throwing darts in the rear. There was a raised platform for music performances, usually accordion or brass as in most taverns, that was now packed with customers as well. Everywhere lively conversations were taking place, each adding to the din. As his eyes drifted over the tables, Carl felt that he could sense the inner personalities of those squashed around them – whether this was really the case or not: the person who gestured confidently but inside was a nervous wreck; the youngsters who were trying to act older than their age; and the old guys who were just kids at heart and could never grow up. And even here he saw something he'd been paying attention to lately – extravagantly conspicuous persons with no substance, and quiet, ordinary-looking folks of possibly huge consequence – angel food cake and pumpernickel bread. He wondered briefly where he fit in this spectrum, feeling oddly like a puffed pastry of the no-substance variety as he did so, and turned to watch a large drop slide slowly down the window pane.

Surveying the crowd again, his eyes lit on a pair of gentlemen leaning over some scattered papers laid out across their small table who were oblivious to all but the words they were exchanging, not in a heated manner as in a political discussion, but in a more constructive manner, like they were planning for an important voyage. He noticed that they were drinking coffee and not beer, which made them stand out even more. The one with his back to Carl was gesticulating and turned slightly while explaining some point to the other, and Carl recognized Albert from the few days before. *Oh, shit! I forgot about his violin!* immediately came to Carl's mind, and his reverie collapsed. His thoughts were back on work. He tried diligently, over another beer, to enter the same relaxed mental space he'd just enjoyed, but knowing that the warm and calming session was over, he finished his beer, put on his coat, and headed back home which was at least downwind this time.

CHAPTER 3

He'd finalized most of the easier jobs, and was now working on a violin that looked like someone used it as a hammer – the bridge had been smashed and had driven a jagged hole into the top of the violin. That someone had been Michael, a first-year student of Master Ehrlich's in the higher-grade school, and Carl shook his head as he remembered the conversation.

"Can you please tell Herr Veblen how this transpired, Michael?" Master Ehrlich had asked when Carl had dropped in to pick up the case and the boy had happened to be in the music room at the same time.

Michael was much shorter than the other boys his age and had large blue eyes that seemed to never blink. Something about the shape of his ears made Carl think of an elf when he'd met him. Michael had stared straight at Carl and had said, "I couldn't reach my lunch bag." Then he'd smiled slightly, "The case looked stronger than it was."

"I should say so!" Master Ehrlich had nearly yelled. "Cases are not footstools!"

Carl had left with the broken instrument, disappointed with the destruction but at the same time thinking, *I wonder what I would have done at his age if I couldn't reach my lunch bag?*

Carl was now in the process of fashioning a new top from one of the blanks he'd obtained from Old Carl. The neck removal had come first and had necessitated steam directed through a small hose and needle into tiny holes he'd drilled at strategic points. The steam heat had loosened the glue, and he had worked the expanding joints with a thin knife until first the neck and then the destroyed top came free of the sides and back.

There was a noise outside, and he looked up as Peer came bounding down the stairs, stumbled, and almost fell through the glass door. Flecken gave a start. "Be careful of that glass, Peer, we don't want blood all over the violins," joked Carl.

Peer shrugged and smiled. He was a tall and gangly fifteen-year old Carl had taken on as a shop helper. *Perhaps someday he'll be interested enough to become an apprentice,* Carl often thought, since school was definitely not his forte. Peer had quit the primary school as soon as it was allowed and said that he preferred to work with his hands rather than with his head. He had good features except for two traits: dishwater blonde hair that ran amok defying any comb, and teeth that crowded and twisted to stay in his mouth. He had shot up at least a hand in the last year, and for his teeth's sake, Carl hoped that his jaw would follow suit.

Handing him Michael's old, broken top, he had Peer use that as a template to copy the sigmoid-shaped 'f-holes' located on either side of where the bridge had been, onto the blank piece of wood he'd just carved and shaped for the new top. It was important to him that the f-holes were an exact match of those on the previous instrument. His apprenticeship years ago had taught him that the shape and placement of the holes was a crucial component in the overall sound of the violin and some experimentation on his own and later experience repairing finer instruments had verified this for himself. He also had Peer trace the shape of the f-holes onto a piece of paper. He had some favorite templates that he'd copied, and although they varied from one to another only slightly, each one, he thought, could bring a unique tone to the instrument. He'd later compare this f-hole shape from the student violin with those accumulated templates and see if it needed to be added to the collection.

With the top of the violin removed from the body and the interior of the back and sides exposed, Carl set to replacing the now damaged thin inner linings or bands of wood that ran along the upper and lower edges of the sides, where the sides met the top and back. *I hope this is worth it,* he thought and shook his head at the shoddy workmanship that had gone into the initial construction. He'd previously bent and carved the new linings into contours matching the shape of the violin. Checking for a proper fit, he then smeared hot liquid horse-hide glue onto the upper portions of the sides, and quickly clamped the linings onto the fast-setting adhesive along the inner top edge. Satisfied with his work, he placed the topless body onto a storage shelf for the glue to rapidly gel and then slowly change to a crystalline hardness overnight.

Peer had made himself some hot cocoa on the stove and was beginning to sweep up the shop. Carl, however, had him first clear a space on the worktable and cover it with a clean cloth so that he could finally set to work on Albert's violin, Lina. He took the instrument out of its case and gave her a closer inspection. With better light, he could see immediately through the f-hole that the sound post, a small dowel set inside the violin to help support the bridge, was not in the correct position relative to the bridge. Carefully examining the bridge, he could see that the string placement along the upper edge was poor, and that it was the bridge itself that was not in the proper position on the top of the violin. Tilting the bridge into the light revealed the small stamp from a Viennese company, and yet Lina was an Italian violin. *Strange, but not uncommon,* he thought.

He completely unwound the strings and removed the bridge. It was of high-quality workmanship and made from a nice cut of maple. Carl had several pre-shaped bridge wedges that only needed minor tweaking to place on violins, but he also had several blanks of maple and enjoyed fashioning his own bridges from scratch as well. Common with all bridges, this Viennese model had two "feet" and symmetric oval patterns cut out of the sides. Carl admired the workmanship on this specimen and wondered how it had possibly come to be on Albert's violin.

Carl took whatever opportunities he could to teach Peer something about violin repair, and to try and keep the boy interested in his work. He called Peer over to explain to him about proper bridge placement, and why this one on Albert's was unacceptable. "Peer, come look at this," he said as he held the bridge up to Albert's violin top. When Peer was at a good vantage point, he continued. "See here, in the proper light you can tell that the shape of the feet of the bridge don't match the violin contours – do you see the light coming through at the base where the feet meet the top?" Peer craned his neck and nodded. "Now, if I move it here, it's a better fit, but that's not where it should be placed. It has to be at that sweet spot where the scale length is perfect and all notes played in normal fingering positions will be in tune." He set Lina down and plucked a different violin from a wall-rack and played it as it was and then moved the bridge slightly and played again. "Hear the difference?"

"Definitely," said Peer hardly surprised, "it's not in tune."

"Right. I know if Albert's bridge had been bought as a replacement, the installer would've matched the shape of the feet to the soundboard to make a complete transfer of pressure and sound onto the violin in the correct position. But it's like he didn't even try, and I think that's odd."

I wonder why Albert didn't mention that he'd had some work done on Lina? he thought. *And I didn't do such a great job of keeping his attention,* as Peer moved off in a distracted manner to continue with his sweeping.

The terrible fit of the bridge was the cause of the muffled sound she'd produced. He was about to begin shaping the bridge for the proper fit when he realized it would be better to explain the situation to Albert and have him decide if he wanted a new bridge, or to have this one installed properly.

◄ ■ ►

The cobbles on the street glistened from a light drizzle, and he had to wait for a passing horse cart and then a screeching trolley before he could reach for the cold and wet lock and handle on his shop hatch. There was no sign of the big white and black cat, Flecken, who usually appeared about this time. He threw open the entry doors and was walking down the steps when he sensed someone behind him and turned to see Paul who grinned down at him and said, "I'm not usually up and about so early in the morning, but I had to meet a friend at the train station and show him the way to the art school. I hope this isn't an inconvenience showing up just as you're opening."

"Hi, Paul!" said Carl. "No problem at all - just let me turn on the lights and fire up the stove, then I'll be able to look at your instrument."

Carl set about his morning routine for opening up the shop and cleared a space on his workbench for Paul to set his case. When the fire in the stove had been lit and caught, Carl opened the case and examined the German-made violin that he'd been maintaining for the past fifteen years. After some time he said, "Good news. I can really see nothing on the violin that needs my attention. The bridge is solid; the strings are worn, but still, they're in very playable shape." He played a brief melody, listening intently, and then made some long slow motions with the bow. "I do notice, however, that the bow could use a new set of horsehairs. It's getting a bit thin, especially on the nearer side. I can recommend a good bow-man whose shop isn't too far from here."

"Well, that was quick," said Paul. "I'll definitely get the bow restrung soon, and thanks, Carl - this gives me confidence going into the performance."

"You're welcome anytime," said Carl and they both turned their heads towards a rasping noise coming from the other side of the door. Carl stepped over and let in the be-draggled cat.

"He still hasn't found his voice, has he?" asked Paul. "Hello, Flecken," he said as he reached down and patted the damp fur on the now-purring cat.

"I don't expect he ever will," said Carl as Flecken noticed the warmth of the fire and quickly curled up below it, licking the rainwater off his side. Carl then turned to his friend. "You know, you've really grown into yourself, especially over the last five years, Paul. What are you now? Twenty-six?"

"No, twenty-five," replied Paul.

"So, what did you mean when we were down fishing for grayling about not performing in the future? I can't believe with all your natural and growing talent that you'd choose to stop. Are there any problems I can help with?" asked Carl.

"No, no problems, and I guess it's not strange that you should ask. Or that you might be disappointed," said Paul perching on a nearby stool. "I recently spent three years at art school in Munich, as you know, and that's left me in a quandary about whether to follow the path of art or of music. People have pegged me as a musician, and I'm embarrassed to say that I even heard the word "prodigy" when I was growing up. But as much as music is my true love, it's diminishing as a passion. I feel in my gut that I need to move in a completely different direction to feel fulfilled... no, inspired."

"What do you mean?" asked Carl.

"Well, do you like the more modern music – Dvorak or Mahler for example?" asked Paul.

"Yes, very much so," replied Carl. "To tell the truth, there's a huge swath of modern music that I can't immediately understand, but once I've heard a piece from one of the newer composers and let it sink in, I find that I actually enjoy it. I even like playing their compositions on my own when I can find the sheet music. Don't you?"

"No, that's not the case with me at all," stated Paul, much to Carl's surprise. "I play their music in almost every concert but, as much as I try, I can't move my sense of appreciation beyond Bach, Telemann and Mozart. I can play the works of those three for hours – centuries if need be – but I simply can't seem to grasp what the newer composers are about."

"Maybe that will come with time," suggested Carl.

"I don't know," said Paul. "Their creations just don't speak to me. It's like the language has changed, and I have no translation. I even find myself wondering if this modern stuff is truly music at all. And strangely enough, I'm a young man who should keep up with the times – it's like I am trapped as an old man, musically.

"However, on the other hand, I've always loved to draw and now I'm finding entirely new directions opening up to me. I've been concentrating seriously on art these last couple of years in Munich and now that seems like the right fit for me. Like I can take this new form anywhere I want to go, whereas with music I'm feeling so stifled. You should see, or perhaps you have, the explosion of creativity that's happening on canvases across Europe?"

"Yes, and I've seen some recent exhibits that I have a very difficult time liking or understanding. I just can't see what they're painting – all those dabs and swishes - as art ... But the old masters - ah," sighed Carl with downcast eyes and a shake of the head. "I'd absolutely love to be able to draw or paint like them. It seems that I can almost feel the world with my eyes sometimes, you know? But you wouldn't believe what comes out on my sketch pad. There're no polite words to describe it."

"Well, do you have some examples that I can look at?" asked Paul. "Perhaps I can offer some suggestions or help."

"No," sighed Carl. "That wouldn't be possible."

"Have you tossed them?" asked Paul.

"No, not all," said Carl with a little smile, "but I should."

"If you change your mind and want any tips, let me know," said Paul, to the exaggerated shakes of the head by Carl. They left the conversation at that.

"Really looking forward to your performance," said Carl as Paul headed up the stairs.

"Thanks, Carl, and thank you for looking over my violin," said Paul. "I'll try and give it my best effort as always," as he stepped out of view.

◄■►

As they'd agreed through messages exchanged beforehand, Carl met Albert at a point on the Kornhausbrucke – a bridge spanning the Aare River north of their houses. There was a nip to the air and the end of twilight was clear and still. In the distance an evening train whistled and, nearer by, the clop of horse hansoms and the sputter of autos rose and faded. Carl was headed to his friend Lukas' home for dinner that evening, and Albert to a meeting with friends, but they'd agreed to rendezvous at a spot where their paths converged.

"Getting colder, isn't it?" asked Carl as they shook gloved hands.

"Do you want to go and get a coffee someplace warmer?" asked Albert.

"Sorry, but I have a few minutes before I need to get to my friend's house - not really enough time to sit and talk over a cup," said Carl.

They decided to stand and look out over the river as they chatted. Some of the brighter stars reflected off the river's surface far below, broken up by ripples from a small rapid.

"So, you had a new Viennese bridge installed on Lina?" asked Carl. "That might account for the big change in tone you're hearing."

"No, I haven't had any work done on that old girl for years," replied Albert. "Why do you ask?"

"Because the bridge is a different make from the violin and it isn't even seated properly," said Carl.

"A different make?" asked Albert. "How could that be? No wonder she sounded so strangely."

"Yes, she would do that. And you're sure you didn't have the new bridge recently mounted?"

"Of course, I'm sure," said Albert, slightly offended. "In fact, I rather pride myself on being very observant." He then lightened things up again with a slight laugh. "And yet, I didn't notice that the bridge wasn't the same at all, did I?

Admittedly, I only tried to play her the one time when I discovered the sound changed so much."

"When was this again?" asked Carl.

"After I'd gone to a friend's house to play some music. The four of us get together and practice nearly every week, and this time it was at Geron's house. He had quite a crowd, and we performed for them as a lark. Actually, it went fairly well, and Lina sounded fine at the time."

"Well, if you're sure it's Lina, she definitely came home with a new bridge."

"Yes, she's my violin," said Albert. "A new bridge though? It was swapped after I'd played? What would be the point in that?"

"I have no idea," replied Carl, and they both thought about this in silence for a time, but there seemed nothing more to say by way of conjecture. "Do you want to keep the same bridge or have a new one fitted? It's a nice make, but since we don't know where it came from maybe a new one would be better. I can either order one from Italy, put on one from my stock on hand that would make a good match, or fashion one myself from scratch."

"How much are we talking about?"

"Oh, twenty to thirty francs, regardless, but the least expensive would be one of my stock bridges."

"Well, let's try one from your stock then. Let's see how that sounds." They agreed and stood looking down over the river moving past quietly in the dark. Albert's gaze slowly shifted higher and higher and, when Carl noticed, they were both soon looking at the gauze of the Milky Way and stars beyond. "It never ceases to amaze me," said Albert. "The light from those stars has been coming at us for maybe 10 years from the nearest star that's been measured, to who knows - perhaps hundreds of thousands of years, or even more, from many of the others. It travels all the way through space, dodging planets, stars, rocks, and dust - really anything out there that can stop or deflect light. It travels at an incredible speed and is rushing towards infinity, or to the edges of the universe if it could catch up with them. Nothing slows it down. Nothing can approach its speed. And then, bam! It stops - right here on our pupils. Never to go anywhere again."

Carl, looking in the same direction, involuntarily blinked his eyes. The stars suddenly seemed in much sharper focus than they had just a few moments before. Carl was feeling some urgency to get to the Lukas house on time, but this didn't seem the right opportunity to do so, and he was becoming interested in what Albert had to say.

"On a bright night in the winter, you can turn around and see the faint shadow of the place the light never reached," continued Albert. "And in the daytime, we don't notice the glow from the stars because of the sun, but it's there none the less. I feel honored to be able to see it sometimes – like a gift from someone incredibly far away whom I'll never meet."

"How do they know the distance to the stars?" Carl felt compelled to ask.

"They use the parallax..." Albert turned and momentarily evaluated Carl. "They use trigonometry and have now catalogued the distance to quite a number," Carl nodded in reply as Albert continued. "Standing here and gazing up, it's impossible to tell which are the nearer stars and which are very far away since they each are a different size and shine with a different intensity. Some might be very bright but incredibly far away, and some might be close but relatively dim. What looks like a flat sheet before us is really very vast in depth."

Carl raised his arm to point. "And very dense in places," he said indicating the heart of the gauze of stars.

"Yes," continued Albert. "In fact, there are astronomers who've postulated that the band of stars you're pointing at in the Milky Way really comprises a huge swirl of stars called a nebula and we're looking at it from an edge facing back into the center. But just think - if we are in our own nebula or galaxy, then it's not a huge leap to guess that there are probably other galaxies that contain millions of stars just like ours. We could in reality be seeing lights from billions of points, but we're not even aware of it. And who knows how long some of that light has been traveling since it started out?" Albert suddenly pulled out his pocket watch and held it close to his eyes to be able to read the hands on the darkened Kornhausbrucke bridge. "Oh! I see it's time I started out, too."

He said his farewells, and Carl stood for a moment alone on the quiet roadway. He was intrigued by what Albert said – he'd learned some astronomy in school and enjoyed looking at the stars occasionally, but had certainly never thought of them in the way that Albert had described. But he also found himself slightly annoyed by the way Albert seemed to lecture him. *Maybe he's a teacher*, thought Carl, *and that's just his way*. Suddenly remembering his own appointment, Carl headed off to the Lukas home. Hurrying now into the more lighted streets of the old town, Carl thought that he should really ask Albert what he did for a living – he was convinced the man must be a lecturer in some school, probably the university.

CHAPTER 4

The next morning, Carl steeled himself to face the stack of ailing student violins, reminding himself that he could only care for them one at a time. Now came the detailed task of adding purfling to his current "problem child" born of Michael's bad decision in reaching for his lunch.

With the arched shape of the new top of the violin largely carved and the outline firmly established, it was time to add the thin decorative and protective laminated strips that were inlaid just inside the border of the top of the violin. He would love to have Peer be able to do this on his own, but still didn't entirely trust the young man with sharp implements around valuable wood. He cleared two spaces on the workbench for Peer to follow his actions – only Peer's attempts would be on the old destroyed top that had been taken off the violin, rather than on virgin spruce.

"Hey, Peer," said Carl. "When you're done mixing that shellac, would you come over here? I've set up a station where you can try some cutting."

"Cutting?" asked Peer excitedly since he was rarely allowed to work with the shop tools.

"Yep, we're going to cut up some violin tops," said Carl with a grin.

Peer was soon over to the workbench and began toying with one of the chisels.

"OK, Peer," said Carl, getting the boy's attention as he held up the old top. "This violin already has a purfling stripe, and I'm going to show you how it was installed. See here how it's the same distance from the edge of the top all the way around?" Flipping the top over he continued, "And notice that it doesn't go all the way through? The stripe is set into a narrow groove, and we use this to do it." Carl held up a purfling cutter and then took Peer through the process, Carl on the new top, and Peer on the one that was being replaced.

They'd both cut the fine, sharp lines defining each side of the purfling channel with the cutter, and then with a very fine chisel, Carl cut out the spruce between the two lines forming a narrow groove. In Peer's case, he was essentially digging out the old purfling.

While chiseling the channel, Carl was aware that his hands had lives of their own. They'd been cut and scraped enough times with sharp or abrasive tools that they seemed to know how to keep out of the chisel's path without him being conscious of the fact. Every time the direction of the chisel changed, the placement of his hands – especially the one holding the wood in place – changed as well. He'd tried repeatedly to caution Peer about the sharpness of the tools, but the boy would have to find out the hard way and have his hands learn on their own. Peer, tongue sticking out of the side of his mouth in concentration, made it through this exercise without a laceration, although there were some near misses.

"Good job, Peer," said Carl when they'd finished. "What did you think?"

"Yeah, that was fun," said Peer. In the next moment he asked, "Did you hear that they're setting up a fair in the square across from Parliament? Johann and I are going to see it after work."

"No, I hadn't heard," said Carl amazed at the quick change of direction capable in a young mind.

For the next task of the day, Carl turned to Albert's new bridge and wanted Peer to observe this as well. After a few minutes of attention, the boy seemed just as interested in petting Flecken and watching the legs and feet of the people passing by on the street, which was all he could see of them from his position down in the shop.

Carl chose one of his stock bridges and began to match it to Lina's curvature. Taking measurements, he found that he needed to bring down the height of the bridge, and simultaneously make the feet match perfectly with the top. He placed an abrasive cloth rough side up on the soundboard where the bridge was meant to be placed and then painstakingly moved the upright bridge back and forth across the cloth. From the shape of the sawdust left by the tracks of the passing feet of the bridge, he could tell when the full width of the feet were meeting the contours of the instrument top. He kept sanding until the bridge was at the proper height. Peer had by now become utterly bored and had been mindlessly playing in the shellac, so it was already well stirred. Carl applied a few coats of the shellac to the bridge and let it dry - the bridge was finished.

Turning back to Albert's violin, he reconfirmed that the sound post, a concealed round dowel, was in the correct position. He wanted to make sure that nothing else was amiss on the instrument. The post's purpose was to connect the top of the violin to the back and physically transfer the vibrations of the bridge directly from the bridge and the soundboard to the back. It was well placed near the foot of the bridge on the treble side, or the side with the thinnest strings. The post was tight enough to be held in place by friction – not glued; he knew they could sometimes become loose when the violin was de-strung, but this post appeared to be well fitted and needed no adjustments.

In the meantime, Peer had begun to clean up after him, but noticed his friend Johann waiting at the top of the stairs. "Johann's here!" shouted Peer as he threw open the door. Carl said goodbye as Peer tripped up the steps and the pair were off.

◄ ■ ►

"Hi Max," said Carl as he stepped into *Zum Bären* for a beer after work. Built in what had been an old storage cellar, the tavern was amazingly bright and lit from above by a high series of windows during the day and by huge wooden candelabras during the evenings.

"Hello, Carl! How are you?" asked Max wiping the countertop after having just filled a stein for a patron, cutting the foam off the top with a knife. "What can I get you?"

"Just one of your free beers would be great," said Carl with a smile.

"Now, now, you know the sign says 'Tomorrow'," Max grinned. He reached for a stein and pulled the tall ceramic beer tap for the pilsner that Carl usually ordered. "Peer sure seems to be happy lately. You must be treating him well at work."

"That's good to hear, but who can tell with him? At least he puts up with the chores I give him," said Carl. "But sometimes I suspect he just stays for the cocoa."

"He sure loves it, doesn't he? No, really, he's been talking about how he likes to work on violins more and more lately."

"Well, that's good news!" said Carl. "I keep hoping that I might have found an apprentice..."

"Not so fast," laughed Max. "I need someone to be able to take over here after I retire!" Max and his wife Frieda had assumed the business from his father and had run the tavern for nearly 30 years. Childless, they'd provided the stability that Peer needed when he'd entered foster care and they'd taken him in.

"Well, hopefully that won't be too soon," said Carl. "This place has been here forever."

"It must seem that way to you," said Max. "I still remember you being brought in with your parents when you were just a tyke. That, and you showing up to drag your father home when you were a little older." Frieda appeared at Carl's side with a tray of mugs for Max to fill.

"Hi Carl!" she said giving him a matronly peck on the cheek. "Haven't seen you in here much lately."

"Hi, Frieda," Carl responded. "Nope, it seems like since summer I've been too busy to do anything but eat, work, and sleep."

"Well, to tell you the truth," said Max as he set another mug on the tray, "I'm glad that we don't see you as much as we saw Josef."

"Max!" said Frieda. "That's not very nice."

"No," said Max, correcting himself, "I mean we love to see you, Carl, but I'm just happy that you're not as beer-sodden as your dad was. He, Old Carl, and Hans Klee used to go through a barrel a night amongst them, I swear."

"I know," said Carl remembering the smell of alcohol and sawdust that seemed to increasingly permeate his father's clothing the older he became. "And it looks to me like Old Carl is still at it."

"Yes," said Max, shaking his head as Frieda took the tray away. "He changed taverns to one closer to his workshop, but I hear he's still a regular there. At least Hans has become a little more temperate. Everyone has to have beer, but too much too often is just not healthy for anyone."

The door was opening more and more frequently as people got off work and families arrived for early dinner. Max was becoming too busy for a sustained conversation. "Poor Old Carl," he said putting his hands on the counter and ignoring a patron who'd come up to the bar with an empty glass. "He was never the same after his wife died. She was his rock. You never really knew her that well, but Eva was the perfect combination of your mother's sweetness and Ida Klee's determination. And as beautiful as they come. They loved each other so much and were always the life of the party. What a shame!" He took the glass and filled it as Frieda came up with another tray. "The poor guy never recovered and turned to your father and Hans for support, which they gave him here every night."

"I know," said Carl taking a long drink of his pilsner. "I was just at the age when I could understand Old Carl's loss of Eva and be included in the group, and then dad died."

"We were sorry about your father, but maybe it was for the best that you hadn't yet joined their club," said Max. "Who knows where you'd be if you'd kept at it like those three?" Frieda subtly pushed the tray of empty steins toward him. "Talk to you later," as Carl nodded and moved off to make room for others at the counter. For a moment he had an image of his father bellying up to the bar with them and could hear his boisterous laugh echo in his ears.

CHAPTER 5.

The raucous din was deafening to the point where Carl could hardly think. The class bell had clanged and, as the doors flung open, a deluge of noise, patent leather, and bodies poured out of every doorway into the hall. He felt lucky that he wasn't in the main corridor, but was instead in the music room just off the central stairway, and that the music room was apparently not in the direction of any of the flood. He'd delivered a collection of 12 violins to the music instructor who'd then presented him with two more cases for him to take back to the shop. The cart man who'd helped him with the delivery wasn't so lucky with his timing. He'd just stepped out into the hall to return to his cart on his way to his next consignment, but made the mistake of freezing in place when the bell rang. Carl watched, mesmerized, as the poor man stood immobile like a worn-out wind-up toy soldier in the middle of the hall as what seemed to be hundreds of shouting uniformed students swirled around him. His eyes, nothing like the dull ones of a wind-up soldier, were wide with panic, or perhaps wonder. He was most certainly deaf by now, as well. After a few minutes, the flash-flood abated, the cart man stumbled to the exit, and Carl could finally make out what Master Ehrlich was saying.

"... with absolutely no idea where it came from."

"Where what came from?" asked Carl.

"'Where what came from?' Haven't you been listening, Carl? Honestly, you're just like my students – they act like I'm just flapping my lips."

"No, the noise from the ..." Carl sighed. "Oh, never mind."

"Never mind what?" asked Master Ehrlich. "That an orchestral quality bow suddenly just appeared in one of my classes?"

Carl was about to say 'What?' again, but decided on a different direction for his side of the conversation. "I'm sorry I got distracted by all of the energy of the students. What was it you were saying about the bow?"

"Well, to repeat myself," said Master Ehrlich in a somewhat exasperated tone. "The second period was tuning up a week ago, and you know how hard it is to hear each instrument with all of the extraneous noise those kids are making." Carl nodded and made a face. "Anyway, I was leaning over each violin to hear the pitches when I glanced down at Jan Rauss's violin. I realized that it wasn't the violin that caught my eye; it was the bow. As you well know," he then digressed, "the entire period's violins and their bows are owned by the school, well, really by the trustees of the school, oh - and those instruments are next in line for maintenance, by the way. Anyway, that means they should all look exactly the same."

"Yes, I'm well acquainted with those violins and bows," said Carl patiently.

"Well, I must say, I was utterly shocked that he possessed such a fine bow, and immediately demanded that Jan hand it to me and explain where he'd acquired it. He went red, stammered, was getting visibly upset, and I realized he had no idea at all what I was talking about. I asked him again how he had come by the bow, and he said that it was the one assigned to him with the violin, and I said back to him that that was impossible. When he was near breaking down, I said that there had obviously been some mistake, and retrieved a spare bow out of the storeroom and gave him that one instead. You should see this bow that he'd been playing with – well trying to play the violin with," he ended with a sad smile.

He unlocked the drawer of his desk and brought out the bow, bouncing the taught hairs against his other hand a few times. Carl immediately thought that the Master had a very good eye. At a cursory glance, it appeared to be an ordinary bow, but as he leaned closer he could see more clearly the quality laminations at each end, a pinstripe running the length, and a very intricate but miniscule flower of mother-of-pearl and abalone inlaid in the frog on the tightening end. He took the offered bow and admired the workmanship and the quality horsehair with which it was strung. This was definitely not a student-grade bow. He noticed an "A" stamped into the tightening screw, but whether this was from the metalsmith or the bow maker, he couldn't say.

"How do you think it came into Jan's hands?" marveled Carl. The Master raised his hands and shook his head. "When did he get it?" Again, a shake of the head with raised eyebrows.

"This is perplexing," said Master Ehrlich. "I've already spoken to the administration about it. The only thing that makes sense to us is that it was stolen. But I highly doubt that it was filched by Jan based on his reaction and knowing the kids as I do. He's just too young and innocent to have done something like that. The administration wants to tread lightly here since his father is rather prominent in the city, as you may realize."

"Well, you're certainly correct that this isn't a student-level bow. Good luck in finding out how he came by it." Carl was gathering the carrying cases of the two violins in need of attention when Master Ehrlich stopped him with a hand placed on his arm.

"Well, as a matter of fact, the administration, at my suggestion, was wondering if you would be good enough to help us."

Carl turned to him and asked, "And how would I do that?"

"We," Master Ehrlich paused and adopted an imploring look. "We want to avoid the police and we thought that you might be able to determine where it came from, or if a similar bow had been reported as missing. This is the kind of incident that we're just not able to investigate, you understand, being the school which Jan attends and all," proposed Master Ehrlich with dwindling volume during the last sentence.

"I don't really know anything about theft or how to even begin tracking down the owner," Carl protested. "And furthermore, violin bows are out of my area of expertise."

It was as if the halls had again filled with students, this time overwhelming the Master who acted as if he couldn't hear a word, and Carl ended up saying that he would see what he could do, departing with the bow and two violin cases.

"Maria is going to wonder just what I was thinking," lamented Carl. "Obviously, I'm not."

◄ ■ ►

"Honestly, did you think this through, Carl?" asked Maria as she fashioned her long brown hair into a tight bun. "The schools should have both more resources and time than you do for something like this. Do you even know where to start?"

"Well, no," answered Carl. "But I got the impression that even if I can make a few enquiries, that's more than the schools are able to do. They seem to be pretty intimidated by Jan's father."

"Oh, and you aren't" asked Maria.

"Well, I've never met the man, and never expect to," he answered. "What do you want for breakfast?" Carl then asked, quickly changing the subject. "I picked up some fresh eggs yesterday." He disappeared into the kitchen and started poaching some eggs and frying a slab of bacon while Maria began sorting the stack of papers covering one side of their small dining table. Maria had arrived as arranged on the last train from Zurich the night before, and he was glad whenever she could squeeze in a weekend visit. One of them would usually make the trip to see the other at least once every few weeks, but to Carl her visits to Bern were especially important since she was the bookkeeper for the both of them, and the paperwork could be overwhelming if she was away for too long. Maria usually brought school papers to grade as well, so it was always a working holiday at best, but at least they were together.

They chatted over breakfast and then Carl left her to the bills while he cleaned up the dishes, went down to open up the shop with Flecken, and then Peer entered a short time later.

While Peer saw to his daily chores, Carl completed a final fit of the bridge on Lina, brought her up to tune, and played a little melody. She sounded very good to his ears, and he was certain that Albert would be pleased with the results. He couldn't compare the sound now with how she had played before, but was hoping her tone was at least equivalent. He had Peer detune her, apply some lemon oil to her fingerboard and rub it in well, and then polish her body, neck, and peg head. Tuned up once more, she was placed carefully in the case for later delivery.

The door opened with a tinkling, and Maria backed in with a tray bearing bowls of hot potato soup and apples for lunch. She set the tray on the workbench and then walked over and gave Peer's hair a ruffle.

"Hi, Peer," said Maria. "How have you been?"

"Fine," said Peer looking down at his feet but with a big smile on his face.

"How are the Bergmans?" she then asked. "Are they treating you well?"

"Yes, ma'am, very well," replied Peer raising his head with adoring eyes to meet hers.

"Well, make sure and tell them that we're willing to help out if you become too much of a handful for them, will you?"

"Yes, ma'am," said Peer.

"And you won't become too much of a handful, will you?" she asked with a laugh and again tousled his hair.

No wonder his hair is always a mess, thought Carl with a shake of his head. Then he caught Maria's smile oddly turn down for the briefest moment and he knew the look. She was wondering what a son of their own would have been like. He gave her the same sad smile back.

Flecken had jumped down and was rubbing up against Maria with his raspy squawk of a 'meow,' interested in a lunch as well.

"Hmmm, potatoes and apples are probably not to your liking, huh?" asked Maria. "Luckily, I brought you these," and she put a couple of cubes of cheese down near the stove which Flecken happily devoured. She gave him a pat and then headed back up to the apartment with the empty tray.

Later that evening, after they'd finished dinner, Maria suddenly asked, "It's still early, do you want to play?"

Carl jokingly began to unbutton his collar. "Sure!" he said.

"You know what I mean!" said Maria giving him a gentle shove on the chest. "That can wait till later!"

They put on their coats, Maria gathered up a folder of music, and Carl grabbed his father's violin case from under the bed. They didn't have a piano, but Maria loved to use a free keyboard whenever she had the chance. A small choir chamber attached to a nearby church had a piano that was almost always available, and the two of them set off to see if the room was unoccupied. The night was chilly, and they stayed close together on the short walk to the church. Duet music filtered out into the nave for an hour after they discovered the piano was not in use.

◄ ■ ►

On Sunday, Carl and Maria took a stroll through a local park and then ate an early dinner at their favorite restaurant *Der Sturm*. They'd purchased concert tickets months in advance for the season-opening performance of the Bern Symphony, and both were excited to attend. Maria had arranged her classes so that she could remain that night in Bern and then catch the first train back to Zurich the next morning.

Arriving early in the white columned music hall, they checked their coats, climbed the steps to the balcony seats, and watched as the auditorium began to fill. "Interesting," said Maria pointing to her program near curtain time, "I'd forgotten that Herr Schelle was going to be the conductor tonight. This should be good."

"Yes, I remembered seeing his name when the schedule was announced this summer," replied Carl. "I think he's the best guest conductor that the symphony invites." Maria nodded in agreement. They both appreciated Herr Schelle's approach to the music and the orchestra. His conducting style was to remain in the background until he was needed, and then provide just enough guidance to maintain control and direction. In contrast, the principal conductor, Herr Grass, was much more energetic and showy. Although he could occasionally pull more out of the musicians, his own performance on the podium became a distraction rather than letting the music take form and speak for itself.

Autumn and winter demanded more indoor activities from the city's residents, so this was the first symphony to play after a summer of lighter fare in smaller venues. "Isn't that Paul?" asked Maria as the orchestra seated itself, pointing to the front row of violins.

"Yes," said Carl. "He said that he's signed on to the symphony for this year at least, but I was a little shocked when he told me that he wants to quit music and devote his time to drawing. Had you heard that?" Maria shook her head as Herr Schelle raised his baton.

Beethoven's 6th 'Pastoral' Symphony seemed the perfect piece for the season with its memories of summer and storms of autumn on full display. They fell into the music with the first teasing notes. The opening, with its swirling repetition, intimated how the work would progress, and towards the end of the first movement the circular sweeps folded in on themselves and overlapped like wind gusting through the grasses and trees. Time had seemed to disappear until they were suddenly on their feet with the rest of the audience in thunderous applause at the conclusion.

They waited after the concert to search out Paul and congratulate him on his excellent performance, but there was such a crush of audience members and instrumentalists that they decided this would be too difficult. Donning their coats, they walked home together arm-in-arm down the frosty lamp-lit streets.

"Wasn't that good?" asked Maria as she tightened her arm against his. "I know it's meant to be about the countryside, but for some reason the opening this time reminded me of Goethe's 'On the Lake' where he describes the twinkling sunlight like stars on the scattered waves and the breezes blowing through the bay."

"Yes, I thought it was an excellent concert," said Carl. He was continually amazed at what Maria could draw out of performances, especially those that he either didn't understand or felt were too familiar. "So, maybe you can explain the time signature of the second movement? I tried to follow, but it was like a quick waltz, but not really in waltz time."

"I think it's a 12/8 tempo," said Maria. "Think of it as triplets played over a four-beat measure."

"Ah," said Carl counting a beat on his fingers, "Now I see it. You know, in this performance I was totally taken with how much Beethoven played with time in the Pastoral. There was that pause at the beginning, and then the total halts when the birds sang, and later a trumpet blast and then the storm completely stopped the music."

"That's funny, I noticed the same thing, Carl, so maybe it was how Herr Schelle handled the orchestra. I was also struck by what godlike power a composer really has, doesn't he? In most baroque music, we can be guaranteed that the tempo will remain constant and beat out the same time until the end of the piece. We're lulled into thinking that the universe he creates is constant, however, in reality the composer can play with time as much as he wants to. You know," she continued in another vein, "I so loved how he wove in elements of country life – the opening vista and birds, the babbling brook, the peasant dancers, the storm. I've started working on a book about landscape poetry and music, and I think this concert might be the real anchor for that."

As they walked on, Maria began to describe the difficulty some of her science-based students had in understanding poetry. As she talked, Carl found himself thinking about what time really meant in music and realized that time, to the listener, could be deceptive. The melody could proceed at an unhurried, leisurely pace surrounded by lightning fast *arpeggios*, but the tempo would be perceived as slow, and a melody could be very fast with a slow tedious bass line, and the listener could pick out that tempo as being quick. It was when the rhythms of the melody and accompaniment were blended or exchanged, like in the final movement they'd just heard, that the listener would find himself in a state of suspension, riding along with no temporal compass and waiting for resolution. As he listened to Maria, he had a strange feeling that maybe time was changeable and free of the pocket watch, at least in the concert hall.

CHAPTER 6

A few days after Maria had returned to Zurich, Carl rose early and delivered two violins to Master Ehrlich – he'd wanted to be in and out of the school before classes began – and so had arrived just as the sun was coming up. He found the music teacher wrestling with music stands in the middle of the room.

"Carl!" he said in welcome. "That was a fast turnaround for those violins – please go ahead and set them on the desk."

"Yes, it turned out that they were easy repairs," said Carl as he made a space on the only free area he could find. As Master Ehrlich worked his way toward him through the chairs and stands, Carl looked at the violin cases lined up against the walls, in some places two and three deep. "How do the students ever find their own instruments?" he asked in wonder.

"Oh, they know them," said Master Ehrlich, "and besides they're numbered..." he suddenly paused and, speaking more to himself than to Carl, groaned, "Oh, Ehrlich, you old fool! I'm sorry, Carl - we have an inventory with records of which instrument goes with each student. Damn! That list should help show us which bow Jan should have – just a minute," and Master Ehrlich left the room to go fetch his records from the administration office.

Master Ehrlich hustled back into the room with several ledgers in hand. He immediately apologized for not remembering his records in the first place. Leafing the pages and scanning the ledgers he finally said, "Here we are. Two years ago, Jan was assigned violin number 32 that Heinzman had the year before, and the bow should have the same number."

Neither of them remembered a number etched on the newly discovered bow – only a letter stamped on the screw, but Carl said he'd make sure there were no numbers of any kind scratched on it when he was back in his shop. Then, just to be sure, they searched through the bow cases from all of the violins that hadn't been taken home for practicing the night before and found none labeled with the number 32. "Well, I'll keep my eyes peeled here," said Master Ehrlich sounding overwhelmed, "but at least we have it documented now that if the discovered bow has no number, it does not belong to Jan. Please continue to help us find its rightful owner though." Carl said that he would try, but thought to himself that he hadn't a clue as to how that could be done.

◄■►

It was crisp in the shadows and warm in the sunshine as Carl walked back to his workshop feeling that it was good to get some exercise and be out and about while the weather near the onset of winter was still so pleasant. Approaching the shop, he could just make out Peer sitting by the stove with his constant companion – Flecken was curled in his lap. By the time he descended the steps and opened the shop door, Peer was sweeping around the work bench and Flecken was stretching. Carl smiled to himself.

Carl had installed a smaller stove in his shop that he used to heat an attached medium-diameter metal pipe. He had Peer light a fire in that firebox and while the stove warmed, he filled a long narrow tray with water and set it and the thin purfling strips on the workbench. He was going to make a black/white/black pattern and he cut the strips to their approximate lengths before drops of water tossed on the heated pipe bounced back off and told him that it was now hot enough to create steam.

Carl was quietly humming as he immersed himself in the task. Wood bending was an amazing process and took some skill to get it right, but now it seemed like second nature to him. The wood used in instrument construction was very stiff and would normally snap when bent – depending on the species it could break very easily. The trick was to move the wood gently back and forth against the hot pipe until it suddenly became very elastic and could move into any shape with relative ease. Too much pressure too soon might cause a break, lingering over the pipe could scorch the wood, and uneven pressure could twist the piece. Carl began to work on the new purfling strips, alternating between dipping them in the tray, bending them on the pipe, and checking the bent strips against the channel they were to be set in until finally the shape was right and the fit was made. After finishing that, he still had some more time, and so he next tackled the finicky job of cutting the ends of each group of purfling with a mitered angle so that where they met at each end of the "C" shaped waist would result in a perfect point. Satisfied, he gently pressed them with some glue into the waiting channels, but in some spots a couple of taps of the hammer were required for a good seating. With the last inset in place, he leaned back and admired his day's work. *But is this like putting rouge on a pig?* he wondered when he remembered the poor workmanship that had gone into Michael's school violin in the first place.

◀■▶

He'd walked to a nearby square in the early evening, and again Carl found two opposing pages in the sketchbook spread open on his lap – one with his attempts to sketch the buildings of Bern as they tumbled down to a sharp bend of the Aare, and one filled with his rambling doodles as his thoughts wandered. He was concentrating on the building sketch, amazed again at his inability to capture the proper perspective. His rubber eraser was just about to rub out an entire section of the drawing when a hand was on his arm and someone said, "Wait."

Somehow Carl was not surprised or even embarrassed by the interruption and looked up with curiosity to see Paul staring down at his efforts.

"What's wrong with that?" queried Paul. "It looks like an excellent start to me." With a sour face, Carl held up his sketch so that, from Paul's viewpoint, it lined up with the section of town he'd been struggling with.

"Not even a close match," lamented Carl. "There's absolutely no resemblance between what I've started and the scene below. In fact, if there was such a thing as a reverse perspective, this would be it. The slope down actually looks like it is somehow moving uphill - and look at this building – it looks like it's jumping out of the page!"

"No, no, that's good! Just fill it in and it'll be fantastic!" exclaimed Paul.

"Now, there's no need to be rude," started Carl.

"Wait, I'm being serious," said Paul. "You should never abandon such a fine beginning."

Carl was flabbergasted. "What are you talking about, Paul?" he asked. "This mess bears no resemblance whatsoever to reality. It's obviously a far cry from the scene we can both see with our own eyes, and far removed from anything a real painter would accept."

"Carl," said Paul. "You're looking at paintings the way that I look at music – do you mind if I sit down for a moment and explain?"

Carl's feathers were a little ruffled, but he'd known Paul for years and appreciated that he'd recently been to art school. Carl nodded and off-handedly waved at the empty spot next to him for Paul to take a seat. Paul settled himself into the waiting chair and leaned back casually. "Let me guess, the reason you like the old masters – Rembrandt, Van Dyke, Vermeer – is because the more realistic or like a photograph the painting is the better. Right?"

Carl nodded, shrugged, and said, "Well, of course. The more realistic *is* the better – that's the point of art, isn't it?"

"Ha!" laughed Paul. "If your idea of what comprises art is stuck in the last century! There are new masters since then, you know, and they're taking us in new directions."

"Now, wait," replied Carl, "you're saying that just because art has changed, maybe even for the worse, that we need to change how we view it? The recent stuff is just a fad, don't you think? What if we just don't like it?"

"Take my case," said Paul. "I now see that my appreciation of music is anchored in the last centuries and I view it in exactly the same way as you see the visual arts. When I hear compositions that don't stick to a strict time sequence or veer off with no apparent melody, it drives me absolutely mad. But that's only because I can't let the form progress – it has to be 'real' to me or similar to how I've come to love it, to be valid. Otherwise, it's just an unformed mess that has no predictability."

"Exactly what I was saying about art," retorted Carl.

"But I know what you mean," said Paul nodding furiously in agreement. "Now, take your drawings for example. You're stumped by trying to make the perspective match what you see with your eyes, thinking that this is the proper way to draw." Carl started to speak, but Paul raised a finger to stop him. "What you need to realize, and what I've recently come to understand, is that whatever perspective you have is the correct one. There's no 'true' perspective that lies out there – it's your own viewpoint that's the valid one, and that perspective is beautiful and what *you* must be true to. Any way you choose to portray reality is the right way to render it. We all try and capture what we see in a drawing, but why is a copy of an exact photograph the best? Really, what you should focus on is how you feel about what you see or imagine and try and capture that instead."

Paul picked up the page of doodles. "Look at this," he said. "No one in the entire world has created anything like these images, and it probably portrays more of your inner world than anything else you could try and depict. This is absolutely valid art, and actually quite good."

"God," said Carl. "I think I might understand what you're saying, but that'll never change my opinion that this is absolute rubbish. It looks like we're both stuck in the past; you with music, and me with art."

Paul nodded and sat back with an oddly satisfied smile. He thumped the sketchbook with his finger. "This is not rubbish," he said adamantly.

CHAPTER 7

Albert had said that there was no reason to bring the repaired violin all the way to his apartment since he wanted to get out of the house anyway. He'd suggested that, as before, they meet at a spot that was somewhat equidistant between their two homes, and *Zum Bären* fit the criterion. The sun had set when Carl washed up his dinner plates, locked his apartment, and fetched Lina from the shop below. It was a peaceful evening, but dark – cool with no wind and high clouds.

Carl greeted Max and ordered a beer from Frieda as he awaited Albert, and the man and the beer both arrived at the same time. Business was first, so after Albert ordered a bock beer suggested by Frieda because it had just been brewed for the season, Carl opened the case and took the violin out for him to examine. "Lina!" Albert exclaimed. Without a qualm, he took her up, grabbed the bow, stood, and played a little lilting tune to the amusement of the rest of the tavern patrons who clapped loudly at the end.

"We need to hire you!" shouted Max with a laugh from behind the counter. Albert grinned in appreciation and gave a lady-like curtsy in reply. He then sat and more seriously bent his ear close to the body of the violin and bowed both lightly and deeply on each string. With another grin, he set Lina in her case and said, "You know, she sounds a little better than when she left."

When Carl started to say, "Well, I should hope…" Albert smiled more broadly and said, "Of course meaning before that odd occurrence with the other bridge. No, this is fine work, and I love how Lina sounds now!"

Seeing the case being snapped shut, the group at a nearby table suddenly shouted for an encore and Albert was up to the task. He played a more somber piece with dramatic flairs and ended in a deep, sweeping stage bow. He laughed at the applause and then indicated with his hands that he was done for the night. When he sat back down, he carefully tucked Lina away and then said, "Carl, it still bothers me that someone tampered with her. Do you know anything about that Viennese model of bridge that you just replaced?"

"No," said Carl, "I wasn't familiar with the company, but I ran into Herr Zenger who's a local luthier and he said that he's seen a few of their bridges before when he worked in Munich. Has anyone else you've played with mentioned anything strange with their instruments?"

"I asked them that very thing two nights ago. I borrowed my friend Michele's violin so that I could play with a quartet, and everyone thought it very odd that my bridge had been swapped for another. No one has a clue why that would have happened."

They then talked a little about the cost of the replacement, and both easily came to an agreed amount of twenty francs.

Carl said, "I enjoyed our little chat above the river the other night, but I have to ask, what is it you do for a living? Are you an astronomy professor or something? You seem to know a lot about the stars and light."

"Oh, I wish I was a professor," said Albert. "I've finished my courses at the University in Zurich, and I'm in the process of writing my Doctoral thesis, but right now I'm just a working stiff."

"You mentioned the university in Zurich? My wife Maria is working there! She teaches the literature courses - I don't suppose you know her, Maria Veblen?"

"That's funny, my sister's name is Maria, but we call her Maja. Veblen? No, the name isn't familiar to me. Of course, I haven't been in Zurich for four years so..."

"Oh, then that explains it," cut in Carl. "She's only been there for two years so you couldn't have crossed paths." Albert shook his head in agreement. "She seems to really enjoy the University," continued Carl, "but it's my hope that we don't end up moving there. I mean Zurich is fine, but a little big for me. Maria's getting attached though, I can tell."

"Ah, I loved Zurich," said Albert as his beer arrived and Carl took a few sips of his own. The noise level in the tavern had not yet risen from the dinner conversation level to the more boisterous drinking conversation level, so they were able to enjoy a discussion at their leisure without straining to be heard.

"I'm sorry about the digression, so then, what is it you do now?" asked Carl.

"I miraculously landed a clerking job in the Patent Office here, and I review submitted designs and decide whether to accept them for patent or else I refer them on for further work. My area of expertise is primarily electrical equipment and concepts – something my father was involved in, as it happens. It's an acceptable position for now, but, as I say, I'd hoped to maybe teach, or find appointment to a more academic post."

"In astronomy?"

"Oh, no, not really. I'm more intrigued by light than by the stars themselves, although they are amazing things, aren't they?" Carl nodded as he sipped his beer. "My main interest is in physics," continued Albert, "in how everything is put together or interacts, and in the way things behave at the elemental level. So, I guess the Patent Office job is vaguely related to that in some ways." He paused and stared off across the room. "I have to say, the slow pace there does give me time to think about the concepts I'm really interested in though. Like the workings of light, for example - now, there's something that's worth spending some mental energy on."

"What's it about light that you find so interesting?" asked Carl, now intrigued.

"Oh, light's a tantalizing little puzzle!" Albert said immediately leaning forward. "To ponder how it's produced, how it propagates, how it acts. For instance, did you know that…" Albert appeared to physically catch himself by the collar and pull himself back in his chair. He took a deep breath, a sip of beer, and with a little smile said, "Sorry about that. I need to watch myself. I've been absolutely consumed by this subject lately and I've almost nattered my friends to death on the topic. One fellow at work won't even speak to me about it anymore. Light's an obsession for me right now, and I have a hard time putting it aside – forgive me again, Carl. We should talk about music or something of interest to you – your work, perhaps?"

"Well, I love music, but I'm also more than happy to talk about things I know little about," said Carl, and then with a sheepish smile continued, "and the older I get and with the more advances in science there seem to be every day, there really is an ever-increasing amount about which I'm woefully uninformed, I can tell you. I'm not a scientist like you, you know."

"Actually, by admitting that, you're smarter than most professors I know!" exclaimed Albert laughing loudly enough to catch the attention of the people at the next table. Then in a lower voice, "We all really know so little about so much, don't we?"

There was an awkward silence and then Albert took the initiative. "Well, if you don't mind then – I'd be happy to talk about light!" Seeing Carl's approval, he smiled and took a few sips of his bock. "Well, for some background, you probably know from school that light propagates itself as waves?"

Propagates? Carl thought for a moment. "Ah, travels," he said aloud and grinned at Albert over his own beer glass. This time he was more prepared for a lecture and was drawn to Albert's take on the world.

"Yes, travels... travels," Albert said again more quietly before he continued. "Of course you know light travels as waves, because that's what the teachers were all taught, and so when we learn that from them, we believe we know it as a hard fact. But I've been thinking that we may be partially wrong about that assumption. You see, at the heart of it, we don't really know what light is, fundamentally, and so we hypothesize about it based on the properties we observe. There was an important experiment done by a man named Young about 50 years ago making it evident that light is a wave. Do you know this experiment?" Carl paused and then shook his head. "Well, Mr. Young did something with light that's very similar to what we can see with wave action on the surface of water. If you make two sources of waves, say by dropping two stones into a pond, or by letting the waves from the ocean come in through two openings in a jetty, each source will make a series of waves in arcs like a fan, and you'll see a pattern where the arcs meet and the waves interact. Where the crests of two waves converge, they amplify each other, and where a crest meets a trough they negate or interfere with each other. The resulting effect seen from above shows dead or calm spaces where the interference has occurred."

Carl nodded for him to continue.

"Mr. Young passed light through two very thin vertical slits and, low and behold, rather than two vertical slits of light on the other side, there appeared a pattern of light and dark bands – dark where there was interference from the troughs and peaks of two waves canceling each other out. This is exactly what should happen if light propagates itself as a wave."

Albert smiled and dramatically rubbed his hands together as if in anticipation of a welcome meal. "That's all well and good, and so we think we know what light is. However, there are things that light does that make me wonder. Just a few years ago, Herr Planck, a physicist in Berlin, published a paper on black-body radiation that explained observations about light that don't support it being a wave."

"Wait, I think you just lost me," said Carl. "In fact, I know you did - black-body radiation?"

"Sorry," said Albert and paused. "I think another beer will help," and he drained his glass.

"Another here, too," piped up Carl as Frieda came over at Albert's upraised hand. Albert started to speak again but appeared lost in thought until she returned with their foaming beers. "Max says these are on the house for the fine concert," said Frieda warmly.

"Then, cheers, Frieda," and they both raised their mugs in appreciation as she ducked with a smile and moved over to another table.

Albert's thoughts were already back on physics. "I think I have a good example," he said as he stood, leaned over the table, and stuck his finger into his bock. He pulled the wet tip out and then drew a flat line with a dome-shaped bump in the middle on the tabletop with the brown liquid.

"Let's say that this graph or line is based on actual measurements we've made about the relationship between energy and light frequency – and we don't need the details for this – it resembles a wave-shaped hill. Now, the perfect model or equation would match this shape exactly for each measurement of energy we put into it. But, historically, physicists have had to rely on an equation that matches this shape very well - up to a certain point." And he wetted his finger again and traced the lower section of the hill, from the flat ground and then going up one side.

"But near the top, the equation keeps going straight up, like this." His finger zoomed up to Carl's beer glass across the table. Carl reflexively moved his stein out of the path. "The more energy put in, the predicted frequency goes through the roof – where your beer was. So, the formula clearly doesn't match reality, which is this bump way down here. Does this make sense so far?" asked Albert.

"I think so, and like you said - the goal was to find an equation that did match the hill?" asked Carl.

"Exactly!" said Albert sitting back down. "And Herr Planck did just that. He came up with an equation that perfectly matched the measurements scientists have taken. But the problem for him was that, up close, his hill was really made up of a series of steps, like the Great Pyramid, and he was left scratching his head about why this might be the case. The assumption has always been that the relationship we were looking at was smooth, like a wave, and not stair-stepped.

"In my own investigations, I now think that the equation makes perfect sense if light is visualized as packets of energy - just like the blocks that make up the Great Pyramid. All of the packets of the same energy make up a level of the pyramid, and all the levels together make up the pyramid itself."

"But what about waves and that experiment with the slits?" asked Carl.

"Perplexing, isn't it?" asked Albert. "Oddly, I now realize that light acts as both waves and energy packets. It still fits all of the properties of waves, but also is made up of individual particles or energized packets, and so it matches Herr Planck's formula as well." Albert sat back and held out his arms. "Imagine! Centuries ago Isaac Newton thought of light as particles, then the evidence seemed to point to it being a wave. Now I'm thinking it may be both!" He let his arms fall down to his lap in conclusion. "But enough for now, I'll tell you more about a few other theories I've arrived at some time later, if you like." Albert grabbed his stein and took another sip of beer leaving foam that clung briefly to his moustache.

"That would be wonderful," said Carl. The conversation switched to banter about the coming winter weather and their families. Albert agreed to play Lina and to get in touch with Carl if she needed any more adjustments.

"By the way, I assume you play the violin as well as work on them?" asked Albert.

"Of course, just not that well," replied Carl modestly.

"You see, we could use a fifth violin on some of the pieces we play in one little group Lina and I meet with," said Albert. "If you're interested, I can talk to the rest of the fellows the next time we gather and see if they want to fill in the extra parts to make it a quintet."

"Well, I haven't played with a group for some time, and become nervous around solo parts, but if it's third violin, it would be fun to get out and perform some," said Carl.

"Well, then I'd say you're in, but I'll let you know what the others think. And thanks again for the great work on the bridge so I'll have a decent instrument to play," said Albert, as they got up, donned their coats, and walked together out into the crisp evening.

CHAPTER 8.

Lingering in the apartment over breakfast, Carl finished reading the newspaper and then leaned back staring out at the shaded street. The morning sunlight was just hitting the opposite building at the highest point and he watched two pigeons fly up and perch on the windowsill that was newly illuminated. He found himself wishing that Maria was with him more often. He missed her presence and her love, of course, but also her advice. They needed to have a more in-depth discussion about their finances, and to really sit down and decide on their long-range plans for living together in either Bern or Zurich, or continuing on with their current sub-optimal situation.

A knock on the door startled him. Peer was trying to try to see inside through the exterior reflections with cupped hands against the small window on the door. *Damn, I'm late in opening up the shop,* thought Carl, *and Peer is never this early.* Then he yelled, "Come in, Peer!" and threw his assistant the keys for downstairs when Peer opened the door. "Oh, and here's a little something for that good-for-nothing cat," he said smiling as he grabbed a bowl of chicken scraps he'd set aside from last night's dinner and handed it to the boy. Carl cleaned up from breakfast and headed down himself soon afterwards.

Peer had the fire in the stove started, and Carl returned to the new top for the student violin that Michael had destroyed. He took a curved scraper and slowly brought the surface of the exposed, roughly seated purflings down to the level of the rest of the soundboard. He showed Peer that there were a few gaps remaining in spots between the edge of the purfling and the spruce top and had him make a mixture of glue and sawdust and work this into any tiny spaces that he found. After this glue mixture dried, he had Peer sand the top carefully on both sides.

When Peer was finished and called him over, Carl picked up the top and using his thumb, gently deflected it in several locations – looking to see how much the thumb pressure could move the surface especially in the area where the bridge was to be placed. Holding the top by the rim, he also tapped in several spots, trying to detect how the tone of this wood was going to sound. The top was now ready for a bass bar to be glued to the underside, reinforcing the flexible spruce against the downward pressure exerted by the thickest strings on the bridge. The bar would run from tip to tail and spread the vibrations of the bass notes out along the entire top, adding responsiveness, especially at the lower registers.

In a slow but necessary process, Carl carved the bar to match the inner violin shape and glued it in, forcing some extra upward bend to counteract the opposing pressure exerted by the bridge when the strings were installed. When the glue was dry, he took a small plane and gently removed much of the height of the bar at the tip and tail ends to minimize the weight, creating a domed shape in the process. Some tapping on the other side told him when he had about the proper amount of wood removed from the supportive bar.

He'd been so engaged in this work that he'd completely missed lunch, though he had joined Peer for a cup of hot cocoa while the glue was setting. Now the shadows were already long again outside, and Johann was waiting eagerly for Peer to finish up. Carl gave Peer his weekly wages, and Peer was gone like a shot. Carl trudged slowly upstairs to make dinner.

◄■►

He had no idea where Flecken disappeared to each night, nor how the cat seemed to know when he descended from the apartment. As soon as he stepped onto the street, Flecken appeared from nowhere and hopped up on the shutter doors. Carl shooed the cat aside and opened the shop, waiting for Peer to arrive and get set up for work. Once the boy was in his apron and the cat was settled under the warming stove, Carl made sure that Peer had enough jobs and tasks on hand to stay busy for the entire day, if necessary. A friend of Carl's who owned a stringed instrument store across town had been in touch and wanted Carl to help him evaluate a batch of violins he'd purchased at auction earlier that summer in Vienna.

Süd Hoffman acquired his nickname because he came from Southern Germany, and the name had stuck. Carl found it odd, but perhaps that's what nicknames were for – tacking a quirky descriptor where it fit. The name of his store was even 'Der Süden', or The South, and the door was open when Carl arrived. Süd called him into the back room where Carl found him surrounded by crumpled newspapers and packing crates. Together, he and Carl toted ten violin cases into another less cluttered room and opened each one. They all were fine looking instruments, and for Carl, they offered a welcome relief from the hum-drum school violins he saw in plenty at this time of year. He lifted, rotated, and plucked the strings of each one in turn and realized what high-quality craftsmanship was in front of him.

Süd and Carl each chose a bow, and one by one, picked up each violin and played – one at time, in a duet, or at once as the mood took them. After an hour, they agreed that one violin stood out far above the rest. They took turns trying out different melodies on it while hitting all of the registers. Carl picked up and played each of the other nine while Süd played the exceptional instrument and each time they nodded to themselves.

"That is a very special violin you have there, Süd." And Süd beamed in agreement.

They sat in silence for a time as Süd's wife had brought them some coffee. Carl was suddenly surprised at how tired he felt and welcomed the large mug.

"Listening to that violin made me think of a poetic analogy," said Carl.

"OK, let's hear it," said Süd.

"The other violins are beautiful and a joy to play. I'd say that they're like a rushing stream that's both fun and lively, but where it's difficult to see the rocks underneath. This violin is like a deep cool channel with a still surface and so clear that you can see everything from a pebble to a boulder underneath."

"Exactly!" exclaimed Süd. "Every tone comes out crystal clear."

"Almost like it was made by that Strad what's-his-name," joked Carl and they both laughed. But both jumped up at the same time to recheck the label within.

The name on the label, as they both knew it would be from checking previously, was Storioni, and Süd was acquainted with some of the instruments he'd made at the beginning of the last century. To look at, the instrument was plainer than the others, but sonically it stood out above them all. Examining the violin closely, the wood appeared to be of even a lesser quality than that of the others, but somehow Storioni had created something magical out of it.

Süd was eager to open a bottle of wine to celebrate, but Carl said that he wanted to wait until he'd examined each violin to see what, if anything, was needed to have them ready for sale. He spent another few hours on the lot and came away saying that several needed new strings and polishing, and a few needed new tuning pegs, but not a single one required any major work. Since the auction had taken place in Vienna, he also looked for any bridges that might match the odd one he'd found on Albert's violin, but none were from that maker. Joining Süd in his living quarters above the store, he handed him a list he'd made for reference.

Süd was overjoyed and, while Carl had been working, had asked his wife to set an extra place for dinner - so he invited Carl to join them. Carl was exhausted but also energized by the day and happily accepted the invitation. After thanking Süd's wife for the lovely meal, the two sat next to a warm fire and enjoyed some more of the wine that had been served with dinner.

Süd groaned as he lifted his feet up and onto a stool. "I'm turning 55 the day after tomorrow, if you can believe it, and I feel like life is catching up with me. When I was a boy, each day in the summer seemed to last the whole summer, and now each year literally shoots by with the blink of an eye as they say. The contradiction is that I'm now plodding through that blink rather than sprinting. How about you? How old are you now, Carl?"

"Thirty-seven," said Carl. "And I know what you mean. I can't believe that I'm already settling into my middle age when I'm still eighteen inside. My young shop-helper, Peer, can get bored after two minutes with nothing to do, and I get down to the shop and look up and the sun's already setting."

"Ha!" laughed Süd. "I'm still eighteen too, so maybe we're really always the same age!"

"Yeah," said Carl. "Without the stamina, hair, or looks," and he smiled sadly into the fire. "How is it fair that violins just get better with age?"

◄ ■ ►

The bells outside were tolling the noon hour when the chimes on the door tinkled and Albert stepped into the shop just as Peer was leaving. "Hi Carl," he said.

"Hello, Albert!" greeted Carl. "It was good to see you the other night."

"Yes, I really enjoyed our talk, too. Well… my talk," and he grinned as they shook hands. "I thought I'd drop by during my lunch break and pay for the great work you did on the bridge. Lina is very happy." He walked over to the workbench. "Hey, nice shop," he said as he admired the top that was Carl's latest project. "This looks fascinating. How long have you been working on violins?"

"Since my teens, at least," Carl replied. "I followed in my father's footsteps, so I've been making sawdust since he first allowed me into the shop. Maria and I have been situated in this spot for the last six years or so and business has been good." He patted his stomach as it made an unseemly noise. "Say, if you haven't had lunch yet, would you care for some sausage or cheese and some bread?" asked Carl. "I myself am starving."

Albert paused for a moment and then said, "Sure, that would be great if you're making some for yourself - that would save me a stop at home on my way back to work." He sat down on the nearest stool and passed his fingers over the carved spruce. "I'm afraid that the only things I can build are in my own mind," he said admiringly. "And nothing concrete has come out of it yet."

"And the things I build in my own mind turn to vapor," joked Carl. "I'll be right back."

"Oh, and here's the money I owe you," said Albert getting up and handing over twenty francs as Carl opened the door and was about to head up the stairs. Albert wandered absentmindedly around the shop, and Carl soon returned with a tray of French bread, sausage, cheese, mustard and tomato.

Albert was standing near the stove with the bulk of Flecken cradled in the crook of his arm, the cat's back legs and tail dangling out behind. "I found your shop assistant, and he's certainly got some mass to him," he grinned.

"Lord knows how he found me," said Carl. "He snuck in one day when the door was open and adopted us as his home base. You'd think he would've been happier at the cheese store, wouldn't you?" throwing a bit of sausage on the floor.

"Looks like he does pretty well here!" said Albert and set Flecken down for his treat.

"Well, we didn't start out to spoil him, but it looks like he has us trained. Here, help yourself."

"This is a really impressive workshop," said Albert as he constructed his sandwich, following Carl's lead. "I can see that it would take years to arrive at the point of such craftsmanship. That, and the dedication to stick with it."

"It's funny," replied Carl, spreading mustard on a slice of bread. "I've never really taken the time to consider anything else. It's probably the only thing at which I'm the least bit competent, and trying other occupations would have only led me back here to this same job."

"Hmm," mumbled Albert around a bite of sandwich. After a swallow of some water he said, "I wonder where I'll end up? I seem to have antagonized all the professors I've ever studied under so that I can't get recommendations out of any of them, and yet I'd really like to be one of them. Isn't that funny? I don't think any of them would want me to join them at the university though."

"It's probably not as bad as you imagine," offered Carl.

"No, I think that some of them really hate me," smiled Albert. "It's gotten to the point where I sometimes wonder if perhaps my surname and Jewish heritage have something to do with it. It's either that or the fact that I love discussion and debate - but not being lectured to. Truthfully, I know I have an issue with authority figures. Maybe as a lecturer myself it wouldn't be so bad, but perhaps I'll end up having to avoid universities all together." He sighed. "For the present though, this Patent Office job is actually becoming comfortable for me, although I can't picture myself in it forever."

"It seems to me that you're not at an age where you have to worry too much about acquiring a permanent position just yet," said Carl. "I had no real choice in the matter, but I'd think that you'll have many possibilities open to you. How old are you, by the way?"

"Twenty-five, and with the time it took to land even this job, I really wonder about those possibilities," reflected Albert as he continued with his sandwich. "I'm also becoming aware that my carefree student days are now behind me. My mere acquaintances are melting away, and I'm left with only a few remaining stalwart friends. My life's narrowed down, on the outside, to work, home, and music, but on the inside, there is only physics. There's not much space for many more people or duties in it anyway."

"Well, if you ever do have the time, I, myself, would love to hear more about your physics. It's interesting that you're hoping to become a professor, because I find that instead of just talking about the subject, you're actually trying to explain it to me, and I appreciate that. Not that I necessarily understand all of what you say, but it provides fertilizer for other thoughts to grow."

Albert nodded, choked a little on his bite, and laughing said, "Hopefully not like horse shit!" After a coughing fit he continued. "You know, I have two friends that I discuss my thoughts with in detail, and Mileva also enjoys digging into the weeds, so to speak, but I rarely have a chance to explain the theories in more general terms. It's also good for me to step back and say simply what I mean in plain language. Like occasionally cleaning the mirror."

Carl finished his sandwich and consolidated the fixings back on the tray. Albert looked at his watch and commented, "Well, back to work," yet he took his time closing the watch cover and held the timepiece in the palm of his hand for some moments. "Well, back to work," Albert repeated with a sigh, slowly returning the watch to his pocket. "Everything is about time lately, at work and in my mind. We've suddenly had a flurry of patent applications about various methods for synchronizing the clocks across Switzerland, especially using electricity. A few even consider using light to do it. Anyway, they make for very interesting applications. Thanks so much for the sandwich and the chat," said Albert as he headed for the door. "Say, we should try and take a hike some time, if you'd like. I have to warn you though, that I can be known to drift away from conversation when I'm out in nature."

"Certainly, I have a flexible schedule and there's nothing I like better than a walk in the woods," agreed Carl.

A patent clerk, thought Carl later as he was doing some sanding. *That's funny – to me Old Carl looks like a luthier, Max looks like a tavern keeper, and Paul looks like a musician. Maybe because they all act the way I expect them to, and somehow their personalities fit their jobs. But Albert? I'd never have guessed he was a clerk by just looking at him – I'm still betting he'll end up being a professor.*

CHAPTER 9

The next morning, angling the top he'd fashioned for Michael's violin in the available light, Carl checked for uniformity - that the curves comprising the dome shape were smooth and the wood was unmarred - and was satisfied that it was ready to be glued to the body. He slowly carved the slightly exposed linings on the sides to match the angle and shape of the matching top, checking the fit after every few passes of the plane or the sanding block. When the join was finally perfect, he applied hot hide glue to the top of the sides and linings and situated the new top in place. He then quickly arranged a series of wooden clamps around the perimeter and tightened the screws uniformly, solidly fixing the top to the original student violin body, and then set the assembly aside for the glue to dry. The image of this top - dinged, scratched, and marred in future years jumped into his head, but he immediately quashed the thought.

Noting that the shop was relatively clean and knowing that he was going to be out for the afternoon, he let Peer off for the rest of the day. With an unexpected yip, Peer threw on his coat and was up the stairs with a barely audible "Thanks!" before he disappeared. After puttering around on some of the other violins, and feeling satisfied with his progress, Carl set his focus on the mysterious bow. He snatched up the bow case Master Ehrlich had given him, chased a protesting Flecken out the door, and locked up his shop; he'd decided to take the bow to the police station located next to the Kunstmuseum, and grab a late lunch along the river on the way. He headed toward the banks of the Aare and then west on Brunngasshalde. Just before reaching the Kornhausbrucke Bridge, now busy with day-time traffic, he stopped in a café and bought a roll stuffed with thick slabs of cheese and mustard and sat for a spell at one of the outdoor tables, watching traffic and munching on the crusty bun. He'd also bought a milk coffee and washed the roll down with it. A light wind that was tugging at the looser pieces of clothing on passersby also quickly cooled his coffee so that it wasn't as satisfying in the end as it had been at the beginning. Warmed on the inside and now chilled on the outside, he continued his walk to the station.

A police officer with the regulation brass-buttoned double tunic and short hat with a fan of fluff sticking up at the front directed him to the main desk. He thought there was something commanding, but at the same time silly, about the uniform. The desk officer listened to his query and then led him to the sub-commander's office – the officer in charge of thefts.

At first glance, the sub-commander appeared to be one of those people who lacked vigor and had drifted and finally settled into an eddy in his job. He was thick, had a huge mustache, and turned his eyes in a slow manner towards the door when Carl entered. Carl expected a disinterested and slow interview.

"Mortensen," said the sub-commander standing quickly with both a ready hand and smile. Carl was taken aback and chided himself for making rash assumptions as he shook the man's hand. The look on Carl's face made the officer assume that it was the name that caused the confusion. "Swedish," said Mortensen, "my parents moved to Bern when I was a child and we've stayed here ever since."

"Ah," nodded Carl. "It's a pleasure to meet you, I'm Carl Veblen."

"A pleasure to meet you, as well. What can I do for you?"

Carl set the violin bow case on the desk, opened it and extracted the bow, and then related the story given him by Master Ehrlich. He ended by explaining that the school didn't want to be overly involved since young Jan had a well-connected father.

"Yes, I'm acquainted with Ratsherr Rauss, and he has been known to flex his political muscles on occasion. So, to sum up - we don't know the origins of this bow, when it appeared, or how it came to be in Jan's possession? And we know that it is valuable," Mortensen had ticked these off on the fingers of one hand as he spoke.

"Yes to all," said Carl.

"Hmm," said Mortenson, dropping his large hand onto the desk. "It does seem like the best course of action is to see if anyone is missing such a bow, whether lost or stolen. If you wait here, I can check to see what's been reported to us in Bern as well as the rest of Switzerland. If the bow disappeared in another country, it'll be difficult to find out much unless it was incredibly valuable."

"I wouldn't say that it was overly costly – more than a student could afford and less than a maestro would find valuable," said Carl.

"Then let's hope that something's been reported here in Bern," said Mortensen, who turned and disappeared from the office for ten minutes. "Well," said Mortensen as he reappeared holding some pages of police briefings and squeezing back into his chair, "We've recently had two reports concerning violins in Switzerland. One instrument had been registered as stolen in Zurich a few weeks ago. Let's see," he said, reading, "the report says it was very valuable and made by Meinel in Germany. The bow is missing as well. The other violin was declared as missing here in Bern back in May, but was located soon after. I remember being briefed on that case by the investigator before it was rediscovered in the house. The report doesn't say, but I'd assume that the bow disappeared and then was found again along with the violin.

"Casting farther afield, we also heard of two violins stolen from an orchestra travelling by train from Rome to Milan this past July. No accompanying information was available about those thefts however."

"Thanks," said Carl a little disappointedly. "I don't know the origin of the bow, but Jan has apparently had it for well over two weeks, so it couldn't be from the German violin, and it doesn't appear to be of the caliber to match that violin anyway. But perhaps it did come from the orchestral violins in Italy. Is there a way to check on that?"

"I can run it through the normal channels, but we are not likely to hear anything for some time," replied Mortenson.

Carl thought for a moment about other possibilities, but it seemed that there was nothing more to help them with the problem at hand. "Thank you for looking into this, Herr Mortensen. I'm not sure how to proceed from here, but if you uncover anything else about stolen violin bows, could you get in touch with me?"

"Most assuredly, Herr Veblen," said Mortensen. "I also want to be informed if you learn anything. I'd hate to taint the reputation of a young student and by extension his father the Councilman, and so would do nothing unnecessarily, but I'd have no recourse if you found out it was stolen," said Mortensen, and pointedly met Carl's eyes. "It goes without saying that these things have a way of resolving themselves without police involvement," he then winked. They shook hands and Carl headed back to his shop with a bow case that somehow felt a little heavier.

◀■▶

The bell in the clock tower up the street had rung four times, and Carl was unable to get back to sleep. His mind was on the jumble of violins to be worked on in the shop below, and the image of each instrument was accompanied by a note of urgency from the school or person who'd dropped it off. Rather than mentally reviewing the list of waiting repairs to himself repeatedly, he rose and fumbled in the dark for his heavy sweater and the light-switch in the kitchen that brought immediate illumination. He was happily aware of the strange satisfaction in now having electric lights. Kindling a fire in the stove, he readied the coffee pot, and then sat next to the open cast-iron grate waiting for the room to warm and for the coffee water to boil.

He picked up a book and tried to read, but it didn't hold his interest, so he searched the darkened sitting room and found his sketch pad and a pencil. Back at the stove he drew some lines with the intent of sketching the town square from memory, but soon was absentmindedly scratching away at abstract forms. His thoughts had gone back to the pleasant memories of Süd and the wonderful Storioni violin.

That instrument had been entirely crafted from what would have been cast-off pieces of wood by other luthiers. Carl suddenly realized what a visual builder he himself had been. In approaching all of the violins he'd made as an apprentice and prior to dedicating himself to repairs, it had been the outward appearance that had mattered most to him, and the sound, although important, of course, had been secondary. Here was Storioni's instrument - not visually stunning, but sonically unparalleled. He now saw that his personal criteria for appreciation in an instrument had shifted with time – perhaps aligning more with what his father had been trying to teach him all along – to seeking a balance of form and function, appearance and sound.

How odd, he thought. *Part of the reason I gave up making instruments from scratch was because I'd set seemingly unattainable standards for myself, and yet here I've committed my life to repairing mainly second and third-rate violins. Something about this just isn't right.* They'd struggled financially the first few years of the business, but now he was busy enough that he occasionally had to turn potential customers away. Still, despite his daily contact with instruments, he suddenly felt like he was never fully in touch with any of them; had no real investment in them. Not like when he was absorbed in his own creation from start to finish.

The coffee was boiling, and so Carl poured himself a cup, dampened down the stove, and sipped at the coffee while he got dressed and then spread some strawberry jam on a slice of bread. Holding coffee and bread in one hand, he went out of the apartment and down to the shuttered doors on the street. Setting the cup to the side with the bread on top, he opened up the outer shutters and then took his early breakfast down into the shop with him.

Building another fire with wood scraps from the previous day, he went over to his supply of maple wood that was in an uneven stack against the back wall. Starting at the top he worked his way down the pile, examining and tapping each book-matched set or single piece as he went. Near the bottom of the pile was a piece that was too thin to be sliced into a book-matched pair, but still appeared to be wide and thick enough for a violin back on its own. He picked it up and tapped it as he was about to set it aside, but noticed that the resulting tone was bell-like. He took the piece, with a dark knot at one end and the beginning of a large crack along one side, and set it on the bench. He found a template outline for a violin back and placed it on the wood, maneuvering the template until he saw that it would just fit across the useable portions of the maple.

He was suddenly excited about the prospects of crafting a new violin for himself rather than simply repairing what others had made. Perhaps Old Carl had been right in continually trying to push him into building instruments of his own. And he'd known his father's wishes before he'd died – to carry on his love of the craft, even though it was his perfectionism that had partially driven Carl to instrument repair in the first place. He was busy to the extreme, but for the first time in a long while he questioned whether he really felt fulfilled in his repair business. Carl decided then and there that he needed some creativity in his life, and that building his own instrument was a good start. *But how will I ever be able to carve out the time?* immediately followed on the heels of this decision as he weighed the piece in his hand and then set it on the floor next to the stack.

CHAPTER 10

Carl had stopped by the cheese store, the green grocers, the wine shop, and was now in the bakery kitty-corner from the Munster Cathedral when he heard strains of music. He was choosing some baguettes from a basket and mindlessly absorbing the melodies coming to him from a distance when he suddenly realized that this was the concert Paul had mentioned a few weeks previously. He hurriedly grabbed some of the baguettes, quickly paid the cashier behind the tall glass cases, and ran out the door toward the cathedral.

Under the strange stone frieze depicting Saint Michael and visions of heaven and hell, he pulled open the main door and then gently squeezed through the right access off the small entry vestibule. He felt awkward toting two bags of groceries in with him and tried to keep them out of sight. As his eyes adjusted to the dim light, he soon made out the towering gothic arches of the massive cathedral which, truthfully, he never visited unless there was music present. He crept up to an empty pew, carefully stowed his bags, and was lucky enough to enjoy the majority of Paul's performance. Paul was playing Mozart backed by a chamber orchestra which included a nice execution by a young lady on a clavier.

Paul played expressively, but didn't resort to showmanship in either the quiescent or exuberant sections in the pieces. He was a natural musician and seemed to intuit when to lag just a bit behind or jump ahead of the rest of the orchestra adding an extra dimension to the music.

At the conclusion, there was a well-deserved standing ovation from the small crowd. Paul bowed graciously, but tactfully avoided all but perfunctory greetings amid the praise bestowed on him from the church officials and members of the public as if he were in a hurry to meet someone. Carl patiently waited for most of the assembled audience to disperse so he could give Paul his thanks for the invitation and to congratulate him on his performance. As he hung back, he noticed a young woman who'd been seated to the side and was also staying on the periphery.

When he finally found Paul alone at last and approached him, the young lady was doing the same. "Fantastic job as usual, Paul!" said Carl as he neared his friend.

Paul grinned and shook his hand as he said, "Thanks, Carl, and I'm glad you could make it."

"Um, did you notice I was a little late?" asked Carl sheepishly.

"No," said Paul lightly, "you must have snuck in!" and then turned to the woman whom he briefly embraced. "Carl, this is Lily, a very good friend of mine and an excellent pianist," said Paul by way of an introduction which resulted in Lily suddenly blushing. "Lily, this is Carl, an old friend of the family and the person who's kept my father's and my violins afloat over the years. Carl's father made my father's violin, and Carl also plays very well."

"You're too kind, Paul, given my level of skill," said Carl. "It's very nice to meet you Lily. Do you perform here?"

"No," replied Lily. "I'm living in Munich and met Paul when he was studying there. I come to Bern when I can to visit him and keep him honest."

Now it was Paul's turn to blush, and he grinned. "Well, no need to worry about me on that account, dear! But I love that idea about honesty - it's what life's about, after all. Be as true as you can to the inspiration that drives you forward, that's what I say. And speaking of which, I've been trying to convince Carl that his drawings are heading in the right direction for this kind of honesty, but he sees only failure in them. What do you think we can do to make him see the light, Lily?"

"Have you seen Paul's work?" asked Lily helpfully. "He's taking his drawings in a completely new direction. I haven't seen your efforts, Carl, but who knows? Maybe you are, too. Perhaps looking at Paul's art could help you see that his vision may not be that different from your own?"

"Please," pleaded Carl. "I don't know why Paul keeps thinking of me as an artist. I'm just a technician - I can repair almost any stringed instrument in town, however, if I try anything creative like art, I can't come up with anything that looks like... well, anything."

"Now, don't say can't," said Paul, "Perhaps you mean you're just untrained?"

"No, not even that," replied Carl and then deftly turned the topic to Lily's visit and her impressions of Bern. At this point they were alone in the cathedral and the sun was setting outside. Their footsteps echoed as they walked, chatting, through the chamber.

"Say, Paul," said Carl as they exited the church. "Have any of the musicians you know reported a bow missing? An exceptional one has turned up, and we can't seem to locate the owner."

"Not that I'm aware of," replied Paul. "But I'll ask around and let you know if I hear anything."

"Thanks," said Carl and they parted – Carl schlepping groceries to his apartment, and Paul and Lily arm-in-arm.

They were almost out of earshot when Carl heard Paul shout to him from across the square. "Carl!" Carl set down a parcel and waved back to show that he heard. "I just re-membered that my father mentioned a violin had disappeared from one of his classes!" Paul yelled through cupped hands. "A valuable one!"

"Thanks!" Carl hollered back, and they gave each other a final wave.

Well, thought Carl happily, *it looks like our little bow mystery might finally be solved!*

He stopped by the nearest post office and sent a message to Master Ehrlich to get in touch with Hans Klee about the missing bow.

◄ ■ ►

Carl had intentionally made the new top for Michael's lunch-bag violin disaster oversized and now he needed to round the overhanging edges to match the looks of the original back. This was a nerve-wracking process because the slightest nick or scrape to the sides would mean completely sanding down and refinishing both the sides as well as the top. *What am I thinking? Why am I wasting my time with this?* he suddenly wondered as he remembered the poor quality of the violin in the first place. Deciding that he should let Peer have more hands-on experience, he turned it over to his assistant to scrape the red-brown varnish from the sides as well. Not watching where the sharp corner of the scraper was, Peer put a few dings into the sides, but no real harm was done. Carl had him sand them until the small gouges disappeared and the sides and top were ready for the final finishing processes.

Peer had prepared some fresh blonde shellac by mixing the raw flakes in alcohol and stirring over several days until the shellac was completely dissolved in the alcohol. He strained the shellac mixture through a fine cloth to remove the insect parts and impurities that were always a component of the raw flakes. With a white cotton cloth, he wiped the strained shellac over the top and sides of the violin and set this aside to dry, following up with a second coat a little while later. These two coats soaked into and sealed the wood as the last stage before the final finish coats could be applied.

After lunch, Carl had several customers stop in to collect their instruments or to drop others off for repairs. Since he had a backlog of invoices to prepare, he braced himself and spent an hour on paperwork for his recently completed and current jobs, and then organized their tax and rent files so that Maria would have an easier time dealing with them when she was next in town.

Somewhat overwhelmed by even these simple clerical tasks, and the late afternoon sun being out so wonderfully, he grabbed his sketchbook and headed towards the river. He found himself crossing the Nydeggbrucke Bridge and, because it was just off the main road on the opposite bank, decided he'd visit the bear pit – something he hadn't done in quite some time. It was a popular tourist destination and thus to be avoided especially in the summer, but the late autumn crowds were minimal. The bear pit actually consisted of two adjacent basins, each five-meters deep and nearly circular except where they met at a stone building separating the two. Each pit was about 15 meters across and surrounded at the rim by a fence to keep people and bears apart. The central structure, shaped like a miniature castle, held offices reserved for staff at the top with the bottom level designed to cage or shelter the bears. As he neared the pit, he saw that the cubs had been segregated into one of the halves, and there were tourists down among them feeding them carrots. Some of the young bears seemed to be almost as big as the smaller children, and he wasn't sure he'd allow his own child, if he had one, to be in such close proximity to them. In his mind, he briefly saw a young son scampering among the cubs, and this brought an unexpected pang of regret – something that was becoming rarer as their childless years had progressed.

Along with a small crowd of on-lookers, he gazed down from above watching the visitors in the pit feeding and try-ing to pet the cubs, but then with an increasing melancholy he moved to the other half where the adult bears had been isolated, and where there were fewer people viewing them. He found a spot providing a good perspective and thought he'd try and sketch a bear for distraction. Leaning for a time against one of the fence supports, he felt less gloomy and thought that he had a good facsimile started, which surprised him, when there was a tap on his shoulder.

"Not bad!" said Albert appreciatively, "I didn't know that you were an artist, too."

"Oh, hey," said Carl, self-consciously closing the sketch pad and moving it behind him having again unexpectedly revealed his poor attempts. "Just doodling. I couldn't resist getting out and enjoying the remainder of the sun on this beautiful day."

"The same with me," said Albert. "Mileva is taking little Hans Albert to the doctor for a check-up, and I thought I'd enjoy a walk after work before they get home."

"I've been avoiding the bear pits since there're so many tourists here during the summer, but it's not so bad at this time of year."

"My thoughts exactly," said Albert.

"Those and many others, I'd guess!" said Carl with a smile. "Anyway, I love it that we're in a season when much more of the city opens up for walking in peace and quiet." After a pause he asked, "Say, you don't mind do you?" Albert gave him a questioning look and then chuckled as Carl reached up and scraped what was either some of Hans Albert's breakfast or Albert's lunch off the lapel of his jacket.

"Thanks! What a slob I am!" laughed Albert, brushing at the remainder. "Now that you mention it, the crowds really have thinned out, haven't they? It makes me glad we aren't the home to one of those new ski areas sprouting up in the mountains – we'd have even more vacationers pouring into town during the winter and have no break from them at all. And everyone needs a break now and then." After gazing out over the pit for a moment Albert said, "Speaking of breaks, this has been a very strange year for me, and a real relief from the couple of years leading up to it – it's almost been like a vacation, now that I think about it."

"Oh? How so?" asked Carl.

"I might have mentioned at your shop that I'd become extremely frustrated with being overlooked for several positions that I'd applied for until I finally landed the Patent Office clerk job last year. The baby was on its way at the same time, and I had no work available, so I threw myself into physics and was pushing hard to complete my doctoral degree and carve out some original work in the process. I think I nearly had a nervous breakdown," said Albert looking down into the bear pit. "And Mileva could hardly live with me."

"But things are better now?" asked Carl.

"Oh, much better," replied Albert. "When the Patent Office job came along, I devoted myself to the post and focused solely on its requirements. With the help of my boss, I learned to write with more conciseness and accuracy, which has turned out to be a huge bonus. To be honest, there wasn't much time for thinking about physics when I first started. Paradoxically, as I settled in, I started to relax more and stopped trying so hard on all fronts. I'd even lapse into long daydreams and nearly fall asleep on the job during the less-busy periods.

"Then one day I suddenly had the insight into a different way of looking at one problem I'd been struggling with. That breakthrough led to several new conclusions, and it's as if things are clicking into place with almost no effort on my part aside from the initial struggles. Oh, and except for working out the math – which is not always that enjoyable, and I'm really not very good at it when you come right down to it," Albert confided with a wry grin.

"What was the breakthrough that you had?" asked Carl.

"Ah, it had to do with the photoelectric effect," said Albert.

Carl blinked and asked, "The what?"

"The effect that light can have on certain metals," explained Albert.

"You mean heating metal up, like when it sits out in the sunlight?"

"Similar - but that's a good example of the cause and effect," said Albert. He gave Carl a meaningful look, stepped back, and then in a theatrical voice said, "Your choice now, Carl: return to your drawing in peace or have me prattle on about light."

Carl laughed and tucked his sketchpad firmly under his arm. "Prattle on, sir. Prattle on," in a matching tone.

"OK then," began Albert with a shrug of his shoulders. He paused for a moment and then continued as if there had been no joking exchange. "It's been shown that there are metals that will react to light under certain conditions, and not just by storing and radiating heat energy. These metals release electricity, or charged particles, when illuminated. Charged or ionized particles are excited and thrown off of, or knocked off of, the metal by the light shining on them. This effect has been observed for some time, but I've discovered a twist that makes me look at light in a completely different way – sort of how I talked about it at the tavern – light as particles."

He looked over at Carl as if for permission to continue and received a nod in reply.

"It's been perplexing to experimenters that the results we see from the photoelectric effect haven't matched our expectations, especially with the assumption that light is acting like a wave. One would think that the more intense the light source, the more charged particles would fly off the metal, wouldn't one?"

"I'd suppose so," answered Carl since this seemed reasonable.

"Well, you'd be correct – but with some important exceptions. You see, the different frequencies of light correspond with the colors we see, the colors of the rainbow, and there is a certain amount of energy associated with each frequency. Red light at one end of the spectrum has less energy than blue light at the other end. Experiments with those photo-reactive metals have shown that you can increase the amount of light shining on them, such as low energy red light, to very high levels with absolutely no effect on the metal whatsoever. However, above a certain energy level or color band, even a small amount of, say, blue light will cause a charged particle to fly off the metal. This is hard to explain with the tools we currently have at hand, but as I said before, I believe that light is actually composed of individual energy packets that behave like waves and particles at the same time. It's these energy packets, if above a certain threshold of energy, or frequency, that strike the metal and in turn release a charged particle."

He noticed a slightly blank look on Carl's face, then gazed down at a large black bear ambling over to some apples that had been thrown down by a tourist, and then finally at the stone-block sides of the enclosure. "Ah!" he exclaimed. "A good mental picture of this might be like attackers laying siege to a castle. They can shoot arrows at the walls all day long without leaving any real marks, but if they bring in a ballista which is much more powerful, the bolts or stones it throws will soon start chipping away large chunks of rock. Nothing happens to the ramparts until more energy is directed at them. To the photoelectric metals, a particle of blue light is like the bolt from a ballista.

"I'm just finishing a paper where I expound on this... oh, not the arrows - the light packets - and I predict that for a certain frequency there will be a greater number of charged particles coming off the metal for each increase in the intensity or number of packets coming from the light source." He paused for a moment. "But it's actually what I've deduced from this that I find to be far more exciting."

"Well, I think I get the main point of what you've said so far. It's easy for me to visualize little bits of light knocking off little bits of metal. So, what's this new thing that's excited you?" asked Carl.

The crowds around the cubs were beginning to thin, and a clock tower nearby struck five o'clock in the afternoon. Albert's head swung toward the sound of the bells. "Uh oh,

I'd better head back home to be there to help with Hans Albert when Mileva arrives from the clinic," said Albert.

"I'd better get back, too," said Carl. "I'll walk with you up our street." They headed towards home away from the bear pit and across the stone-arched bridge spanning the Aare. A Yenish gypsy occupied his customary spot at the foot of the bridge, playing his violin for passing tourists. Albert was drawn to the music and stopped at the little bottleneck created by the performance, becoming absorbed in one of the gypsy's tunes. He tapped his foot in time with the song and dug into his pocket for some change as the next tune started up. Tossing the coins into the open case, he immediately switched gears back to physics. As they continued across the bridge, Albert was focusing on the conversation more than on his surroundings and so it was up to Carl to step off the sidewalk to make room for the people coming across the bridge in the opposite direction. He found it a little maddening, but could see that Albert was concentrating heavily as he spoke with expressive hand gestures.

"It suddenly came to me while I was pondering the photoelectric effect: we're used to thinking about speed as a relationship between distance and time, right? – so many kilometers traveled in an hour? And we're familiar with the practical application that the more energy you can put into something, the faster it will go. If we want a faster train, we build a bigger more powerful engine; if we want an arrow to go faster and farther, we make a stronger bow that's more difficult to pull back, like the ballista.

"Ah, but now we come to light," continued Albert. "With the photoelectric effect, the only way to increase the number of charged particles coming off the metal is to increase the number of energy packets being directed at it. We can increase the number of packets at any frequency, but they all travel at the same speed. There appears to be no conceivable way to increase a packet's speed, even though we can do that with any physical object. So, the speed of light has a limit."

"Now, remember that light also behaves as a wave ..." Albert stopped suddenly on the crowded sidewalk and turned to look back at the Yenish player who was now almost out of earshot. Several people came to a halt behind them, immediately making Carl feel uncomfortable. "You know," said Albert, "there must be a better way for someone to be compensated for such excellent music," shaking his head. He then turned back to continue towards home, and they danced around a little as they now faced a woman pushing a pram with four children in tow. Albert continued once they'd moved past, "Light behaves as a wave. A Scotsman named John Clerk Maxwell used mathematics to describe a single wave equation that combined separate equations for both electricity and magnetism – an electromagnetic wave, and his equation indicates that the speed of this wave is constant in a vacuum, and this, coincidently, is the speed of light. Interestingly, this speed holds for any electromagnetic wave – not just light, but infrared and radio waves as well, like the ones used in Marconi's new device. All of these waves move at the speed of light and are in a perpetual state of flux, changing between electricity and magnetism. The magnetic phase creates electricity and the electric phase creates a magnet, each pulling the other along nearly instantaneously.

"But as we know, when we measure the speed of something, it depends on the speed we're traveling at, too. Experiments so far have shown that even with the speed the earth travels around the sun, there's no difference in the detected speed of light from a star whether we're nearing the source or moving away from it. And this consistency is part of Maxwell's equations as well. But at the same time, this seeming invariability in the speed of light is perplexing – are our measurements wrong and the speed does change as we move, or are the equations correct and the speed is indeed constant? So, that's left me pondering another question."

Another? thought Carl, tempted to make a joke in order to slow down Albert's rapid train of thought, but instead he asked, "What's that?" genuinely curious as they reached Carl's apartment and stood in front of one of the circular fountains nearby.

"What are the implications of light speed being a constant, regardless of whether we are stopped or moving? What does that really mean?"

Carl was now glad that he hadn't attempted a joke because he could see the seriousness of the question to Albert, and now he was left wondering about the answer as well. At the same time, Albert looked up the street at the clock tower and suddenly seemed to deflate. "Well, this is when I'd better head off," he apologized. "Thanks again for taking an interest in my ramblings."

"Any time," said Carl, genuinely. "As I said before, I thoroughly enjoy listening to your thoughts, and now I want to hear the answer to your question."

"I'll fill you in next time - I always love to pontificate," smiled Albert. "See you later."

"Oh!" said Albert suddenly slapping his forehead. "Carl, I'm sorry I forgot to mention that the music group said that they'd love it if you could join us!" said Albert. "When I find out the time and place of our next gathering, I'll let you know."

They waved at each other as Albert headed home and Carl climbed the steps to his own apartment. He tried to think about Albert's question, but without any mental images to help him, they were just words floating in space, and he gave up before he reached his front door.

CHAPTER 11.

The blonde shellac had hardened on the new violin top for Michael's violin, and after a light scuff-sanding, the surface was ready for the process known as French polishing. This was the task at which Peer excelled, much to Carl's surprise. For some reason Peer, to whom boredom came so easily, loved becoming immersed in the endless applications of finish and would hum to himself and become engrossed in his work for hours at a time.

Carl was glad he'd taught Peer the process, and it gave him an odd feeling of fatherly pride that Peer was now able to work completely independently. His own father had been too much of a perfectionist to allow his son anywhere near the final stages of finish application on an instrument, and yet Carl knew that Peer, a non-apprentice, did a much better job than he himself was capable.

He shook his head at this thought as Peer took up a ball of cotton cloth and added drops of shellac until the ball was soaked, but not dripping, with the varnish he'd colored with a few drops of madder red dye. Peer then smacked the ball against the back of his hand to form it into a pad with a flat surface and added one or two drops of olive oil to the flat area. He then worked this shellac and oil mixture across the violin with the flat pad until the shellac was depleted, where-upon he'd add more shellac and a few drops of oil, continuing until the entire surface of the violin had received a thin, even coat.

Peer followed this routine interspersed with periods of drying and cleaning the surface for a week or two on each violin until enough minute shellac layers had accumulated to make a beautiful, deep, and protective finish. As Carl worked on the other student violins that needed new tops, backs, or sides, Peer would rotate through a series of violins at various stages of French polishing. It was clear to Carl that Peer revered this part of his job and would catch him holding a violin up to the light at different angles to admire the depth of the finish and the luster it brought out in the wood underneath.

Today, there was a break in the routine, which was to become a routine in itself. Carl saw Peer glance up from his work, as usual, towards what could be seen of the street up through the windows of the entry door. The boy then suddenly dropped his application pad on the workbench, rushed to open the glass door, and ran up the steps, only to immediately shrink back down until only his eyes and forehead were visible from the street.

"What's up?" asked Carl with concern as he walked over to join him.

"Shhh," said Peer.

Carl looked in the direction that had grabbed Peer's attention and saw an elderly woman stopping at the Rosselli's storefront across the street accompanied by a young woman, or perhaps an older girl. The girl was tall, slender and, when she turned to look up the street, he saw that she had deep brown and somehow intense eyes. She was beautiful.

Carl first nodded and then as he turned back to the shop door, shook his head. *The boy's in for trouble,* he thought with a grin.

At the threshold, the grin disappeared as Carl stood and surveyed the student violins with an unexpected sigh at the familiarity of the task at hand. Remembering his recent resolution to build his own instrument, he was about to set this more mundane work aside and begin shaping the back of his own violin, but his conscience stopped him, and he dug out another more profitable case from the pile.

◄■►

Out later for some supplies, Carl's thoughts were on the list of the day, but as he approached a street intersection, he became aware of raised voices beyond it. He reached the street corner and as he turned towards the altercation and into the sunlight, he could blinkingly make out the profiles of two figures, one taller and round and the other stocky. One silhouette was pointedly jabbing a finger into the chest of the other. Both then stood with what looked like hands on hips and heads leaning towards each other. The voices became more strained as he drew closer. Then the stocky one with what appeared to be a full beard began poking back at the taller man's chest. Carl was just about to cross the street to avoid the ruckus when he could make out the individuals involved – Hans Klee and Old Carl; he should have guessed. Each was as stubborn, and prone to flaunt it, as the other. He stayed on course and, as he was nearing them, they both suddenly erupted into laughter and slapped each other on the shoulders. Old Carl disappeared into the tavern they stood before and Hans remained on the sidewalk with a smile on his face and shaking his head.

Noticing Carl as he approached, Hans said, "That old coot will stick to his misgiven opinions as much as I'll stick to my well-informed facts! There is no convincing him!"

Smiling, Carl nodded and said, "Well, that's what makes Old Carl, Old Carl." *And what makes you, you,* he thought.

They shook hands, and Hans thanked him for the grayling he'd given Paul weeks before. Hans Klee as always was direct, commanding, spectacled, and sporting an impressive white beard that reached down to his fourth shirt button. He had a shock of remaining white hair that frizzed out above his ears and complemented the beard.

"Here I am thinking that Paul should stick to drawing instead of fishing, and I was only recently thinking that Paul should stick to music instead of drawing," said Hans. "You heard he is going to give up performing?"

"Yes," said Carl. "He does seem excited about his decision."

"Yes, but what a turn of events – how can you possibly fathom this younger generation? He has such talent with the violin, but then suddenly decides that's not for him? I was dead set against this 'art' whimsy of his, but Ida wouldn't hear of deflecting it, even though music is her passion too, and she's still giving voice lessons. 'He must follow his heart,' she said. Yes, and my pay checks floated to Munich with him."

Hans gave a heavy sigh. "I'd always imagined Paul following in my footsteps with music and maybe even teaching one day, but now either I'm too worn down or I'm starting to see that he might actually be aware of the path that offers him the greatest potential. At least I hope so. It's just too bad that I'm not possessed with the wherewithal to understand what the hell he's doing."

"I recently chatted some with Paul," said Carl. "And the way he talked, I could see nothing but an open world for him as far as his drawings are concerned. I'm sure he'll be fine. Like you, I'm a fish out of water where that new art scene is concerned. By the way, Paul mentioned that Ida is doing well. Please give her my best."

"She's unchanged, thank God – but I wish she'd give me her best," lamented Hans as he shook his head. "Sorry, I didn't mean that. It's perhaps the same in all families – the children can do no wrong and the husband is trying his best, but it's never enough?"

"Yes, that's probably so," lamented Carl. "Say, I just have to ask about the violin bow. So, I can return it to its proper owner then, can I?"

"What bow?" asked Hans looking perplexed.

"The one found by Master Ehrlich. He did get in touch with you about it, didn't he? He's given me a valuable bow that seems to have magically appeared in the hands of one of his students, and I heard that you had a similar bow go missing."

"Oh, that bow!" said Hans. "No! As you say, he thought that it might have come from a violin that disappeared from my classroom, but ours was found by the student's parents the very next day."

"No one in your classes is missing a bow then?" Carl asked wearily. "He's asked me to help look for its proper owner."

Hans pulled some on his beard and then shook his head. "No, none missing, but that doesn't sound right, does it?" he asked. "To have a stolen item appear and not know the source, instead of a known item disappearing to an unknown destination. I don't think I've heard it's equal. You're going to need some luck with that one."

"Thanks, then," said Carl with a visible drop in his shoulders. "Could you please let me know if anything strange concerning new or missing violins or bows comes up in your school?"

"I will, Carl," said Hans. "I'd like to see that bow for myself sometime, too. Make sure you give my love to Maria and greetings to that stuffy Master Ehrlich, as well." He turned in the direction of home, but apparently deciding that the tavern was the better choice, disappeared within its doors.

The next morning, Carl faced the fact that it was past time for him to sharpen his tools and reorganize his workroom. It was getting to the point where it took him fifteen minutes just to find the calipers he needed to make a measurement. It wasn't that Peer didn't keep the floors litter-free and swept, it was that in Carl's own work he created messes that hid even more clutter. He started with the bigger tools and helped them find their proper storage places and within an hour or so he and Peer had regained a clean workspace and had filled a bin with sawdust and shavings in the process. Flecken, at first entertained by all of the activity, soon tired of being moved and shooed from spot to spot and rowred to be let outside. The remainder of the morning and early afternoon was spent sharpening and honing chisels and carving knives. Carl always hated the time that it took to carry out this monotonous task, but it made his work so much easier when he did.

There was no longer a guild for instrument makers in Switzerland, but most of the builders in the city were members of a loosely-knit group that met once a month at *Zum Bären*. Carl bundled up and walked to the meeting, but had misjudged the time it would take and arrived just as the proceedings started in the large back-room reserved for events and gatherings. As usual, Old Carl had the floor and had begun a long diatribe about the lack of competent apprentices and was bemoaning the fact that in the good old days apprentices were not paid, but had to earn their way into the ranks of established luthiers.

Carl found a seat next to Lukas, his friend and a quiet member of the group, and set his coat down. "Hi, Lukas," whispered Carl. "I really enjoyed dinner with you and your wife the other night – thanks so much for inviting me." Lukas nodded with a smile and Carl worked his way to the tub of gluhwein that had been set up by Max at the rear of the room. He filled a cup and wound his way back to his seat. Lukas whispered something about Old Carl's already having drunk half of the tub, and listening to Old Carl, Carl winced his agreement.

The bulk of the meeting was taken up by presentations from the three local families who were supplying Bern and its wider environs with tonewood - European, or red, spruce for violin and guitar tops. These families had for generations planted, nurtured, and harvested a rotating crop of lumber providing a sustainable and consistent product to builders. The relationship between the suppliers and luthiers was largely amicable and synergistic with infrequent breakdowns based on prices or outside competition. There had been a long period of peace between the two, and based on the presentations, that appeared to be continuing. Carl's was not a big enough business to buy directly from the families, but the conduit through larger businesses like Old Carl's worked very well for him.

As the meeting was breaking up, Carl stood and asked for everyone's attention. Not many but the nearest heard him, so Lukas clinked his glass with a pencil, and the room quieted down. Carl explained about the violin bow that had been discovered without mentioning that a student had come by it, and he held the case aloft asking if the members could take a moment and see if any of them recognized it. All who examined it agreed that it was a fine bow, but no one thought that it looked familiar. The only opinions regarding the bow's origins were by the two members who built bows themselves. One was of the theory that it came from Italy and that the maker could be Arassi, a well-known craftsman from Genoa. The other was of a mind that it was by Aculon from Tours in France. Both agreed that the "A" could also, however, be the metal stamp of the screw maker. Carl thanked them and said that he would try and get in touch with those two bow makers.

Old Carl had nodded off during the main part of the meeting, and after struggling into his coat, had thrown his big arm around Carl's shoulder as they were heading out of the main door of *Zum Bären*. It reminded Carl of his father and having to fetch him from this same spot as a child.

"Those taverns just get too hot. It's a wonder that the whole place didn't fall asleep," said Old Carl as they plodded back together along the lamp-lit street.

That was the extent of the conversation as Old Carl bounced off Carl and the sides of buildings as they made their way to Old Carl's house. Dropped keys by Old Carl delayed things at his doorstep, but soon Carl was off to make his own way home. Old Carl slowly transformed into his father in his mind, and he remembered his trepidation as a child wondering how a similarly inebriated Josef would greet his wife each time they entered their house on nights such as this.

◄■►

Early the following morning, Carl was back at Old Carl's shop and Gustav was the only person he could find when he first entered. "Good morning, Gustav," said Carl. "Where is everyone?"

"Beats the hell out of me," Gustav replied. "Dieter was sick yesterday, so he's probably still at home, but Old Carl and the others haven't shown up yet."

"We had a meeting last night, and I doubt that you'll see Old Carl till the afternoon," explained Carl.

Gustav looked at him questioningly, but then he gave a nod of understanding. "He won't be in a very good mood today then will he?"

"Nope," said Carl. "That's part of why I decided to drop by this morning. I need some more red spruce for tops. Do you mind if I go through the supply?"

"Not at all, Carl, help yourself," said Gustav as he turned back to his carving.

Carl took his time and rearranged some of the stacks as he sought out two book-matched pairs for the student violins that were next to be repaired. After selecting two sets, and replacing the remainder of the pairs, he was picking up the dust-covered set that had always remained on the top of the stack to protect the others, when it clumsily dropped out of his hand. Landing on edge, the set gave off a surprisingly clear ringing sound. He picked the pair up checking for damage and then blew and wiped off the dust that covered them. Not only were they unremarkable in appearance, they had images burned in from stickers that had laid on them in years past. Turning them over and looking at the cleaner unexposed sides, Carl saw an average tree ring count in the grain, in fact there were some gaps in growth that made the grain uneven. *No wonder this had always stayed on the top,* thought Carl. He was about to put the slices back in their normal spot when he remembered both Storioni's violin and that he had set aside a very resonant piece of maple for crafting his own violin. Tonally, this set would be the perfect match to the maple. Hesitating for a moment, he added this to the other two sets and slid them all in his satchel.

As he said goodbye to Gustav and was heading out, Old Carl came striding in – much to their surprise. "Hello," smiled Carl as he patted his satchel. "I've been robbing you blind again."

"You and everybody else!" bellowed Old Carl as he squinted through red eyes.

"I owe you for three more spruce tops," said Carl.

"Maybe I should have you work it off, rather than pay me?" asked Old Carl with a cough.

"No, I might like that so much, I might decide to stay," replied Carl as he pushed through the door.

"Really?" asked Old Carl as the door quickly closed on that possibility.

CHAPTER 12

Albert had contacted him with the time and location of the chamber music group. After supper a few nights later, and a small beer to calm his nerves, Carl followed the directions given to Herr Besson's house, the host of the week. He knew why he was nervous. He seemed to play his violin just fine when he was by himself or with Maria, in fact he played effortlessly, but when he knew that strangers were within hearing, his fingers seemed to suffer temporary paralysis and the easiest phrases became Chopinesque complexities. On the balance though, he knew that playing in a group would be a good way to conquer this problem, and he really did like the chance to perform with other people – something he hadn't done since two of his good friends had both moved away several years before.

The Besson's house was immaculate and ornate, and a servant opened the door for him with a flourish when he knocked. He could hear instruments being tuned deeper in the house and was led past a wide staircase, through a long hallway with several adjoining rooms, and into a very large secondary parlor. The first thing he noticed on entering the book-lined room was the thick carpet which helped absorb and mellow the instruments' sounds. Herr Besson even had a *quartett pultaufsatz* or a four-sided music stand in the form of a small decorative table. Carl was offered a cognac by the servant and then was introduced to the other players. Geron, whom Albert had mentioned earlier, was affable and turned out to be a harried parent of three girls finally free to relax in a man's world. The viola player, Thierry, was from France and was teaching conversational French to students at the same school where Geron taught music. Herr Besson who played cello was polite but reserved and preferred to be referred to as Herr Besson.

At Albert's suggestion, Carl listened to the others play a quartet by Bach while he reviewed the sheet music for the compositions in which he would play a part. One was by Telemann, and he was luckily acquainted with it; the other was one of Dvorak's and he had never seen, nor heard it before. Carl couldn't help it, but as was a habit of his, he'd already formed impressions of each of the men based on their playing styles as he listened: Thierry was dynamic and adventurous, while at the same time remaining sensitive to the others; Geron was perhaps a little too forward or showy for his true ability; Herr Besson was regimented but provided the necessary foundation for the piece; and Albert was expressive and very intuitive in how he played Lina. Carl was curious, as always, to see how his impressions would match the men.

As the third violin, he felt confident with the Telemann piece and had fun playing it, and he felt like he didn't totally butcher the sonata by Dvorak. They were happy to have him as part of the group and said that he'd be welcome anytime. After chatting and a rare cigar, which he feigned to smoke because he had never acquired the taste, the group said their goodbyes and thanks to the host.

Walking back towards home with Albert, Carl said, "That was so enjoyable, but I'm not sure that my apartment is large enough to reciprocate as host and make it at all comfortable for everyone."

"Mileva and I are in the same cramped situation, and the other three seem very happy to rotate among themselves, so that won't be a problem. I also play in a trio with my friend Michele, and the three of us can't even fully bow a note without hitting each other or a wall in my apartment. The other three in this group realize that not all of us are able to entertain and seem to enjoy it even more so that they can. No need to worry," said Albert.

"Whew, well then, this is something that I can look forward to. Thanks again for inviting me."

"Of course! I don't know if you could tell in listening that you've already added to our depth and now we can expand our repertoire to include quintets, or even alter some quartet pieces. We're all excited to have you - and we'll have the added benefit of including someone who can fix what gets broken," Albert said with a smile and patted Carl on the back. "You know, I can't imagine my life without music, and Lina has really become my muse. Playing her always seems to enhance my thought processes which these days are only focused on physics," he paused. "Which brings me around again to light..." And he broke out into a chuckle. "I'm just pulling your leg. I'm not totally obsessed."

"Oh, but I'd say you are!" Carl smiled. "But a little obsession isn't such a bad thing, I don't think." They walked for a moment in silence and then Carl said, "Remember, you promised to summarize your thoughts for me? So, I have a question."

"Oh?" asked Albert. "What's that?"

"When we talked earlier, you started going on about light particles rather than light waves, and then later about charged particles being knocked off in the..." He thought furiously. "Oh yes, the photoelectric effect. How can anyone possibly know anything about these tiny bits since both are so small and, I assume, there's no way to show that they're even really there? Otherwise, everyone... um, other scientists, would know about them, wouldn't they?" asked Carl.

"What a happy coincidence, Carl! I've been wondering the same thing myself, since everything I've said up 'til now depends on these particles actually existing, doesn't it?" asked Albert. "I'm just now writing an article where I'm able to prove that atoms, or those tiny bits, do, in fact, exist," said Albert. "First, of course, I had to reason it out in my mind and then through statistics in the paper."

"I've heard of these atoms, so I assume that scientists already know about them," ventured Carl. "But proving is probably another thing?"

"That's been the problem. There are still many respected scientists who don't believe in the existence of atoms since, as you say, we can't see them and have no real way of detecting, measuring, or counting them," said Albert. "An Austro-Hungarian, Herr Boltzmann, developed some exceedingly beautiful mathematical equations based on the assumption that atoms do in fact exist, but he wasn't able to simultaneously offer any proofs or verifications. For this he was roundly criticized, or I'd say thrashed, yes, thrashed by others for daring to assume their existence in the first place. I believe he committed suicide, but I'm not sure if it was a result of the heated backlash he received to his theories or not." Albert shook his head and walked head down for several paces. "Causing a suicide... I hope not all new theories will be treated so harshly."

Taking a breath and regaining momentum he continued, "There's a well-known problem, in physics circles anyway, known as Brownian motion. In the previous century, a botanist named Robert Brown was studying pollen grains. Some of these grains are exceptionally tiny, requiring him to examine them under a microscope. So that they wouldn't blow away or stick to the slide, he suspended the pollen grains in a drop of water. It was a surprise and very frustrating for him that the pollen grains wouldn't remain still. They'd suddenly jump as if they were alive or being pushed by something unseen. The pollen grains would travel in a zig-zag pattern with no way to predict where they would move next. Many who believe that atoms exist thought that it could be their actions in the water that caused the motion, but there was no way to prove it. A single atom couldn't move a pollen grain, you see, but the combined random actions of a large number could. The motion is also evident when you carefully place a drop of dye in a bowl of water – after a time the single drop has diffused across the entire bowl making it a uniform color. The apparent motion of atoms causes the minute ink particles to become evenly distributed throughout the liquid."

"So, this shows that the atoms live in water?" asked Carl.

Albert stopped momentarily in his tracks, staring straight ahead. He looked over and smiled at Carl as he began to walk again. "Ah," he said, "I see. Actually many scientists, and I myself, believe that atoms *are* the water. Atoms of different types make up everything you see – the river, the bridge, you, me."

"But they have to be alive to move, don't they?" asked Carl.

"I don't think so," said Albert. "They all move just by their nature, but the movement is miniscule in solid objects and more pronounced in liquids."

Carl shook his head. "But now you have two things to prove – that they exist, and that they move."

"I think I have. I was at my desk one day when suddenly I saw both Boltzmann's equations and the Brownian motion problems simultaneously – with the clues to a solution. In the next few days I'd worked out an equation that predicts either the distance a particle like a pollen grain will travel, given the liquid, or calculates the number of atoms in a liquid based on the size of the particle and its motion. I'd been able to step back and use statistics to explain the overall pattern rather than trying to predict an individual particle's actual movements.

"Now that I've mathematically proven the existence of atoms to myself, it's laid the groundwork for me to tackle several problems physics has been struggling with for a long time. I've been investigating the nature of light and the inexplicability of the photoelectric effect that I talked with you about, and also how light is related to our concepts of time and space." He looked over at Carl. "Pretty heady stuff, you might be thinking."

"Oh, it certainly is that," replied Carl with a nod. "Even grasping what an atom is. And that they're all moving without being alive."

"You know though," continued Albert, "beyond the ideas themselves, it's equally amazing to me how our thoughts progress, isn't it? One leading to another. I've found that my occasional daydream-like state at the Patent Office, without snoring I might add, was very productive for my insights. At first, I was afraid that not concentrating on a problem meant that I was giving up on it or failing. Now I find it's almost more advantageous to let my mind wander where it will at times, even on the job. My boss just loves me for it, by the way," he winked.

"I might not fathom half of what you say," said Carl, "Especially the atoms and statistical stuff. But I do know what you mean about coming up with ideas even when we aren't aware that we're even thinking about them. Just the other day..." They'd arrived at Albert's house, and he could see Mileva waiting at the window two stories above which also grabbed Albert's attention. They both waved up at her, and she held Hans Albert higher for them to see him. Albert waved even harder.

"I want to thank you for letting me jabber on so," said Albert. "It really does help me to try and organize my thoughts so that even a new friend might be able to get a glimpse of my ideas."

"I'm glad that you have such faith in me, but with this discussion, I'm afraid I'm still a little in the dark," admitted Carl.

"Don't worry, some things take time to sink in," said Albert. "Even for me," and he shook his head as Carl gave him a doubtful smile. Albert climbed the stairs to his waiting wife and son while Carl headed for home with the strange sensation that his body was abuzz.

CHAPTER 13

Maria had an extra day off because of some saint's holiday in the university, and Carl had met her at the train station that morning. They'd strolled slowly to the apartment, catching up on what each had done during the previous two weeks and stopping at a café for coffee. In the afternoon, Maria settled into paperwork while Carl collected three of the remaining student violins that had only needed minor adjustments and set off to deliver them to Master Ehrlich. Making his way from the tram stop, he entered the school in blessed silence since it was a student holiday here as well, although he'd been informed that the teachers would still be present grading exams and papers. "I have four of the violins requiring serious attention to still get to you, but one is nearly finished, and the rest should trickle in over the next month," said Carl as Master Ehrlich greeted him and cleared a space for at least one of those he'd brought on his cluttered desk, while Carl set the other two on the floor beside it.

"Wonderful," said Master Ehrlich. "Thank you for trying to keep pace with us. Unfortunately, I have another one that needs some work already – and it's in pretty sorry shape. And then there are still the violins from the class that Jan Rauss is in."

"Ah. How I love the school year," said Carl somewhat sadly. "Oh, I stopped by the police station and talked to them about the violin bow. There were two violins that had gone missing or were stolen recently here in Switzerland, but neither fit the time frame matching when Jan had the bow. There were also two reported as stolen in Italy, but we may never hear anything more about those."

"Then what the police know isn't going to help us, is it?" asked Master Ehrlich.

"No," replied Carl. "I also showed the bow to our luthier's association, and no one had seen it before. Two of the bow makers suggested companies in Italy and France, and so I'm trying to contact them. Otherwise I'm not sure what more I can do."

"Well, there's certainly no rush, so don't be discouraged but please keep at it," said Master Ehrlich. "If we ever should discover that the bow had been stolen, things will get very messy around here. Please try to keep us posted, and thanks for treating this with the delicacy it deserves. Um, you were discrete with the police, weren't you?"

"Yes," said Carl, "although the police have their own way of dealing with matters of theft."

Master Ehrlich nodded solemnly.

Carl took the additional violin and was heading for the exit as Master Ehrlich was opening the case and playing one of the violins he'd just delivered. "Great job as usual," he shouted as Carl made his way out through the front entrance. Carl was off with a shout of thanks that echoed down the halls.

The unseasonably pleasant weather was holding, so Carl walked rather than wait for a tram. He tucked the violin case under an arm and sticking both hands in his warm pockets, strolled back to the shop. It was late afternoon and, as he was passing Kleine Schanze Park with its small pond, he took a little detour to the right to the viewing area facing south of town over the Aare River valley. In the distance, the sharp white Alps stood out starkly against the clear blue sky. Turning around to continue his route to the shop, he spied Albert slowly emerging from the park with another man. He said hello as they approached, and both men stopped and stared at him for a moment as if just awaking.

Albert blinked his eyes and then said "Hello, Carl! Let me introduce my friend Michele. Michele, this is Carl Veblen, the violin maker who repaired Lina."

Carl recognized Michele as the man he'd seen engrossed in a conversation with Albert at a tavern some time back. "Pleased to meet you," he said as they shook hands.

"We were just discussing physics – remember how I was talking to you about the nature of light? Well, we've been digging in a little more deeply into that subject. You're welcome to join us if you're headed this way," pointing towards the center of the city while holding a paper with complex mathematical formulae scratched on it.

Carl nodded "Sure, that would be fine."

And so they set off, but after a few pleasantries and inclusions of Carl in the conversation, the discussion soon became much too obtuse for Carl to track and much too intense for them to notice if Carl followed. The trio stopped suddenly as Albert stabbed at one of the equations, emphasizing a point for Michele who nodded but came up with an alternate view as they began walking again. After passing the square across from the Parliament building and staying with them for a few blocks, Carl peeled off down a side street with a small wave and barely caught their attention as he left. They continued on to parts unknown as far as Carl was concerned.

Carl set down the violin case in a corner of his shop and checked on Peer. Everything was going well, and he made a mental note that he needed to buy more cocoa – and soon, at the rate the boy drank it. He carefully picked up another soundboard he was currently shaping and thought that it was progressing nicely. When he tapped on it, it was beginning to sound a little like a violin top should. Flecken rubbed against his leg and Carl, with some effort, lifted the big cat, petted him, and then set him on his favorite perch above the stove before diving into another project.

The workday finally over, he headed happily upstairs, leaving Peer to continue with his finishing as long as he liked. "Hi Maria!" he called out as he entered their apartment.

"In here," she called back. "We have a nice bank draft from the viola reconstruction you finished in July." He stepped into the small parlor, and she was waving the check before setting it on one of four piles on the crowded table. "And it looks like Herr Obermeyer has increased the rent again. It's not much, but his excuse this time is his own tax increases. Since when do we have to pay for his lack of foresight?"

"I don't know, Dear," said Carl only thinking that he was so happy that she was the one taking care of the bills.

Startling them both, Peer rapped on the door and motioned through the glass that he was heading home. They both waved back. "It's too late now to make dinner, at least a proper meal," said Carl. "Why don't we go out to eat?"

"That sounds heavenly," sighed Maria, shoving a pile of papers to the middle of the table. "Then we won't need to clear this mess off to make room."

They locked up the apartment, and Maria stood under the covered walkway while Carl made sure that the stove in the shop was damped down before bolting and locking the shutter doors for the night. "Hey, what about Flecken?" asked Maria, "I didn't see him come up."

Carl realized that he may have just barred Flecken inside, so he unlocked and went down again to check. The cat was nowhere to be seen. "He must have left with Peer," said Carl joining her.

They sauntered the few blocks through the surprisingly warm, breezy evening to *Der Sturm*, a place that was never too crowded and felt like a second home to them. As usual the restaurant was half-full, and they chose a small table near the back. Carl suggested they order a bottle of wine, and Maria chose a French red for them when asked by the waiter who was soon back with the wine and to take their orders. Carl asked for some bread and hard cheese to go with the Burgundy. "Is the game hen in season?" asked Maria.

"No, unfortunately not, madam," the waiter replied. "Perhaps you would both enjoy the spaghetti with venison meat balls that is our special tonight?" They both agreed that it would go well with the red and would be fine.

"Have I told you about Albert, the one who's violin suddenly acquired a new bridge?"

"Oh, you told me about the violin when I was here last time, but I didn't remember the man's name. He's the Albert you mentioned in a letter who invited you to join his quartet?"

"Yes, he's the one, and I played with them just last night," said Carl. "I had a lot of fun, and they said I could join them anytime. I walked home with Albert afterwards and have had some interesting conversations with him. He works at the local Patent Office and is absolutely obsessed with physics. He can be the type that sort of lectures while he talks, but there's an intensity and intelligence in the man that's really refreshing. I also get glimpses of a good sense of humor."

"Is he married?" asked Maria.

"Yes, he has a wife and a new baby boy. I forget the son's name right now, but the wife's name is Irmheld – no, Mileva. Anyway, he's very engaging and brings up subjects that I never would have thought about in a million years. Atoms, light, the stars – it's like attending a university course, but at the same time I'm flattered that he tries to explain the stuff to me. I honestly don't know how he does it. He's twelve years younger than me but really has his hands full. He has two – no three – jobs since he works for the government, is finishing a doctorate, and doing his own research. Plus, he has a family to think about with a child not even out of diapers. I don't know where he gets the energy."

"Wow," said Maria. "I'd like to meet him sometime. I'll bet his wife is overwhelmed as well. But still, to have a child..." and the conversation hung for a space.

"I know, honey," said Carl, and then partly to change the subject, "Oh! I just realized that Albert's about the same age as Paul, and the two are very similar in many ways: they're both bright, energetic, and very focused on their interests – Albert in science and Paul in art. They're also both musicians and make sure to set aside time for music. I wonder if they're acquainted? If not, we definitely need to find a way to remedy that!"

The spaghetti arrived, and they took their time eating, watching a fire being built in the fireplace.

"I know you'd like children, honey," said Carl, "but it's not that we haven't tried. Who knows why it hasn't happened, but we have a good life regardless, don't we?"

"I suppose so," sighed Maria, rallying herself. "We do have a good life, and I probably wouldn't have the job I do if we did have kids."

"And I honestly don't know if I'd have the strength for one now anyway," said Carl. "We're not getting any younger."

He toyed with what was left on his plate. "Hey, do you want to hear something I've been thinking about lately? It's probably been influenced by being around Albert." Maria smiled and nodded in reply. "I was in a tavern the other day by myself, just watching people. Now, this is an oversimplification, but I noticed that some people appear to be big in size, money, or status, but are basically nothing but air when it comes down to it. Think of our mayor, or Old Carl, for that matter. They count for little, but they take up a lot of room on the stage. I hate to be uncharitable to Old Carl, and I love him dearly, but he really is all just bluster, isn't he? Especially now that he's gotten older? And that useless mayor who only says what others want to hear, but takes a whole day to do it?

"But then, of course, there are those who at first glance seem ordinary, but in their own way they shine like stars – somehow being noticeable even when in the background. Anyway, somehow that made me think that people are like stars and planets – some attract and some are attracted. Maybe there's some unseen gravity that people possess that attracts others to them and sometimes won't let them go, depending on the strength of the gravity.

"I immediately thought of Jesus who was apparently a mild-mannered man and yet attracted people around him who were absolutely devoted. Christians would say that it was God that provided the power, but I think he somehow had this density and charisma that wasn't outwardly apparent. What do you think?"

"That's funny," said Maria. "My first thought was of Napoleon. He was said to not look like much, but also had this huge charisma that brought a nation to war. Or what about Joan of Arc? This little young woman who convinced a king and led an army? You're right – there's something in those people that isn't in others."

Later that evening, Carl thought about their conversation. He sometimes felt that he had little gravity himself and was constantly being pulled into other's orbits. Perhaps he was more like Old Carl than he cared to admit. There was something about being around certain people that overwhelmed him. It wasn't that he didn't enjoy them, but perhaps this was why he sometimes liked to stay at a safe distance - he could then maintain his objectivity without being overly influenced by their thoughts or personalities. At least, he mused, people-watching from a distance provided the buffer that he sometimes needed to stay balanced.

◀ ■ ▶

Early the next week, he received a message from Mortensen who asked him to drop by the police station at his earliest convenience. The note was short: "Another violin bow has materialized."

Carl spent the morning running errands and in the shop disassembling the newest violin that Master Ehrlich had given him. A student had deeply carved the name of his girlfriend 'Gertrud' into the neck to the point that it was no longer playable.

The weather remained mild, and he left the shop with only a sweater. This he ended up removing during his walk because the mid-day sun was more than enough to keep him warm. The shadows being cast were much longer than those from a summer sun at noon, and it seemed odd to have so much warmth on top of visual cues that spoke to nearing winter.

Mortensen was available, and as soon as Carl entered the room, the sub-commander greeted him and placed a violin bow case on the desk between them.

"Another bow?" asked Carl. "Are they falling out of the sky?"

"No," said Mortensen. "They are falling off bridges. A man walking his dog along the Aare found this underneath the Kirchenfeldbrucke Bridge. The case had been in the water, but to my eye, the bow looks fine."

Carl tried to open the case, but the swollen wood made the clasps tight against one another. With a little extra effort, first one, and then the other clicked up, and he opened the narrow case. Inside was a very ordinary looking bow. Carl picked it up and examined it. To him, it looked like any one of the student bows that he saw every day. "You're right, the water looks like it did no damage. And I'm pretty sure that this is a bow from one of the local schools. Here," he pointed, "it even looks like it had an inventory number etched on it, but that's been scratched so it's illegible."

"I'd kind of suspected it was from the schools," said Mortensen. "It only makes sense that if a student came by a new bow that he'd need to do something with the old one and hide its identity just to be on the safe side."

"I agree," said Carl. "I think I'd better have a talk with Jan, and possibly Master Ehrlich, unless you had that in mind for yourself."

"No, at this point I am simply returning a piece of missing property to the schools," said Mortensen. "But let me know if it comes to the point that I need to become more involved. I'm not keen on letting larceny have its way in the public schools. Oh, and the valuable bow comes back to me until we know for sure its origins. Who knows? We may have other takers in the wings."

"I sure hope so," said Carl, "I'd be more than happy to have it out of my hands. And I'll make sure to relay the outcome of my chat with Jan if anything interesting comes up."

He stood alone in the entry hall for a moment. *Now, how did I let myself become the middleman in all of this?* he wondered idly as he pushed through the heavy front door and out into the sunlight.

CHAPTER 14.

All of Sunday morning the sky had been a contrast of brilliant blue background and near-black clouds scudding low overhead with enough space between to occasionally let the sun flash through. Here and there the bases of the clouds were stippled with the gray streaks from rain or snow squalls.

Albert had mentioned to Carl that he sometimes took short day-hikes out of Bern, and that he'd get in touch with Carl and see if he was interested in joining him. The day before, Carl did hear from Albert about an outing, and the two of them met at the train station just after breakfast for the quick 15-minute rail trip to Thun. Albert had previously warned that he might not be much for conversation, but they chatted amiably on the train.

On the way from the station to the trailhead at the base of Stockhorn Mountain, Albert commented, "You know, I've come to love my job – something I never really expected. I never imagined I'd become a clerk of all things, but here it is Sunday, and I'm not dreading going to work tomorrow. Many of the patents I review are very interesting, and I've found I like working with an applicant to make his submission something that's unique and can stand up under scrutiny. Conciseness is the key. It almost makes me want to patent something myself."

"I guess I'm happy with my vocation, too," replied Carl. "Making wood change into the parts of a violin or a viola can be fulfilling. Especially when you realize that from the lowly student box to the concert stage instrument, they all end up making good to exquisite music, don't they? But this repair aspect of the business can be draining – it means that someone treated their instrument with a lot of disrespect in the first place.

"I decided that to add some enjoyment back into my job, I'm going to start building my own instrument, which is something I haven't done for years. The only thing is, working on my own violin doesn't put bread on the table, and so I find it hard to put in any time into it except on the rare evenings. If I was working solely on my own instrument, I'd be overjoyed to open the shop tomorrow, too. As it is, I find I'm just barely content to do it."

"I'm sorry to hear that, Carl," replied Albert. "You really should pursue your inspiration, whatever it takes. Otherwise, what is there to life?"

"Well, that sounds good to say, but what about expenses and other people's expectations of you?" asked Carl.

"I'd like to believe that those work out," began Albert and shrugged as they found the trailhead and began their ascent.

As they climbed, Albert had started off in that same chatty mood, but was soon looking down at the trail as much as gazing out at the surroundings, and would twist about to say something to Carl, only to turn back quietly muttering a few words to himself in a repetitive fashion and push on. At one point he stopped, lost in thought, and Carl almost walked into him. A later squall had them putting on their hats and hunching their shoulders to the mixed rain and snow, but it soon passed. Carl was becoming mildly irritated with the way Albert hiked. If Carl led, he'd find he had to stop and wait for sometimes several minutes while Albert stood and stared off into the distance or investigated a flower, and if Carl was behind him, Albert would either halt, or get an idea in his head and stride purposefully up the trail leaving Carl panting to catch up.

They finally arrived at a lookout with a broad panorama of the valley that was their goal, and a relieved Carl broke out some bread and sausage, with Albert making himself comfortable against a rock. "Hey Carl, I've almost thought something through, so I hope you don't mind if I complete it?"

"Not at all, Albert," said Carl. "After all you did warn me."

As Carl ate, Albert would take a bite and stare for a long time out over the landscape, and it was usually a noticeable interval before he'd take another bite. Carl sat and enjoyed the tremendous view of Thun and Thunersee, with Interlaken and the lake beyond visible in the distance. He could tell that Albert was deep in thought, though taking in the scenery at the same time.

"I'll be just a minute more," Albert said eventually as he offered Carl an apple from two he'd pulled from his knapsack along with a tattered notebook. This he opened against intermittent wind gusts and scratched out figures intently in it for a full five minutes. He then shut it and said, "Again, thanks! What a view, huh?" as he stood and stretched. "I imagine that a poet must spend days winnowing the words he's written until he's captured his idea in the most concise and articulate verse he could muster. Mathematicians and physicists can fill pages with equations and functions, however, it's always more gratifying to be able to reduce, say, a function with multiple components down to the fewest possible variables. And, in my opinion, it becomes beautiful and almost poetic to take multiple different functions and express the same thing in only a few. Almost like you whittling down a piece of wood to make a violin. I was just able to combine three functions into one, so that was well worth stopping for."

Carl was about to tell him that making a violin was more than mere whittling, but nodded in agreement instead.

"My goal is to take what we know about the universe, in mathematical terms and physical concepts, and carve it down into the simplest and fewest expressions possible to describe everything. That, I really feel, could be my life's work."

Carl sat and gazed at the shifting landscape of sun, clouds, and shadows. "I don't see how, but for your sake I hope that's possible," he said.

"Me, too," agreed Albert.

They both looked out over the hills while the sun and a raincloud were in the right position to form a magnificent rainbow against a jet-black background. For a time, it doubled into two huge brilliant arcs. "Did you know that we're seeing the results of light being bent and slowed down by water?" asked Albert. Carl did a mental double-take since he'd been enthralled at the sight and was just wondering how to paint it. "As the light passes into each rain drop and is reflected off the back surface, the different frequencies pass through at different angles and speeds and so they're separated as we see them in the rainbow bands. But the amazing thing is that light waves that had been bent, slowed, and separated into different frequencies or colors all leave the water zipping out at exactly the same speed at which they entered – the speed of light. Incredible!" With a sudden raising of his eyebrows, he picked up his notebook and wrote for some minutes more.

It was time to head back, and they stowed what they needed into their knapsacks as Carl turned to Albert. "You know, Albert, I enjoy having you lead the conversations because they're always on paths I never knew existed, and I don't know my way. I can't even read the signs because they're in a different language."

"Thanks, Carl," said Albert.

"Now, I hope this won't offend you, but on the other hand, you are absolutely crap at hiking."

This caught Albert by surprise and he raised his eyebrows at Carl while asking, "What do you mean by that?"

"Well, I like to enjoy the view or investigate an interesting plant as much as the next person, but in my opinion, there is a certain pace to a hike – unless you're walking by yourself. If you don't stick to that pace, then the other person is either struggling to catch up or waiting for you to join them. You pay no attention to the other person and just do what you want, so you're frankly frustrating to walk with."

Carl expected Albert to see this as an affront, and so was shocked when Albert burst out laughing. It went on until Carl suspected that he was being made fun of.

"I'm sorry, Carl," said Albert catching his breath. "I told you that I was sometimes not so good at conversation on a hike, but completely forgot to mention that I'm also a terrible hiking companion – unless it's with someone who knows me well!" He wiped his eyes and continued. "You see, when I hike with this certain group of friends, they always demand that I either sing a song, keep up a running conversation, or pound out the time with my walking stick. Otherwise they won't go, or just leave me when I get distracted. They get fed up. I only have one other friend that puts up with my sudden stops and starts."

"Ah, so you knew that you were lousy at it?"

"Yes! But it just slipped my mind when I asked you to join me. I always begin with the best intentions, but then forget that I'm hiking and get lost in my own thoughts. It's really like a disease or mental problem, I'd say."

"Well, that's great!" said Carl.

"Great?" asked Albert.

"Yes – at least you're aware of it, I thought you were just being rude."

"Oh, I can be rude when I want to be!" said Albert. "Just not when I'm hiking with a friend." They both smiled and started back down the slope. "I shouldn't be so bad on the way down," promised Albert as he led.

They passed a rock outcrop, and a hawk came into view circling at eye level. Carl watched as another joined it and, opposite each other, the two birds began twin upward spirals on buffeting air currents. He perceived the two spirals without beginning or end describing where the hawks had been and projecting where they would be in the paths ahead of them, upwards towards the clouds. As he marveled at the durability of this image of twin intertwined lines reaching to the sky, Carl realized that he'd just taken his simple observation of the hawks and made it into something totally abstract; that the human mind continually transmuted nearly every sensation – all that it saw, that it heard, tasted, and felt - into a concept. Oftentimes the transformation was slight – sights and sounds went unregistered or were part of a persistent background in which this tastes sweet; that feels rough; this sounds loud. But occasionally what was perceived produced an exceptional thought or emotion that persisted long after the sensation that sparked it. And even more rarely, the transformation of what someone beheld resulted in a beautiful creation – a country scene like the one they'd just enjoyed recreated in a symphony.

He'd stopped while thinking this, and by now Albert was far ahead. *Now look at me!* he thought, slightly embarrassed, *I hope Albert doesn't notice,* and he jogged down the path to catch up. Following Albert down the trail, he thought that Albert certainly had put him in a contemplative mood. *Maybe that's a little of what it must be like to be Albert.*

◄ ■ ►

Carl finally took a day for himself. It was with some tremendous guilt on his part, and with great glee on Peer's, that he told the boy he need not come into the shop that day, but he would be paid nonetheless.

"Are you kidding?" Peer had asked and jumped high when Carl had replied "Nope."

The guilt Carl felt was in being selfish with his time when there was a plethora of well-paying instruments that needed attention. But he wanted time alone with the violin he was constructing for himself. And he realized that it was Albert who'd made him finally begin to follow his own heart. It hadn't been Albert's words that had been the influence on him, it had been his actions. Despite the declarations Albert made about his love for his job as a clerk, Carl had finally come to see the reality of how he lived his life. The man spent time at work, with his family, with his friends, but the whole time he was really working on his passion – physics. It was obvious that Albert was not really 'here' much of the time and was actually consumed by the true work going on in his head.

With Paul, the choice to follow his dreams was easy. He was still a student with his whole life in front of him and no real financial or social responsibilities – of course he could follow his love for art. But here was Albert, to all intents and purposes a new father and employee, but in reality a man fixed on a single goal. This realization had given Carl the nudge he'd needed. He'd neglected the part of his life that mattered the most and he was resolved to do something about it. He now surveyed his shop with a renewed enthusiasm.

He reviewed the advances he'd made despite his difficulty in giving himself permission to spend the time on the project. The after-work progress was actually quite good. The top and back had been shaped; the f-holes had been cut in the top, the purfling inset, and the bass bar glued in place; and he'd bent and glued up the sides the week before, staying up far too late on two consecutive nights. Now was the time to assemble the body of the violin in peace and quiet during daylight hours.

He wanted to tune the top and the back assembly, something that he only approximated with the student violins that he routinely reconstructed. Tapping the surface and listening to the responses, he began to remove wood from the top itself as needed, especially near the edges, and from the bass bar until the tone he heard matched the F pitch of his tuning-fork. He'd also strike the tuning fork and hold it against the violin top until he heard the best resonance. He then followed the same procedure with the instrument's maple back that he'd carved, only this one he tried to tune to G.

Given the bright tone of both the top and the back, he'd ever so slightly made the f-holes a touch longer than normal and had also placed them a hair closer to the edges. This was said to slightly mellow the overall tone when the violin was finished, and he thought it a good precaution. Immensely satisfied, he then glued the sections up to eagerly await them drying.

In his concentration, he was shocked to see the sun already setting. As he cleaned up the shop, he remembered the first violin he'd built, and yet hadn't built. The project had been with his father, and at each critical step, his father had taken over, sometimes even subtly shoving Carl out of the way while he bent over the instrument. His father had shaved off wood to retune the top after Carl had finished, he had completely re-sanded the violin with a grit that 'would better accept the finish, and besides you left scratches,' and he had reshaped the heel of the violin to change the neck angle more to his liking. Sadly, thought Carl now, he'd accepted his father's meddling perfectionism as normal, and after a decade of criticism had also accepted that lutherie was best left to others. Luckily, he now looked over at the new violin body and felt nothing but contentment with a job well done.

◄ ■ ►

School was in session, and thirteen-year-old Jan Rauss was red with embarrassment from being pulled out of his science class by a school official. The principal had decided not to be involved at this stage of inquiries given the stature of Jan's father, the Councilman, and had warned them to treat the matter delicately. Master Ehrlich joined Carl in the advisor's small, empty office for a discussion with Jan. Once the door closed, and Jan saw the open bow case on the desk, he was as Master Ehrlich had described him previously – distraught to the point of tears.

"Jan," Master Ehrlich lectured, "I'm laying out the situation as we know it, and I'd like an explanation from you in your own words. I'm not going to your father about this yet, but I want to get to the bottom of it once and for all. You're not in trouble unless we find that there's a reason for you to be, so please try and keep your emotions in check. We know that you turned up in class with a violin bow that was clearly not the one given to you at the beginning of the year." Jan began a weak protest, but Master Ehrlich held up his hand. "Now we find a bow and case that look like they could have been yours and they had been chucked into the river. Can you please...." he paused as he remembered. "Ah, yes - we've marked the violins and most of the bows and your number is 32, so all we have to do is verify the number on this bow." However, tilting the bow that had been in the river in all possible angles to the light, neither he nor Carl could make out a number through the scratches deliberately made to obliterate it.

"Jan, this just proves your guilt, doesn't it?" asked Master Ehrlich raising his voice. "You tried to scratch out the number on this bow so that it couldn't be traced back to you! What do you have to say for yourself?"

Jan stared at him in utter disbelief. "I...I didn't even know there were numbers," he began and then gave a sudden wide-eyed start. "If you think I did something bad, you won't tell my father... will you?" and the boy broke down into quiet sobs at the thought.

"We may have to, Jan. We may have to," said Master Ehrlich with a sigh.

"Jan, there's no need to be afraid," tried Carl. "Especially of your father, I'm sure he..." But at this Jan practically convulsed and buried his head in his hands.

"Here, let me get you a glass of water," said his teacher, and he momentarily left the room.

"Now we have too many mysteries," Master Ehrlich lamented to Carl after he'd returned with the glass and coaxed the boy into raising his head and accepting the drink. "Who's bow is the valuable one that Jan had? Where is Jan's bow - although this could still be it for all we know - and if it's not Jan's bow, then whose is it? Carl, I don't want this to take much more of your time, but if you could help us out in clearing up any of these mysteries, we would, I would, greatly appreciate it."

Turning suddenly on Jan in obvious frustration, Master Ehrlich shouted severely, "Jan, you must tell us now if you have any information that might help us out! It will just get worse for you if you're hiding something!"

They waited in silence until Jan finally spoke.

"I...I just don't know," was all he stuttered, and after fifteen minutes of halting statements it became clear that this was indeed the case. Jan hadn't noticed any change in the bow for the entire school year - in keeping with his level of playing, Master Ehrlich whispered after they'd escorted Jan back to his class - and the boy had no idea where the better bow had come from, nor the fate of the ordinary bow with which he must have started the semester.

As Carl was parting from the music teacher in front of his classroom he mentioned, "It just occurred to me that if we have a bow show up that's not in the inventory, and have a bow missing that is in the inventory, maybe we, or you rather, should check the inventory against all of the instruments to discover what else might be out of place."

Master Ehrlich began to balk, but a smile slowly grew on his lips. "That might take a whole period - or two!" he grinned broadly. He told Carl that he'd let him know if anything unusual showed up, braced himself against the building noise, and then picked his way carefully into the cluttered classroom where students were attempting to tune up for the next period.

CHAPTER 15.

His love for his wife easily won out over his desire to spend the weekend working on his violin, and he was going to surprise Maria with a visit to Zurich. He knew that she'd have little free time until the Christmas break, and he also knew that the clamor for repairs wouldn't ease until next summer, so seeing as how it would make no real difference to his workload in the long run, he decided that he'd take a welcome and guilt-free break from the shop.

He boarded the 4:00 train just before it pulled out of the station that Friday and settled onto a bench for the two-hour trip. He'd expected a quiet ride, enjoying the scenery until the sun set, but it turned out that the train car was in a convivial mood. Next to him sat two university students, and across from him a politician from Bern and a teacher at the international school. There was no end of political, economic, political, religious, and political discussions. Carl noted that Bern's useless mayor figured prominently throughout. He tried to maintain a distance from the conversations and gaze out the window, but found himself pulled in and was somehow enlisted as the referee or judge to some of the more heated debates – everyone turned to him for affirmation of their argument. He was able to point out some contradictions, and his nods or grunts seemed to hold him in good stead. As the sun set, their reflections in the window became more pronounced until it seemed that their little discussion group had doubled. The two hours rushed by, and there was a flurry of handshakes and back pats as they disembarked. He was at Maria's flat by 6:30.

Maria sighed and threw her arms around him. "Oh, hi you!" she said. "I get to see you again so soon – but you should have told me you were coming – what if my lover was here?" she asked with a wink. They both chuckled, but Carl stopped abruptly. He suddenly looked serious and said, "What lover?" striding to the bedroom and pretending to search under the bed; and they both broke out into laughter again.

Maria immediately launched into details of the semester and what was on her mind: the problems with a few students and some of the staff, the upcoming restructuring the University was facing, and the possible down-sizing of her department. *This is all a little different than what she talked about last week and described in her letters,* thought Carl. Together they stored what Maria had been preparing to eat by herself and went out to dinner at a nearby restaurant with Maria staying on topic the entire time.

Carl was going to spend all of Saturday in Zurich and then head back to Bern on Sunday's late afternoon train. "I hope you don't mind," she said, snuggling his arm as they were walking back to her apartment after their meal, "but I have a staff meeting tomorrow from ten in the morning 'til two in the afternoon, and I still need to finish preparing my budget, meager though it is, for tomorrow. All because of this damn restructuring! It really is starting to impinge on our teaching and class-loads. Thank goodness it's not happening at the end of the semester when most exams take place."

"That's fine, Dear, I can find something to do in the meantime. Maybe I'll see if Günther has any plans – perhaps a short hike with him would be fun. You and I can do something in the evening. Do you know if there are any performances scheduled for tomorrow?"

"I've had my eye on several," said Maria excitedly, and they decided on a choral piece that was slated the next day at a local cathedral and was free.

While Maria organized her budget details, Carl walked the few blocks to Günther's house to check on his plans for the next day. He'd known Günther when he'd lived in Bern previously, and with Maria now living in Zurich, they were able to keep up the friendship even after Günther's move. Happy to see his friend but wanting to get back to Maria, he breathed a sigh of relief when Günther opened the door with a sleeping child in his arms and a mess in the small apartment. "Birthday party hangover," was all Günther had to whisper. He beamed when Carl mentioned a hike, and they agreed on meeting at the train station at 9:30 the next morning for the short ride out to Zug, a couple of stops from town. It was a favorite hike for them and only took four hours.

Back at Maria's, Carl found her just putting her completed paperwork into a leather folder. "Good timing," smiled Maria, "I just finished."

Carl hung up his coat next to the door and gave her a peck on the cheek. "Günther had his hands full with a sleeping kid, but thought a hike tomorrow would be a great idea, so you don't have to worry about me while you're in your meetings," he said as he sat on the one of the three wooden chairs in the small apartment. "Oh, I forgot to tell you – I'm making good progress towards building that violin for myself."

"That's fantastic, Carl!" said Maria. "You'd mentioned that you'd found some wood that might be suitable. I'm so glad that you're spending some time on your own project."

Carl nodded as he got up and poured them each a small glass of cognac. "I forgot how engrossing it can be to build something new from scratch. I actually closed business for the entire day recently to work on it, and it's the most fun I've had in the shop in a long time. It's so enjoyable, but I know it takes time away from the projects we're being paid for."

"Oh, Carl," said Maria coming over and massaging his shoulders, "I didn't know that the repairs were becoming such a routine."

"Oh, they're fine," replied Carl. "That's what we set up the business for. But this new project sure has sparked my interest and makes the other stuff seem so... I don't know... run of the mill, I guess."

"Well, I'm glad you're doing something rewarding," said Maria. "What made you decide to start a new violin in the first place?"

"I played the most incredible sounding violin that was absolutely nothing special to look at. In fact, I don't know how he did it. The maker, Storioni, chose second-rate wood which should have been a recipe for disaster. But he made it work and the fantastic tone reminded me what making instruments is all about," said Carl and he proceeded to tell her about his visit to Süd Hoffman's and the Storioni violin.

They enjoyed the rest of the evening together, discussing the differences between Bern and Zurich, sipping cognac, and just being near one another once more.

◄■►

On Saturday morning, the couple enjoyed a leisurely breakfast and then left at the same time to their respective destinations – Maria to the university and Carl to the train station. Carl and Günther caught up with each other's lives on the train ride to Zug, and then talked, but in staggered sessions, as they hiked in the hills, interrupted by sightings of birds, vistas, plants, or labored breathing up three steep stretches through the spruce. They both walked at the same pace and were interested in the same features of nature, so the outing was very enjoyable for both. Günther had purchased a new pair of binoculars and loved the entirely new perspective they provided. At the top of their moderate climb, they had an excellent view of Zugersee through the trees, though from their position it was difficult to see Zug itself nestled beside the lake. The snow was becoming a constant and descending feature of the Alps, and today the peaks glistened white in the sunlight all the way down to tree line. Günther sat, filled, and lit a pipe before they headed back down, the smoke swirling around his head and off into the trees. "Oh, Carl!" exclaimed Günther between puffs. "I attended the most fantastic lecture at the university last week! Have you heard of Rudolf Steiner?"

"The name sounds familiar…" began Carl.

"I'm sure you must have, and you should see him in Bern if you get the chance," continued Günther. "He's a member of the Theosophical Society – you know, the one with Madame Blavatsky?"

Carl shook his head.

"Well, Steiner is the most engaging speaker…" as he continued, and they headed down the mountain. Günther told him all about the secret Society masters that were said to be hidden around the world and their belief in reincarnation. Günther had been a fervent Protestant when living in Bern, but since moving to Zurich he'd stepped away from Christianity and had become surprisingly esoteric – joining seances with psychics and meeting with occultists. During his last visit to Zurich, Carl had heard about the *Ordo Templi Orientis,* and now his friend was explaining the tenets of the Theosophical Society. Carl was always amazed at the zeal Günther threw into each new religious interest, but listened with some secret skepticism as they hiked easily downhill.

They made it back down to the station in Zug with time to spare and enjoyed a coffee at the small outdoor cafe attached to the train depot. They'd warmed up considerably on the hike, but began to replace the outerwear they'd shed as a cold breeze built during the morning and now blew steadily down from the mountains. Arriving back in the city, they agreed to try and get together again over the holidays. Carl said that he hoped to make another trip to Zurich soon.

Unexpectedly, it turned out that the evening concert was really a practice session for an upcoming Christmas presentation of Handel's Messiah. This meant that there were several interruptions due to problems with the sopranos on "All we, like sheep" and with the basses on the final "Amen" chorus. They could have abandoned the rehearsal during any of the breaks, but enjoyed the warm, mostly empty church, and had plenty of time to chat quietly while the conductor gave instructions, worked with the instrumentalists, or broke the sopranos up into smaller groups. Finally, separating two sopranos on either side of that section seemed to solve most of the problems there, and the basses were to meet again on their own later that week. Even though it was a broken performance, Carl and Maria left contented.

On the return trip to Bern the next day, Carl had the train car almost entirely to himself and was able to relax and enjoy the scenery and his own thoughts. He spent quite a bit of time thinking about Günther and his beliefs. It seemed no matter what his latest interest, Günther embraced it whole-heartedly. As a Protestant he'd devoutly accepted heaven and salvation through Christ, and now he said that he had indications through dreams and a psychic of his own reincarnation. In a way, Carl was in awe of his friend's ability to believe in anything so completely. Carl's parents had been somewhat religious, and he began his early life attending church with them, but they'd quit attending services when he was about six years old. After that, it had taken Carl years, but he had gradually accepted that he himself was a humanist. He believed that humans were inherently ethical and compassionate and was having a more and more difficult time understanding the need to believe in a supreme deity when remarkable humanity was right here at hand. The more he thought about reincarnation and its ramifications, the more the notion morphed into a concept increasingly incomprehensible to him.

◄■►

Stepping from the train and working his way through the small crowd, he noticed with surprise that Albert was standing alone on the railway platform near the front of the train and seemed to be simultaneously staring both at, as well as through, the still-steaming engine and coal cars. Carl was about to leave the platform for the exit when he decided to go up and say hello to Albert.

"Oh, hi Carl!" said Albert.

"Am I bothering you? What are you doing here?"

"No, not at all. I come here sometimes to think through a couple of problems I've been wrestling with. I was taking advantage of a Sunday evening and was just about to head home when the train came in. Were you on it? Where've you been?"

"I just hopped over to Zurich to see Maria for the weekend, and I hiked one day with a friend in the hills outside of Zug."

"Zurich has some nice paths, but I really enjoy the lake and hiking around Zug, too," said Albert. "How's Maria? The semester's going well?"

"Maria's fine, thanks," said Carl, "but there're apparently some changes underfoot at the university and they've made Maria a little nervous." The crowd in the station was beginning to thin as they stood on the platform. "How's," his mind raced, "Mileva?" asked Carl, his brow almost breaking into a sweat at nearly forgetting her name.

"She's an angel, and she puts up with all of the time that I spend out of the house. I love having a child, but they can create such breaks in concentration, can't they? Mind if I walk you home?"

"Sure, I'd love the company," said Carl. They talked some about Carl's trip, and Carl brought up his meditations about Günther's beliefs and his own more humanistic view. He was interested in what Albert thought.

"I, myself, am a non-practicing Jew," interjected Albert, "which means that I hold god at arm's length. But that said, I can't escape his presence - which I find to be absolutely everywhere. How can we not stand in awe at the mystery of life? Going out for walks in nature like we did the other day, don't you have to wonder how all the details could be so well arranged and mesh so perfectly? All of the multitudinous forms of life occupy even the harshest conditions on the planet – and they all interact and thrive! And not just life - looking at the train tracks and the engine as it came in, it was beyond comprehension that we humans could pop up out of the remnants of stellar debris and reach the point where we could create all of this incredible, intricate, and durable ... stuff. Just think about what all had to come together to create that train!"

"Well, I agree that this earth is an amazing place, and that the life on it is incredibly diverse. But I just can't see any superior being having a..." and Carl held out his own hand with the fingers pointing up, "hand in it. Life just happens – it's nature, it's natural. It doesn't need some divine presence pushing things along. It's just so complex because it's had so much time to become the way it has."

"Ah, but you see, it's that very complexity," replied Albert, "the improbabilities at the large scale and the incredible symmetry at the small scale that makes it hard for me to envision it happening by chance. Think of the atoms we talked about the other day. There are hydrogen and oxygen atoms. Why should they combine to form water – which they do? And if some do, why don't all of them join to become water? And how does water get its properties that are unique from either of those two atoms? I could go on, but the day is late," he said with a chuckle. "The god I keep in mind isn't the personal god of the Bible, but is in the very fabric of all that exists. One that was part of whatever started the whole business going and one that is part of every star that arises and star that dies."

They walked for a time and then Carl replied, "I'm having a hard time picturing an orchestrating hand that isn't a hand. It's like a thought without a brain to think it, isn't it? But since I can't picture a personal god myself, if there was a god, I like your version of him. It's like the music I listened to lately and realized that the composer is really like a god – able to control the beginning and end and the time that occurs in between. I suppose I should give some thought to the possibility of a god that is more like a vast hidden conductor," said Carl.

"Well, I'm certainly not saying that you should believe in god if your thoughts and experience have led you to another conclusion. Only that I can't help but be amazed with every detail I see each and every day," said Albert.

They walked for a while in a comfortable silence. The cold wind that had come down from the mountains near Zurich was here in Bern as well, but they were dressed for the weather and the wind didn't affect their walk. As they neared Carl's apartment, they talked about the next musical get-together, and Carl briefly described the problem with the violin bows. As they parted, Carl patted Albert's shoulder as his friend set off towards home, packing and futilely attempting to light a pipe as he walked past the last streetlamp in the row.

CHAPTER 16

Carl spent the next morning starting to replace the sides of a sorely abused violin. "What one among all of these has not been ill-treated?" he murmured.

"Ill-treat away!" shouted Peer making Carl jump slightly at the unexpected response. "I need to keep my job!"

Carl chuckled at his outburst. Here was one youngster making a living at picking up after the follies of other youngsters. His mind was suddenly elsewhere as he saw the violins he'd been working on as the students themselves. Dozens and dozens that were the same: producing the same tones, with the same playability, the same fickleness with staying in tune, and all with the same common countenance. Only a few in their lives would transform to become a Stradivarius or a Storioni – either immediately recognizable or hidden among their peers and biding their time to emerge as the shining examples that they truly were.

Now, what should I name this one? wondered Carl. He often christened some of the more difficult projects that he knew he'd be spending some time on to try and insert some character into each violin unless he knew the client. It suddenly occurred to him that it was odd that he'd never nicknamed his own violin as Albert had his. *Horst is this one,* he decided at random.

"Carl?" asked Peer, and Carl shook his head as he noticed the odd look the boy was giving him.

"Ah, just thinking, Peer," as he turned back to work.

Constructing the new sides for Horst was a very similar process to forming and fitting the purflings, only on a larger scale. Carl sorted through his stock of long chunks of maple and came up with one covered in cat fur. "I think I've found where Flecken's been sleeping," he said to no one in particular. From this wood, he cut, planed, and sanded slats of maple that were somewhat wider than the depth of the violin. He'd previously made a mold that was the same size as the student instruments - a solid block of wood matching the thickness of the instruments with a hollow in the middle cut out in the shape of a violin.

After preparing the wood slats, Carl ate lunch up in his apartment and caught up on some inventory and billing, grumbling at the continuity of the paper process, and thankful again that Maria really did the majority of the bookkeeping. The inventory revealed that he needed some extra wood stock to repair the neck with 'Gertrud' carved in it that he'd recently been given by Master Ehrlich. He stepped outside, headed down the steps, and then immediately turned back into the apartment to grab his warm coat. Running down to the shop, he opened the door and told Peer to continue with some French polishing, and that he'd be back later as he headed to Old Carl's for the neck blank. Remembering the violin he was building for himself, he made a mental note to check for a potential blank for the neck of that one, as well.

◄■►

Carl had detoured on his way home from Old Carl's to a store he knew that sold horse-hide glue and was passing by the School of Arts and Crafts when he noticed Paul talking to a friend outside the main portico. Both men were stamping their feet in an effort to keep them from freezing as they conversed.

"Hi, Paul!" said Carl as the friend had apparently finished their chat and was hurrying back into the school and out of the cold. He walked up and shook Paul's gloved hand. "Again, I wanted to let you know how much I enjoyed your performance the other evening. Not only did you play phenomenally, as usual, but the acoustics in the Munster are incredible and they added such depth to the music. Oh, and it was a bonus to meet Lily, too. She seems to be a very nice young woman."

Paul smiled and said, "Yes, she's something else, isn't she? It's too bad for me personally that her music requires her to stay in Munich. I think that one of us is going have to move soon so that we don't spend so much time apart."

"I know a little about that," replied Carl. "Maria's living in Zurich during school sessions, as you know."

"Yes, but I'd never realized how difficult it must be," Paul said sympathetically.

"Well, we've learned to cope, and I don't know that it'll be a permanent situation."

Paul stood still for a moment and then, with difficulty wearing gloves, bent and picked up a large folder that he had tucked between his feet. "Do you have a moment, Carl?" asked Paul. "Let's duck inside to get out of this damn wind first, though."

Paul led the way into the main hall of the school. "Since I've been living in my parent's house and also using it for my studio, I normally keep my drawings there," continued Paul. "However, this afternoon I brought some of my portfolio here so that I could present the sketches to Herr Volmar, the drawing and etching instructor." He patted the thick folder under his arm. "I was hoping to perhaps arrange a showing, but it's difficult to find the right venue in Bern. Anyway, he was encouraging about my work, though I have to say not necessarily impressed with what I've done so far - at this stage at least. Be that as it may, I also know that tastes range across the spectrum, and his family has been classically trained – did you know that his father and his brother also taught here?"

"No, I can't say that I know the Volmars," said Carl. "You know, I don't really pay so much attention to the art scene, but I've recently heard good things about your drawings from several sources. I know that your father would be happier hearing more about your musical accomplishments, but it seems that people are beginning to pay some attention to your new vocation, too."

"Thanks, that's good to hear," said Paul. "How about if we find a spot to sit down for a minute. Remember our chat about your drawings?"

"You mean my attempts," corrected Carl.

"No, I mean your drawings," retorted Paul. "You should take a minute and look at these." He pointed to his folder as they walked toward some granite benches at the back of the entrance hall.

"I'm leaving the idea of art as a 'picture' behind and putting more of myself, mixed with perhaps a bit of emotion – or sarcasm and humor – into what I draw, and I think it's really turning into something that's beginning to define me. You should take a peek at these, because with some work and more effort to, well, relax, you could travel on a similar path." Paul sat down on the nearest bench and began to unstring the binding on his folder.

"You should understand," said Carl in a protesting tone but sitting, as well. "I'm an older hobbyist and married to my career of violin repair. I'm never going to travel down another path."

Paul shook his head, but also smiled at Carl. "I'm afraid to say that you don't know what you're missing by not adding a little more creativity into your life. But regardless, have a look at these. Most in this series of etchings I've titled *Inventions*."

Carl spent twenty minutes going through the thirty or so drawings and etchings and revisiting them several times. Paul was silent but attentive the entire time. When he was finished, Carl leaned back and handed the portfolio over to Paul who reshuffled and secured them in the portfolio while Carl gazed down the corridor and watched some of the students strolling by them. He then turned back to Paul. "I don't know what to say," said Carl. "But bear with me. On the first pass, I was wondering what the drawings were all about. They were so unexpected and, as you say, not like a photograph at all. But then going through them again, once I was used to their oddity, I quite enjoyed them. Especially since you added titles to put them in context. I really appreciated 'The Virgin' stuck by herself up in a tree with only birds to admire her, and 'The Comedian' with his true face showing behind the mask. You have a way with portrayal and yet convey some message at the same time. You know that I'm not one for this modern art, but I really like what you've done. And perhaps I now see what you mean when you say that you're aiming beyond a true representation of an image."

Paul began to reply, but Carl quickly interrupted.

"Oh, that's not to say that I really understand your drawings, but maybe I can begin to appreciate those who expand their boundaries a little. It's not for me to do, but I can now envision where you may be headed with your art and, frankly, I'm impressed."

"Thank you, and that's what I was hoping for," said Paul. "Not to convert but to gently nudge you a little." And he grinned and slapped Carl on the back. "As we agreed, we're both stuck in the past in one way or another."

"You know, Paul," said Carl. "Whereas I might forget about a realistic drawing that I saw within in a few days, some of your pictures are very memorable and will stay with me for a long time."

They sat on the bench and talked some about Paul's devotion to drawing, his parents, and his desire to return to Munich to be with his new love, Lily. It was getting late and the two wrapped their coats up tightly as they left the campus and walked into the old part of town; Carl said goodbye as

Paul continued his walk across the river and to his parent's home above the bear park.

◄■►

The next afternoon he was walking - though not in a straight line due to wind gusts - in the direction of his shop after a pleasant late-lunch with Süd Hoffman who'd again wanted to show his appreciation for Carl's work on his set of auctioned violins. The wind buffeted and knocked him about so that he felt pummeled by the time he reached his own street.

Once back in his shop, it took Carl a half an hour to warm up and by that time the light was already gone from the sky. Peer had left for home and had damped down the work stove and done a good job of cleaning before locking up – Carl now glad that he'd decided to give Peer a set of shop keys. Thawing out from the cold made him incredibly tired, but he dared not take a nap. It was too late in the day, and he was one of those people who felt worse after a short doze. Where he'd be tired before the nap, he'd be even more groggy and disoriented afterwards if he took one. It was better to soldier through. He fixed himself an early dinner in the apartment and while the soup simmered, went down and checked once more that the shop was secure for the night. Flecken was waiting there behind the door when he opened it, but showed some hesitation before running up the steps and into the cold dark.

After the hot soup, he lurched through the bitter wind to *Zum Bären* and ordered a mug of mulled wine to finally shrug off the remaining chill of the day. Pipe smoke hung low over the room, but thick as it was, he enjoyed the odors. There were few patrons, so Frieda must have taken a welcome break from serving, and he walked to a solitary table after being given a steaming mug by Max alone at the counter. He waited for the spices in his wine to sink and for the fruit bits to rise and blew on the surface before he took a sip. There was even a cinnamon stick to stir with if he wished. He sat back and began to relax with his cold hands wrapped around the warm mug to thaw them out. Max in *Zum Bären* stuck to the old ways and heated the wine with a red-hot poker, so he knew a steaming mug was only a beckon away.

His mental reflections began by ticking off the many things he needed to take care of in the shop over the next few days, and they went on to wondering what he could do about the discovered violin bow. That bow was becoming too big of a distraction and was eating into his work hours. Slowly his thoughts began to wander, and he found himself thinking about his discussions with Albert, and what he himself had learned in school about what lay beyond this earth. He thought about the planets orbiting around the sun, and moons orbiting the planets. An image of the sun, moon, and planets as people slowly formed, and he realized that this was probably due to his discussion with Maria in the restaurant the other night. He was convinced that there was a kind of physics at work in the human realm.

It seemed, Carl thought, that any collection of people eventually ended up circling around a central individual, one somehow with more pull than any of the others. In the case of two people, as in a marriage, the attraction could range from being equally strong between the pair, to one personality being almost totally subsumed by the influence of the other so that none of the weaker *persona* could be expressed. And suddenly his father was there in the bar with him, and the image brought back memories of his family life. This lopsided arrangement of an oversized individual had been the relationship of his parents, and he saw now that his father had completely dominated and stifled his mother. In his mind's eye was the vivid picture of his big-bellied father holding his diminutive mother in an orbit around him as tight as a belt. As that faded, he felt exceptionally lucky that he had found Maria and that they seemed to strike a sort of balance – like the binary stars he'd heard about.

He stared out over the nearly empty tavern and blew across his steaming mug. The attractive force among people at large was generally very light, he thought, and almost imperceptible in most cases, but could become evident when something important, different, or urgent faced the group as a whole. There always seemed to be an individual whom the others looked to or deferred to in making decisions or focusing them on the problem at hand in a time of crisis. He thought that often this person was not immediately recognizable but would become evident when the occasion arose.

In the cases where the attraction to a person was exceptionally strong, as Maria had thought before about Napoleon, entire nations and the fate of the world could hang in the balance. In the instance of a group with no apparent leader or a weak leader, all it might take was for things to be stirred up on some large scale for a charismatic individual to become the new center and provide the attractive force. His thoughts led him to think of the calamity that could befall the world if someone with truly bad intentions should ever provide this focus, and he quickly moved on to lighter subjects.

He'd hardly drunk more than a sip from his mug of wine when he felt like he'd already had too much. He had Max reheat his mug, just for the experience, took a final warm sip, thanked his friend, and then headed back out into the bracing cold toward home, his father's memory leaning heavily against him as he again battled the winds through the narrow streets on which he had so often guided his father back home.

◀ ■ ▶

The next morning Carl built a fire in each of the shop stoves, one to heat the room and the other in preparation for bending the wood needed to replace poor Horst's broken sides. Peer was a little late, and when he did show up, looked under the weather. "How are you feeling, Peer?" asked Carl.

He was answered by watery eyes, a sniffle, and a handkerchief.

"No cocoa for you today. I'll run out and buy some fresh cider we can heat up on the stove. That and some honey and lemons should soon make you as good as new," said Carl. He didn't really want to catch a cold himself, but wanted to make sure that Peer kept the pay that he knew the boy needed and so didn't suggest that Peer return home.

"Do you remember how to shape the corner blocks for the work on the sides?" asked Carl as he put on his coat. Peer muttered that he thought so, and Carl left him to it.

Returning to the shop and letting Peer heat and spice the cider, Carl saw that Peer had shaped each of the four triangle-shaped blocks correctly, and then he had him set to work in shaping the two rectangular blocks that would go at the head and tail. Meanwhile, Carl finished thinning the six slats of maple that he'd roughed out the day before and cut them to the approximate lengths that he'd need. He then steam-bent, glued, and clamped the side pieces together into the mold using the triangular blocks at the corners defining the "C" waist and the neck and tail blocks at the ends. He especially focused on the critical tail joint first, and dry fitted and then glued the joint when happy that it was tight. When the glue had dried, Carl separated the newly formed sides from the mold and had a free-standing violin shape. It was always at this stage that he was reminded that he was building or restoring an entire instrument and not just working with individual pieces of wood.

They had cheese, bread, tomatoes, and mustard for lunch, piling up loose open-faced sandwiches. It was not the tidiest of meals, but they were both starving so it was satisfying. He'd also brought a little bowl of cream for Flecken, and the cat licked the porcelain until it sparkled. After eating and cleaning up, he had Peer sit next to the stove with his head under a small makeshift tent draped over a steaming kettle and breathe in the vapors. Unperturbed, Flecken remained on his lap the entire time. With the steam and a mug of lemon and honey, Peer was feeling much better in the afternoon. Carl had Peer get some fresh air by delivering a violin to a client and running some messages to others who were wondering about the status of their instruments.

Sipping some tea, Carl took up his drawing pad and thought *You're lucky it's not summer or I'd be carting you out to a view of the river.* Instead, he started sketching some alternative scrolls for Gertrud with the badly carved-up neck. He enjoyed spending some time creating the swirls on paper that could become templates for future scrolls and holding the sketch pad at arm's length, he realized that the spirals were very similar to the doodles he unconsciously drew when distracted.

Having taken a long enough break, Carl donned his canvas apron and was about to resume work on the student violins when he was suddenly inspired to begin carving the neck on the violin he was making for himself. He found the block of maple he'd purchased from Old Carl and transferred one of the scroll sketches he'd just made to the wood. The remainder of the afternoon he spent in contentment carving the maple away until, slowly, the shape of a violin neck and scroll began to emerge.

As he shaped the piece, he thought it was an odd juxtaposition that the violin scroll was a beautiful visual component of the instrument, but contributed little or nothing to the sound, and that the sound post was a simple dowel hidden away inside the body and yet it helped shape the voice of the violin and ultimately the aesthetic experience of the music. The violin could function perfectly well without a scroll, but

not as well without a sound post. Somehow earlier craftsmen had arrived at a perfect combination of visual beauty
and intensely pleasing sound. The ornamentation of the scroll
was in handsome proportion and mimicked both rolled paper
as well as some sea shells he'd seen, and it seemed to him to
somehow complete the violin. Many luthiers had even gone
further in ornamenting their instruments. He thought of a
visit he'd made to a museum in Vienna where he'd seen many
violins including one by Hans Krouchdaler who, two centuries before, had made violins that were beautifully inlaid with
fine wooden patterns on the top and back. The student violins
seemed slapdash by comparison.

◄■►

In the middle of a late dinner he suddenly realized, with a
start, that he'd completely forgotten the next scheduled music
session with Albert and the chamber group. With the thought
that they sometimes ran very late, he wolfed down what remained on his plate and ran most of the kilometer to Geron's
house. By the time he arrived, he barely needed his overcoat
in spite of the cold and climbed the front steps with his coat
flaps open.

It took some time for anyone to hear the door knocker and
that gave him the respite he needed to catch his breath. Two
of Geron's daughters, he found out after introductions, greeted him giggling as they opened the door. Carl was shown in
and found that the group was on the third of five pieces they
were playing that evening. Carl nodded while trying to con-

vey apologies as he caught Geron's eye, and Geron responded with a wink. There were several people gathered in a small audience, and most appeared to be in their teens. Taking Carl's place in the quintet, as the third violin, sat a student - tall with blond hair and flaming cheeks in response to the warm room and possibly from playing in front of an audience.

The piece went well, and during a break Carl had the chance to greet and apologize to the others for being so tardy. "It's not ingrained in my schedule yet," he explained. The next was a quartet arrangement meaning he would sit out anyway, but he'd be able to play in the final number. As the song advanced, he met his stand-in violinist, Friedrich, a fifteen-year-old who quietly introduced Carl to the other students in attendance. They mainly came from Geron's classes, but included in the group were friends from other schools. Friedrich whispered that he was a pupil of Master Ehrlich's. Friedrich quickly packed up his violin as they spoke in subdued tones and thanked Carl for letting him stand in. "No thanks needed," whispered Carl. "You sounded very good."

"Oh, by chance, it's a piece that we're playing now at school, so I could almost play it with my eyes shut. Get me on another unfamiliar composition, however, and I struggle. I wouldn't have even let them try and get me to play."

"Me, too, for scores I don't know," agreed Carl.

The remainder of the evening at Geron's was pleasant. After performing and seeing the other guests out, Geron shut the remaining four into a lavish den, and he completely relaxed knowing that there was a barrier between him and his wife and daughters. There were cigars for those who wanted and brandy for all.

As was becoming usual now, Carl and Albert, cradling Lina, walked home together. Carl wanted to ask Albert more about his visit to the train station the previous evening, but Albert was focused on Mileva and her problems which took Carl a little by surprise.

"Do you ever question how good a husband you are, Carl?" asked Albert.

Carl hesitated a moment at the unexpected question. "Actually, yes, especially with Maria being so far away. It isn't so easy to maintain a relationship at a distance as you might think."

"Yes, at a distance," said Albert and paused. "There are all sorts of distances, aren't there?"

"I suppose so," said Carl.

"Mileva's trying so hard at home, but I can see that she's under all sorts of pressure, and is not always so happy," sighed Albert. "She was in classes with me at the university and sought a degree, but she's had to give all that up when she had our son. It's a strain for her to no longer be in an academic program, and it's beginning to show. Caring for Hans Albert along with the household duties are demeaning to her now compared with her scholarly pursuits and on top of that, she's having problems with her younger sister Zorka - they're growing apart. I know that she loves our son, but being isolated and cooped up with him all day long only compounds all of these other things that are beginning to affect her deeply."

"Well, I'm sure that you're both trying your best," offered Carl. "Maria and I have never had children, but all the parents I talk to say that the earliest years are the hardest."

"They are at that," nodded Albert, "but it's absolutely no help that I'm working six days a week. Look at me. If I'm not working, I'm consumed by my physics problems, and then to unwind I'm out of the house in the evenings playing music."

"It's all a juggling act," commiserated Carl. "From the second we get up, we have to meet our own goals and help others reach theirs. It's just that not everyone can reach their goals at the same time."

Albert was silent as they walked on and then said, "Well, I'm going to try and do better at helping Mileva reach her goals and try and help out more with our son so that she has more time to herself."

Already knowing some of Albert's nature, Carl suspected that Mileva might be in for a bit of a rough stretch in the years ahead unless this newfound concern was stronger than Albert's love of physics.

CHAPTER 17

Carl received a message the next morning from Master Ehrlich. "The inventory is mostly completed - and mostly a disaster. Come by when you can – fifth period is the best," was all it said. As interested as he was in finding out what the inventory had revealed, Carl had a full day ahead of him and knew that tomorrow would be the soonest that he could stop by the higher-grade school.

Just as he'd finished reading the message, there was another knock on the door. A policeman entered with an update for him. "Good morning, sir," said the officer. "Sub-Commander Mortensen said to tell you that an investigator from Italy is going to arrive tomorrow afternoon to examine the bow that had been in Jan Rauss's possession. The sub-commander wants to know if you have any more information that might help with the identification."

"Tell the sub-commander that I've just learned from Master Ehrlich that he's completed an inventory of what the school's students should possess, and I'll let him know if anything interesting turns up," said Carl. *There goes tomorrow afternoon,* he thought as the policeman made his way up the steps to street level. At the top, the policeman stepped aside for Peer who was just coming down. Closing the door, Peer said that he'd slept from the moment he arrived at home yesterday and was now feeling much better. Carl thought that his throat sounded scratchier, but that he did look somewhat improved.

Carl turned back to his work while Peer continued French polishing the many violins still needing completion. He was interrupted several times by customers dropping off violins for repairs and by his friend Süd who would pop in occasionally. Süd could become bored after long periods alone in his own store and had a circuit of friends he would stop by and chat with to break up his day. They had a good discussion while Carl grabbed some leftover potatoes and hot cocoa for a quick lunch. Süd declined the potatoes but joined in a cup of cocoa along with Peer. Carl later felt like he'd rushed his friend out, but had to get back to work.

When the daylight was waning, he tidied up, sent home a dragging Peer who plodded up the stairs carrying the cat, and went through the mail as he locked the shop and headed upstairs to make some dinner. By chance, he had replies from both Arassi in Italy and Aculon in France. Both said that they stamped their entire name on the bow, but Aculon added that there was a screw supplier who did engrave the end of the screw with the letter "A", however, he believed that the English bow maker Samuel Allen might also only use the initial of his last name, and to check with him. Carl drafted a quick letter to Mr. Allen, but was in need of an address to be able to post it.

◄■►

Peer didn't show up the following morning. Carl guessed that he was still fighting his cold and thought it was best for Peer to fully recover anyway. He cleaned up the edges on Horst, the violin with the broken sides for which he'd earlier joined the top and back to the new ones, and was now ready to cut the mortise, or neck pocket, to accept the original neck. He made light markings with chalk on the violin to establish the centerline and make certain that the neck would be properly aligned. He then took measurements of the neck heel to determine the shape and depth needed for the new neck pocket and carefully marked the outlines of the new mortise. Carl stopped here in the process and poured himself a cup of coffee. This next stage usually went well, but he'd had a few instances where his cuts caused a misalignment that could take hours to straighten out and remedy. Taking a breath and setting down his coffee cup, he then took up his chisel and patiently carved out the area between these marked lines, testing the fit with the neck often, until he had a pocket into which he could tightly slide the heel for a perfect joint. With a sigh of relief and satisfied with the position and fit of the neck, he warmed up some horse-hide glue, painted this into the neck pocket, and then positioned and clamped the neck in place.

Closing the large shutter doors, with Peer gone he had no choice but to lock up his shop during the noon hour. He wrapped his winter coat more tightly around himself, as a wind had blown up again overnight, and had an invigorating walk to *Der Sturm* where he enjoyed a hot lunch of sauerkraut, potatoes, and sausage and decided to have a schnapps with it as well since it was frigid outside and he knew that it might be quite a while before he was working back in his shop after his meetings with Master Ehrlich and Sub-Commander

Mortensen. The schnapps made the hike to the school feel more difficult, but less cold. It was a long way, however, and the effects of the alcohol were gone by the time he was knocking on Master Ehrlich's door at the school.

"Hello, Carl!" greeted Master Ehrlich. "This is perfect timing since it's my free period and I've just finished lunch. Have you eaten yet?"

"Yes, I just ate," replied Carl. "But I could almost eat again after that freezing cold walk!" His hands were covering his ears to help thaw them out, and he was stamping his feet to warm his numbed toes.

"Well, let me know if you change your mind about lunch," said Master Ehrlich. "Now, here are the results of my inventory," and he laid a large ledger book out on his cluttered desk after shoving some musical scores aside. They both sat down next to the desk and looked over the columns of numbers. Carl's eyes were still tearing from the cold, and he dabbed at them frequently with a handkerchief held in stiff hands to be able to make out the figures. There were 108 violins listed from both this school and the two other schools that fell under the school district administered by the educational trust.

"I've made indications in the ledger if the inventory for a student, violin, and bow all matched with these little marks," Master Ehrlich said pointing. "There ended up being five numbered violins missing, but since the students in these situations each possessed a violin, it was difficult to know, as I'll explain, if it was the violins or the inventory that was the problem. You see, there were also 22 violins that were misassigned or were sitting in the storeroom. And to further complicate things, since about one quarter of the students own their violins and no longer have those provided by the school, it's difficult to tell when they acquired them and whether the school violin they may have had previously was marked off as returned. In other words, it looks like my accounting over the years may have become a little lax."

Inwardly dismayed, Carl said, "Well, I'm not surprised since every year you have new students, new violins, and repairs I make which change the violins listed in this catalogue. I sure wouldn't envy anyone the job of keeping them all straight."

He received a sympathetic nod from the Master.

"Unfortunately," said Master Ehrlich in a dejected tone as he pointed at the ledger, "this column shows the disaster that has become of the bow inventory. Since the bow cases get separated from the violins, and since once opened, bows get put back in the wrong cases, I wasn't even going to try and reestablish the connections with the cases. The good news is that every violin has a bow associated with it. The figures in this column are the numbers etched onto the side of each tightening knob on each bow when they were assigned to the student. I tried in the first period to sort out where each bow should go and for the most part have come up with a means to rotate bows across periods and the store room supply so that now the inventory is largely correct. I would say 75% anyway, or maybe 60%."

"So, there's no way to really tell what happened to Jan's original bow, or if it was the one found in the river?" asked Carl.

"Oh, didn't I mention? I found it! Number 32 that was assigned to Jan showed up in a case from the next period held by Frank Meyer. Frank had been assigned number 61, and that one hasn't shown up yet. He has the violin assigned to him, but not the bow. It really is just a mess. I'm sorry that approaching the problem from the inventory side doesn't seem like it's going to be any help at all."

No, thought Carl, but he asked, "So maybe this isn't worth pursuing anymore? If no one is missing a bow or has reported one missing, how can we possibly know where the discovered bow came from? I heard from two bow makers that had the initial "A" in their last names, and the bow of interest was manufactured by neither of them. I should also hear later this afternoon if the bow came from Italy, based on an expert who's going to talk with Sub-Commander Mortensen from the police. Otherwise, I'd say we're out of luck."

"I have to agree," said Master Ehrlich with a sigh. Carl couldn't tell if it was from disappointment or relief. Master Ehrlich continued, "I'll explain all of this to the trustees at their next meeting and see if they think there's anything else they would like to pursue. We certainly don't have to worry about a theft if one hasn't been reported."

"One more thing that you might try," said Carl, "is to ask each of the students who own their instruments if they're missing a bow like the one that Jan had. You might even talk to the parents if that's convenient, since the students might not want to admit to misplacing a bow like that."

"Good idea!" said Master Ehrlich, "There really aren't that many personally owned violins involved, and we have parent/teacher meetings coming up soon, which will provide the perfect opportunity to ask the parents."

Carl left their meeting with a weight lifted from his shoulders. Not that it had been that burdensome of a task, but he was glad to be freed from this distraction. Just to follow up, however, he changed his course so that he was walking towards the police station.

Sub-Commander Mortensen greeted him warmly when he was shown into the office.

"It turns out that the Italian gentleman is an insurance investigator. He left just a little while ago to catch the next train on the trail of the stolen violins. He affirmed that the bow that we have was not from among those stolen in Italy. He also said that it was indeed a fine bow, and that he would assign quite some value to it. It appears to be older than we might have suspected, and the age and condition increase the value. He looked it over carefully and surmised that for its age it had been relatively lightly used, possibly restrung with new horsehair at some point, and then suffered some superficially when played by Jan. More than that he couldn't say."

Carl was surprised and hadn't thought that the bow would be quite that valuable. "It looks like you'd better keep this safe until you find the owner," said Carl.

"Wait!" said Mortensen "I thought *you* were going to be the one to track this down."

Carl described his visit with Master Ehrlich and the condition of the bookkeeping, and about the letters from the French and Italian bow makers.

"Damn," Mortensen said with a sigh, "I was expecting to be able to take at least one thing off my plate. I haven't even officially written this case up yet, which means even more documentation and paperwork. Well, thanks for your help, Carl, and if you could do me a favor and keep your eyes and ears open for anything that might help the bow find its owner, I'd greatly appreciate it."

"Will do," said Carl a little too jubilantly. A groan escaped Mortensen as Carl headed out the door.

◄■►

Carl walked home in the late afternoon, and as he passed the train station, who should he notice but Albert ambling along slowly in the same direction lost in thought. Somehow the bent head, unkempt dark hair, long overcoat, and gait were immediately recognizable, even from behind. Carl called to him, and they both fell into step together.

"I see you like your trains," said Carl. "Or is it just a coincidence that I run into you here in front of the station again?"

"I left work early and ended up here on a walk, I guess because I'd been thinking about trains," realized Albert.

"I've been meaning to ask. Were you specifically waiting for the train I arrived on from Zurich the last time I saw you at the station? Or were you thinking about trains in general then, too?"

"Well, you're not going to believe this, but I was actually thinking about trains in relation to light."

"What possible connection is there between trains and light? Well, I guess I should have known it would have something to do with light," laughed Carl. "What that could possibly have to do with trains though, I could never guess."

Albert shrugged and gave a little smile as he strolled towards home with Carl. "It does sound odd, doesn't it? Well, to put it simply ..." and then he stopped. They were next to a cart selling children's toys, and Albert stepped over to it and picked up a red rubber ball.

"Say, do you have half an hour or so to spare?" asked Albert.

Carl thought for a moment about the fact that he'd already lost most of the day anyway and then said, "Sure. Why?"

"It will help me in what I've been thinking about," said Albert as he bought three of the rubber balls from the vendor and then led Carl through the gaping entrance of the train station.

"We'll just make a quick trip out of town and right back," said Albert as he stepped up to the ticket counter and purchased two round-trip tickets to Thun. At that moment, the train boarding whistle sounded, and Albert hustled Carl aboard. They walked through the cars until Albert found the emptiest one in the line and handed Carl one of the red rubber balls as they took a seat.

"Here, bounce this ball while the train is stopped, and keep it up as the train leaves the station and gets up to speed," said Albert.

"Why?" asked Carl.

"It's just a little experiment I've been thinking about," said Albert.

"So, what does this have to do with light?" asked Carl as the ball bouncing began and the trip was about to commence.

"I don't want to influence what we're doing, so how about if we talk about that when we get back?" asked Albert to a shrug of the shoulders from Carl. The two of them bounced the balls and engaged in small-talk as the doors closed, the whistle blew, and the train began chugging towards Thun. When they were underway at full speed, Albert stood and walked towards the other end of the car.

"Hey, Carl, let's play some catch," shouted Albert, and threw the ball to a startled Carl, much to the amusement of the few fellow passengers. Carl missed a few times and had to scramble for the bouncing ball, but otherwise they tossed the ball back and forth, retaking their seats as the train slowed to a stop in Thun.

"Well, that was strange," said Carl as they stepped down from the train.

"Yes, but it should help me just the same," said Albert.

It was a matter of minutes before they boarded the next train headed back to Bern. They sat for a time until the engine gained speed while Albert explained what he wanted Carl to do next. In a few minutes Carl found himself at the end of one of the railcars and peering out of the window facing into the chilling wind. Albert was two cars ahead holding one of the red rubber balls. When Albert drew next to a telegraph pole, he dropped the ball and Carl watched it fall, hitting well beyond the pole as it passed, and bouncing forward as it hit the nearby field. Then holding another ball, Albert waited for a passing pole to reach him and threw the ball towards Carl's end of the train. The ball appeared to drop in the vicinity of the pole and when it bounced, it barely moved forward at all. Then the two swapped positions, and Albert threw the last ball towards Carl in the direction the train was travelling. The ball just about reached Carl two cars ahead when it hit the ground but bounced forward at great speed and nearly paced the train for a few bounces.

"OK, what was all of that about?" asked Carl as the train pulled into the station and the two climbed down from the car.

"It was this," said Albert as they began to walk towards home. "When we were in the train, did you notice any difference at all in the rubber balls as we were standing still in the station compared to when we were running at full speed?"

"No," said Carl after thinking for a minute.

"When we were bouncing the balls, they went straight down and came straight back up. But outside the train, things changed, didn't they?" asked Albert to a nod from Carl. "You noticed that I used the telegraph poles as markers like I said I would?" Carl nodded again. "When I dropped the ball straight down, it landed well beyond the pole that I was beside when I dropped it, but to us it looked like it went pretty much straight down, except for the push of the wind, right?" Carl nodded yet again. "And it was going the speed of the train when it hit. So, to someone watching from the outside, the ball didn't go straight down, but followed the train along until it landed way past the pole."

"Then when we were playing catch inside the train, the balls didn't go any faster or slower in either direction, did they seem to?" Carl shook his head. "But outside, the one I threw towards you when you were behind me seemed to just drop down near the pole, and the one I threw towards you when you were ahead of me was going quite fast and bounced forward at great speed. Well, all of this illustrates two things I've been thinking about," said Albert as they walked between the darkening buildings.

"I've been envisioning a train racing at near the speed of light and what that would mean. The first thing is that no matter how fast the train is going with the windows closed, you can't detect its speed by any clues inside. The actions of the balls or any other experiment you might try won't vary with the forward motion of the train. You can't tell if the train is going at the speed of light or stopped dead still – on a quiet train on silk-smooth rails, of course. All of the measurements you make remain relative to the train you're on."

"The second point is that the speed of light is constant no matter how it's viewed. With the rubber balls, the one I dropped straight down outside of the train was moving at the speed of the train, the one I threw to the rear canceled out the train speed by how hard I threw it and it dropped nearly straight down, and the one I threw forward was going at the train speed and increased by the speed I threw it. If those rubber balls were light, they would all be travelling at exactly the same speed – no faster, and no slower no matter who saw it from what position. And this has huge consequences," said Albert.

"How so?" asked Carl, dumbfounded.

"There are experiments that show that the faster something is going, and I mean at really high rates of speed, the shorter it actually becomes in the direction of travel. So, on our train traveling at near the speed of light, a meter stick would still measure a meter, but it would actually be a shorter meter than one measured if the train was stopped. The train and everything on it would be shortened, but no one inside would be able to tell that it was. OK, now here's the tricky part. We measure speed by distance and time, say 40 kilometers per hour, right?"

After another nod from Carl, Albert continued, "But if we're hurtling along on a train at near the speed of light, our unit of measure for distance has shrunk. So, if the speed of light is a constant value, what would have to change to make our calculation of speed as the relationship between time and distance come out correct where the distance has actually shrunk?"

Carl thought about this as they walked for a moment in silence. He shook his head, but then answered hesitantly and with misgivings about the correctness of the answer, "Time?"

"Precisely!" exclaimed Albert. "Time would have to slow down for us to measure the constant speed of light with a shortened scale of length."

"That makes no sense to me," said Carl as they approached Albert's home.

"I know, isn't it great?" Albert asked as he shook Carl's hand with a huge smile. "I really appreciate your joining me for that little experiment, Carl," and he turned and headed upstairs, already lost in thought.

Carl was bewildered watching him climb the steps. *That sounded like one of those trick word problems,* he thought shaking his head. *I wonder if Albert's pulling my leg this time. That just can't be real, can it?*

CHAPTER 18

Carl began his morning by finalizing the woodwork on Horst, the violin into which he had set the neck. He shaped the end of the neck heel where it met the plane of the back until they matched seamlessly. It looked like an excellent job, and once varnish was applied, no one would know that this violin had been destroyed and now had completely new sides. Peer came running down the steps and into the shop, slammed the door, and went straight to the stove to warm up. There was a sparkle in his eyes again, and he looked much better with a healthy glow about him. After cleaning up any glue that had smeared out of the joint, Carl had Peer set to sanding Horst and beginning the long task of applying the finish. Rather than sending him back out into the cold again, Carl bundled up to run some errands himself.

The clouds were low and the wind was brisk; anyone outside was hidden in a coat and a hat and hustled by in a hurry. Yet as Carl passed a small square, he noticed a figure attempting to huddle out of the wind behind the steps leading up to a small church. A violin lay on the first step next to him which immediately caught Carl's eye, and he realized it was the Yenish gypsy who often played for tourists near the bear pit. Something didn't look right to Carl and as he neared the steps, he could see that the instrument's neck had been snapped in two. The man appeared to be all right, but not the violin. Without thinking, he reached out to examine the instrument when a hand shot out and grabbed his arm while the now-alert man pulled himself away from Carl at the same time.

"I'm sorry," said Carl defensively, "I was only interested in your violin."

"You not have it!" the man nearly shouted in broken German. "Mine!"

"I...I know," said Carl placatingly. "I only meant to see what was wrong with it," and slowly picking it up, he held the scroll-work in one hand and the violin in the other. "What happened to it?" he asked making an exaggerated shrug of his shoulders at the same time to emphasize the question.

"Nothing," replied the gypsy at first, but eventually Carl learned that some drunken young toughs had accosted him the previous evening and stepped on the violin in the process.

"I'm so sorry to hear about this," said Carl sympathetically, "did you call the police?"

The gypsy was immediately shaking his head as he finished and then repeated "No, no Police!" until Carl set the violin down gently and raised his hands for him to stop.

"OK, OK," said Carl. He looked at the violin and then at the man, as he kneeled down to his level in the process. "I can fix it," he said. The Yenish looked at him questioningly, and then Carl took up the two parts and roughly joined them together. "Fix it. I can fix it," he tried. The gypsy's posture and expression slowly relaxed while they worked out that Carl could make the repairs and have it back from the shop to the gypsy fairly quickly.

◀■▶

So, the next major task Carl tackled was rebuilding this neck that had the scrollwork so rudely cracked off. Taking the pieces up, he examined the shattered separation point in the light from the shop door and holding the scroll end and the remainder of the neck in each hand, loosely joined them back together. Except for a few splinters and some small gaps, it would look from a distance like it had never been fractured. Carl knew, however, that if he tried to just glue the two pieces back together as they were, the joint would never be strong enough to tolerate the string tension and would be liable to separate or break again later. It was the peg box, or the open cube holding the tuning pegs, that took the damage, so he'd need to preserve the scroll and insert a new peg box between it and the remainder of the neck.

He clamped the separated section firmly to the bench. Using a fine saw and woodblock as a guide to keep his cut straight, he carefully sawed off the scroll at the exact location and angle he'd determined was best. Turning to the shattered end still attached to the violin, he sawed out a wedge shape into the remaining good wood so that he would have a result-ing "V" as a solid gluing surface for the new peg box graft.

Suddenly, Peer jumped up, scraping his stool with an ir-ritating noise on the floor. Flecken was not impressed with the unexpected excitement and softly yowled from his perch before covering his face with his paw and trying to go back to sleep. From the low vantage point of the shop, Peer could either see the legs of people passing on their side of the street, or the heads of people on the far side. Carl walked over and could see the profile of the girl who'd attracted the boy's attention some days before.

Carl grinned and asked, "Why don't you run out and pick us up some biscuits at Rosselli's, Peer?" He handed the boy a five-franc coin, and Peer went sheepishly up the steps and hesitantly walked across the street to the store next to where the girl was window shopping.

Carl continued the slow process of cutting, chiseling, and sanding a new peg box from the piece of maple he'd chosen for the replacement. Glancing up now and then he saw that Peer and the girl were surprisingly engaged in an awkward conversation. Peer eventually returned to the shop flushed and with a big grin on his face.

"Thanks!" was all he said as he got dreamily back to work.

"Hey, where are the biscuits?" asked Carl.

◄■►

Thierry had sent Carl a rather urgent message wondering if he could make it to a music recital at Thierry's house that very evening. The French teacher was going to be out of town later that week for business and would like to reschedule for tonight rather than miss a practice. The message had included directions to his house. The messenger waited while Carl thought about it and then gave a reply that, yes, he would be able to attend. Carl also realized that he'd better start out soon after work since it was a long walk to the other side of the river. The trek required going downhill to reach the lower bridge and then up a steep slope to the houses on the far side. He finished the chores necessary to wrap up the work-day, locked up, grabbed his violin from upstairs in the apartment, and followed the directions to Thierry's house. He hoped some kind of food might be involved or this would be a long evening.

The walk was beautiful, and frost and ice were already forming at the base of the lengthening shadows. He passed one of the city's many circular fountains with a column in the middle and an ornate figure at the top, this one a knight manhandling a lion. The low sunlight was cold, but bright, and brought out any color left in the browns, oranges, and occasional reds of the few leaves and berries remaining on small bushes along the way. He eventually climbed a street into a very well-kept and much more up-scale neighborhood than he was accustomed to visiting. The house where he ended his walk was smaller than those around it, but very well-appointed nonetheless.

Thierry greeted him at the door, as did the aroma of what he guessed was turkey. He was immediately famished. Being the first to arrive, he and Thierry chatted as he was led to a small sitting room that had cheese and crackers and some wine if Carl so desired, which he did. Carl learned that Thierry was only a part-time French teacher in the schools, and that he was also in a fairly lucrative import-export business with his brother. As the others arrived, he discovered that Thierry needed to make a buying trip to Morocco and Spain and would be gone for two weeks. The group couldn't hide their jealousy and found ways of good naturedly ribbing Thierry all through the evening.

Following the snacks, they played a selection by Beethoven and spent a long time working on a piece by Debussy that they just couldn't seem to get right. In the end, Thierry did not disappoint and served them a small but delicious roasted dinner of turkey, potatoes, and yams. They were provided with brandy afterwards in a den featuring red leather-covered chairs from Spain. The others followed Thierry off to look at his acquisitions from around the world and what he said was an excellent collection of French postcards. Both Albert and Carl begged off and remained contentedly seated in the antique leather chairs.

"Ah, the comforts of home," said Albert with a sad smile.

Carl could imagine him comparing his own apartment with their current elegant surroundings. Albert seemed much more subdued than Carl had seen him before – more relaxed and withdrawn. Perhaps it was the warm room, the company, and the excellent dinner that made him so. Albert took a sip of brandy from a large snifter.

In the absence of Albert leading the conversation as he often, or usually, did they chatted about trivial matters and then Carl said, "You know, I found myself thinking about people the other night. And it occurred to me how much like planets we are."

"Like planets in what way?" asked Albert.

"Well, there seem to be attractions between and among people, just like the planets around the sun. Sometimes it seems to me that there's a type of gravity in everyone. It's especially noticeable that certain people seem to have more of this attractive force. Take Napoleon, for example. What is it that causes certain persons to exert a huge influence on others and cause them to flock and circle about?"

"Good question," said Albert. "You're asking what is charisma? What draws people in?"

"Yes," nodded Carl. "Or is it what they represent or rather their ideas instead of the actual person that's the attractant? Perhaps ideas can carry on long after the person who came up with them is gone, imbued with a form of attraction of their own."

Carl realized that although he enjoyed thinking about this kind of thing, his analytical and mathematical friend might not find it appealing or worthy of the effort.

Then Albert responded, "I'm not sure that attraction by a person is the same thing as the pull that an idea has. But I do like your humanizing physics." Carl had expected him to downplay what he'd said, but Albert seemed to accept it neutrally. They were quiet for a time and then Albert said almost to himself, "Gravity," repeating the word several times as if testing how it sounded. He took another small sip and then reached over and poured the rest of his brandy into Carl's snifter. "I hope you don't mind. I like some things about alcohol, but I can't always seem to get it past my throat – especially brandy. You can have mine," he grimaced and then continued. "Gravity is the one thing that I can't seem to fit into the framework I've established in my own mind. It's always just out of reach. I'm having to resort to fudge factors to make the equations come out, and no one likes fudge factors."

Carl looked at him questioningly and was about to ask what fudge factors were when Albert said, "Oh, yes, um, things we put into equations to make them come out right, even though they make no sense by themselves." Carl nodded and he continued. "We might think that gravity's very strong, living here on earth and falling down occasionally. But it's actually a very weak force. So, it must be amplified in your theory of the attractions among people. When you think about it, there's some gravity in everything, and yet a large rock on the earth can't pull any other objects towards itself because that force is dwarfed by the earth's gravity, and it takes the entire planet to pull the rock towards its surface. And yet gravity is very important in the universe. It operates over vast expanses, and it takes long distances for it to be diminished, and so every large object like a planet or a star is exerting an influence and attraction on all of the other planets, stars, and objects around it."

They sat for a while more. "Yes," said Albert. "I think that ideas are a different kind of thing."

The others returned to the den, and they all discussed the music they'd been rehearsing – Albert saying that he didn't particularly care for Debussy - Thierry's upcoming trip, and what they should practice for the small concert they were going to give over Christmas. They agreed on pieces by Bach, Corelli, and Mendelssohn. Albert accepted a ride home, settling into Geron's carriage with a mellow look on his face, and Carl decided to walk and enjoy the night air.

The evening's discussion with Albert had made Carl reminisce about his parents. It was only through hindsight that he was able to see how strong and dominant a personality his father, Josef, had been and how meek and dependent had been Hilda, his mother. And their relationship, involving a domineering husband, was in step with many other marriages in the town.

Josef had been best friends with Hans Klee and with Old Carl, although in spite of his name, Old Carl had been the youngest of the three. Almost all their meetings were boisterous, and they were together nearly every evening at *Zum Bären*, their favorite local tavern. At home, Josef was either in the shop or continually belittling Hilda, although Carl was sure that they must have had their more tender moments, or he never would have come into being. Despite his treatment of her, Hilda had doted on Josef, cooking, cleaning, shopping, tending the small garden, and mending his clothes all in an effort to keep him happy. To Carl, it had seemed a normal childhood.

After Josef had died, Hilda was adrift. She had lived for another three years following her husband's passing and spent nearly all of her time sitting in the over-grown garden or in the cluttered house, either staring out into space or working on needlepoint. Carl and Maria visited often and had Hilda to Sunday dinner every week, but the conversations were mostly one-sided on their part. Hilda was engaged in their lives, but also seemingly uninterested in her own.

Carl wondered what his mother's life would have been like had she been attracted to someone more similar to herself. Or perhaps she had always been destined to be swept into orbit around the strong, magnetic personality of someone like Josef.

◄■►

The next morning, Geron unexpectedly knocked on the shop door and entered, the bell on the door tinkling as he did so. Carl set down his coffee on the workbench and moved to meet him.

"Oh, so this is what you do," said Geron as they shook hands and he perused the cluttered work space. Carl introduced him to Peer who nodded back in greeting.

"Nice shop," Geron continued.

"Thanks," said Carl. "That was fun last night, wasn't it? What brings you by?"

"Oh, I had a little extra time this morning, so I wanted to let each member of our group know about the exciting change of plans as soon as I heard of them."

"What change? Some coffee?" asked Carl.

"Sure, if you have some," said Geron, and continued as Carl found a cup, wiped out the sawdust, and poured in the coffee. "You know how we were going to have a small Christmas performance at that chapel near the bridge? Well, we're moving it now to Mme. Guiveny's mansion!"

"What?" asked Carl as he shakily handed Geron his mug. "Why?"

"Well, apparently Mme. Guiveny has decided to hold a fundraiser for the holidays and has invited us, as well as another adult quartet, a duet, and several of the student orchestras to showcase the event. She said that she had the idea to invite mainly amateurs and students to perform rather than people who make a living playing music. It's going to raise funds for music education, and she's invited fifty of the most prominent businessmen in town to attend. As a final gesture, she's going to auction off a piano and a violin that she owns and apply the proceeds towards the same cause. Isn't that sensational?"

Carl's hands began to sweat, and he suddenly felt cold despite standing next to the warm stove. He hated performing in public.

"Oh, yes," faltered Carl. "When is this going to take place?"

"On December 17th – a week before Christmas, and a week after schools close for the holidays. For me, that means I'll have a whole week to practice before the performance."

"Yes, good," said Carl. *A month to go of the jitters,* he thought.

Geron continued, "She's really quite a supporter of the arts, you know. Especially music. Every summer she hosts music camps at her mansion and has even set up two different halls for small and larger performances. She doesn't house the kids, but provides full lunches for them while they're there. Any teacher feels lucky to be invited to the camp. I've gone twice, and she really is the most charming person, if not getting a little old and forgetful. I never feel slighted if she doesn't remember my name though. My oldest daughter has been to camp twice playing the clarinet, as well." He set down his still-full cup. "OK, thanks for the coffee. I'm off to tell the others, and I'd better catch Thierry before he leaves. Don't forget to mark your calendar," and with a shaking of hands, Geron was off.

Carl closed the door behind him, telling himself again and again that his was just a supporting role.

◄■►

The new peg box insert was roughed out, and Carl spent the next hour on the Yenish violin, carefully refining the male wedge on that piece to perfectly match the female 'V' he had previously cut into the existing neck. Once happy with the fit of the joint, so that it stayed in place without being held, he applied glue and clamped the two firmly together.

Taking a break and warming his hands over the stove, he thought about the Yenish man he was trying to help. There were few Yenish in Bern compared to other parts of the country but they lived as well as they could among his fellow townsfolk, and he knew that this man wasn't the only one he'd heard of who'd been mistreated. Standing in his comfortable shop next to a blazing stove, he wondered if the man had family nearby, where he slept at night, and how he managed to stay warm. He also vaguely wondered how he'd find him again.

The original scroll to be reattached to the other end of the new box would not receive any stress from the pull of the strings, so doweling would be acceptable. He drilled four holes into the detached scroll and then drilled matching dowel holes in the new peg box. After all was ready, he applied glue to the dowels, fitted them in the holes, pushed the two parts together, and then clamped the whole bundle to dry.

Now he was at a point in the process where Peer could help and learn something new at the same time. The final stages were to finish carving the peg box, drill the holes for the tuning pegs, and then ream them to the proper size. He chose a small chisel and had Peer begin the carving. The chisel slipped badly once and just nicked Peer's hand, so Carl decided that he'd do the carving himself. When finished, he called Peer back over and had him drill out the peg holes with the safer brace and bit tool. Peer then reamed each peg hole to the proper shape which was slightly conical so that friction alone would hold the tuning pegs in place. He had a standardized reamer that shaved minute amounts of wood away from the holes until the drilled initially cylindrical shape became a perfect cone to accept the tapered pegs. Peer did a great job and then proudly carried the neck away for varnishing.

Maybe he really will become an apprentice some day! thought Carl.

◄■►

Carl had rushed to the Post Office to mail some packages for Maria just before closing and decided to follow a return route along the curve of the River Aare on its arc through the city and then to meander randomly along the streets on his way back home. In the gathering dark, he was back on his own street, Kramgasse, when he heard violin music coming from a window that had been cracked open. He glanced up and recognized Albert's apartment as the source of the sound. The lights in the house had not been fully lit for the evening, but there was a soft glow emanating from inside, perhaps from a candle on a table near the second story window.

It took a moment for Carl to recognize the melody that Albert was playing – it was, of all things, the tune that had been played by the Yenish gypsy near the bear pits - but it soon went off in a more melancholy direction and it was obvious that he was playing free-form rather than any set piece. Not wishing to appear obvious or suspicious to the neighbors as a loiterer, he feigned interest in one of the circular fountains, this one with an armored bear in fighting stance at the top of the column. He admired the fountain for as long as he thought seemly, and then went to sit at the edge of the covered walkway across the street out of the lamplight. The music emanating from Lina alternated from following a brisk tempo, to slowing, and at one point a single note stretched out for a quarter minute before finding its beat and the melody again. The original song was left far behind as the tune wove on in a non-repetitive course that was somehow faithful to a certain mood.

Albert was obviously thinking as much as playing which accounted for the occasional falling off altogether of the path of the music, and Carl could tell when his mind was on the notes and when it was somewhere else. *This reminds me of the doodles that appear on paper when I'm lost in thought*, reflected Carl. As he headed home, he was in awe at being able to listen to Albert's thought process in a completely different, non-verbal manner. At least the music he could understand.

CHAPTER 19

Carl had risen early the last few mornings to make progress on his own violin. The scroll was carved, and the neck shaped, and he was nearing the point where the neck and body could be joined. He picked up the light body and tapping here and there was rewarded by a clear ringing tone. Holding it horizontally in front of his face, he blew across an f-hole and heard a pleasant resonance. He'd begun the final sanding when Peer arrived and hung up his coat. Flecken had followed him in, and Peer grabbed the cat and held him as they both warmed themselves by the stove. A low purring resonated from somewhere in the shop.

"How did the party go?" Carl asked as Peer petted a draping Flecken. The Bergmans had asked that Peer leave work early the day before to help them set up for a wedding celebration.

"It was busy, but didn't go that late," said Peer shrugging. "Max let me go to bed while he cleaned up the rest."

"That's good to hear," said Carl, "and the business is going well?"

"Max said that Oktoberfest wasn't the money-maker he'd expected, but that things were picking up now. He said that he has high hopes for the holidays."

"Well, I definitely plan to keep up my patronage," said Carl with a grin. Peer nodded and set the big cat up on his perch, grabbing a broom. "Peer," continued Carl. "Are the Bergmans planning on you joining their business? Do you have any thoughts about what you want to become when you … get older?" He had been about to say, 'grow up', but realized that someone of Peer's age might take exception to that word choice. "You know, a profession?"

Peer swept under the workbench and then said, "Not really." He filled a dustpan and then added, "Don't tell Max, but I know that I don't want to run a tavern. Too noisy and smelly."

Carl resumed his sanding and thought the conversation was concluded.

"I do like this work, though," Peer quietly mumbled. "What?" asked Carl. "Well, that's good to hear. You know I'm glad to have you in the shop – you really are a big help."

"Thanks, Carl," said Peer and Carl thought he detected a small smile on the boy.

The next thing he knew, Carl was finishing up a project and unexpectedly realized that the lighting outside had changed from sunlight to streetlamps. *Really?* he asked himself. He shook out and hung up his apron and was walking over to turn off the lamps and dampen down the stove when he realized that Peer wasn't on the premises. *Now where's he gone? Carl wondered. I don't remember him leaving. And the cat's scampered, too.* Shaking his head at his forgetfulness or inattention, he climbed up the steps out of the shop and closed and locked the shutters behind him. The air was brisk, and he could see his breath as he made his way to the stairway leading to the apartment, rubbing the dust from his hair as he did so.

At the top, he turned the key and opened the door fumbling for the light switch. Suddenly the light came on by itself, and he jumped back when there was a shout of "Surprise!" There stood Maria and Peer both grinning madly in paper hats and waving colored streamers. He noticed that his hand had jumped to his heart. His nostrils were suddenly hit by the aroma of roasting chicken. Maria ran into his arms and said, "We did surprise you this time, didn't we?"

"I'll say!" said Carl hugging her tightly. "I'd wondered where you'd gotten to," he directed at a now laughing Peer.

"How did you possibly arrange this, Maria?" he asked, slowly holding her out to arm's length.

"I had no classes until late tomorrow and was free today, so I thought it was the perfect time to slip into town and wish you a happy birthday," she said gleefully. "I snuck in after you had lunch and then caught Peer to clue him in on the plan when he ran an errand this afternoon."

"And now it's time for presents!" shouted Peer as he ducked into the kitchen and brought out a pitcher full of beer. "My parents wanted to donate to the cause from the tavern, and they send their best."

"Well, tell them thank you!" said Carl as he poured them each a glass – a smaller one for Peer.

Maria handed him a bundle wrapped in cloth. Inside were two sets of new violin strings. He could see immediately that they were the newly available variety where two of the strings in each set were gut wrapped around a steel wire core. "For your new project," she said and gave him a kiss. "And maybe for the next one too."

They settled in to a steaming meal of roasted chicken and Brussels sprouts combined with lively conversation, and then they saw Peer off before the hour grew too late. Opening the grate to the cook stove, they brought over two chairs and watched the flames turn to embers while they talked and bathed in each other's company.

◄■►

Maria was sifting through the bills and his work-log the next morning when she raised her head. "Carl, what's this - two days spent on 'scroll repair'? I can't find the billing for it."

"Oh, well I couldn't charge him," commented Carl as he was pouring them coffee.

"What? Why ever not?" asked Maria indignantly. "If you put in the time you've simply got to charge for your work, Carl. We can't really afford for you to be just giving your services away."

"Well, honey, there is no way that he could pay for it," began Carl, and rushing through before she could respond, "you see there is this Yenish that plays down near the bear park..." After his explanation of the gypsy's misfortune and Peer's tracking him down to return the finished violin, Maria got up from the chair and embraced her husband. "You're a good man, Carl. Not so good with finances, but passably good," and they both laughed.

Maria was off to Zurich later that morning, but Carl thought that it was one of the best visits they'd had in a long time.

◄■►

A trio that Paul belonged to was performing in a small concert hall, and as Carl entered, he saw that the attendance was unusually light. He was surprised to find Albert and Mileva seated off the aisle to the right and went over and sat in the free seat next to Albert. They exchanged greetings, with Carl leaning over to lightly shake Mileva's hand, and then Carl asked about the poor attendance.

"The opera is performing *La Traviata* tonight and is sold-out. This, on the other hand, is free, and we found a baby sitter for the evening. Mileva and I are making a night of it and just had an excellent dinner at a nearby restaurant."

Mileva leaned over with a grin. "Just like the old days, except all I can do is worry about Hans Albert," she sighed.

"Well, if this is a good performance, it should take your mind off your son at home," said Carl hopefully. Just as the lights dimmed, Carl asked if either of them knew Paul. Both shook their heads, and Carl pointed out the figure in the position on the left of the trio.

The performance was more than good, and the light crowd gave an appropriately loud applause. As Albert and Mileva began to gather up their coats to leave, Carl asked if they could wait a moment and said he thought that they would enjoy meeting Paul. They agreed, and the three chatted with coats hanging over their arms until the trio appeared from back stage. Paul noticed them and walked up, greeting Carl and shaking his hand.

"An excellent performance as usual," said Carl. "Paul, I wanted to introduce two friends of mine, Albert and Mileva Einstein. And this is Paul Klee," continued Carl as he gestured toward the violinist.

"A pleasure to meet you both," said Paul.

"Likewise," said Albert. "I believe I've seen you in the symphony orchestra, haven't I?" he asked as Paul nodded.

"Yes, I've committed to playing this season with them," replied Paul

"Well, very nice execution here tonight, too," said Albert. "Have you lived in Bern long?"

"Pretty much my entire life, except for some years at university in Munich. I was actually born in Münchenbuchsee, but we moved to Bern when I was only one-year old. My childhood home is coincidentally just around the corner. And you?" asked Paul.

"Well, I was born in Ulm, but spent many years with my family in Munich," replied Albert. "Since then, I applied for Swiss citizenship and moved here from Zurich some years back, and then Mileva made the move to join me."

"Didn't you love living in Munich?" asked Paul. "Especially the area around the Fine Arts Academy?"

"We lived on the other end of the city, and I rarely made it up that far," replied Albert. "Though Munich is fine. Are you married?"

"No, I have a sweetheart in Munich, and she visits occasionally. We'll have to see how things go as regards marriage though. Are you working?" asked Paul.

"Yes, at the Patent Office near the train station. How about you?"

"No, I'm currently living at home with my parents," sighed Paul. "But it does give me time to follow my passion."

"Oh?" asked Albert. "And what is that?"

"Drawing," said Paul. "The peace and quiet at my parent's house, at least when father's out teaching, helps me focus."

"I'm in a somewhat similar situation," said Albert. "Oddly, the Patent Office job gives me time to follow my passion, as well."

Mileva could see that they were both about to launch into long explanations about what excited them and gently tugged at Albert's sleeve. "It's been good to meet you, Paul," she said. "Our son is waiting for us at home, but perhaps you and Albert could meet sometime to continue the conversation?" To her surprise, they agreed to meet later that evening at a tavern near Albert's house. They all left together with Mileva smiling and shaking her head at the same time.

◀ ■ ▶

Carl had difficulty sleeping that night and lay awake initially with random thoughts that soon turned as they would to worries about work. To distract himself, he thought about applying finish to his violin in the morning, and what color he wanted it to be. He was finally just falling asleep when he remembered the piece of maple he'd spilled coffee on months before. *It might be a perfect color!* he realized. *I can't wait to see what became of it.*

Flecken had been sitting on the shutter doors when he came down from his apartment in the pre-light and was anxious to get into the shop. "You might be showing your age lately, Flecken," he'd said to the cat. "A few years ago, you'd still be out on the prowl." By dawn, there were two pots boiling on the stove: one was for his normal cup of coffee, and the other he'd packed solidly with grounds to make the darkest brew possible, the strong aroma filling the shop. He'd examined the coffee-stained maple piece and quite liked the color but preferred it many shades darker. It was hardly traditional, but he'd heard of others using tea, or sometimes coffee, to stain the wood, and was feeling adventurous since no one other than himself would be playing the instrument when done.

Once the coffee had brewed for much longer than normal, he tried some drops on a scrap of wood. It would be nearly dark enough if it were a little more concentrated, so he let the pot boil away for another hour. Happy with the next test result, he let the coffee cool and then, dipping a rag into the liquid, smeared it over all of the surfaces of the violin he'd assembled earlier, wiping extra dampness off quickly with an additional rag.

When the wood was dry, he took the finest sanding cloth he had on hand and lightly rubbed off all the miniscule fibers that had been raised by the coffee liquid, without sanding out any of the color. After being sealed with shellac, his violin would be nearly complete. Only Peer's French polishing remained.

◄■►

The next morning, a customer who'd made the journey southeast from Zurich on the early train arrived unexpectedly at the shop. He'd heard of Carl's inlay abilities and wanted to investigate the options for having the tailpiece of his violin inlaid with a floral motif. Carl was excited to talk with him since inlaying was one of his favorite occupations as a luthier. The art involved cutting shapes out of shell material, such as mother-of-pearl or abalone, and imbedding these into wood. It was a time-consuming task and was expensive – both for materials and labor - and so inlay was not the bread and butter of his business, but it provided him with the most satisfaction.

"Do you have a specific design in mind?" asked Carl, moving some tools and wood scraps from a nearby shelf and finally placing his hands on a folder of papers. He discretely blew off some dust and cat hair before laying the bundle on the workbench.

"I have no real preference," said Franz. "But I want to show off my violin in a subtle way. I know it's an extravagance, but I have a friend whose tailpiece has made me absolutely envious. I thought – Why not? I really need a new violin, but this will help spruce up the one I have until I find the right one."

"Let me show you some of the designs I've done before," said Carl and opened the folder on the work bench.

"Yes," said Franz. "Something like this, but not quite so intricate," when Carl had turned over a few sheets. "Simpler, but along these lines." Turning the sheet over, Carl quickly sketched out an idea, and Franz nodded his head.

"Yes, that design will do nicely," said Franz. "I play with the Zurich symphony, and since I'm always in formal dress, I think my violin should be, too." Franz had brought the tailpiece with him and handed it over.

"My policy is that if you're unhappy with the final product, you won't be charged," said Carl. "But you'll need to acquire a new tailpiece on your own to replace this one."

"Oh, I already have one that I'm going to use while this is being ornamented," said Franz.

They were both in agreement on the project and the price. "I should be able to finish before Christmas," said Carl. "Perhaps my wife, Maria, or I can transport it up to Zurich. She's living there while teaching at the University, and we frequently take the train back and forth."

"I travel a lot, as well," said Franz. "We'll arrange something. Thank you, Carl." He shook Carl's hand and nodded at Peer as he headed to the door, however, curiosity drew him to the violin upon which Peer was applying finish.

"What a unique instrument," he said admiring Carl's violin. "Who's is it?"

"It's one I've just completed for myself," said Carl.

"How I wish I could hear its sound!" said Franz as he stood and watched Peer work.

"I can't wait either," Carl replied with a smile.

◀■▶

Carl was exiting *Zum Bären* when he noticed Albert parting with two friends and heading the same direction on the opposite side of the street. He didn't want to bother Albert, since he knew how preoccupied the man could be, and knew that he might want some time alone with his thoughts. Carl had walked for half a block toward home when he heard Albert calling his name from over his shoulder. "I just had an interesting but nostalgic evening with some old friends," said Albert in a pant when he'd joined Carl. "We jokingly call ourselves the Olympia Academy."

"Interesting name," remarked Carl. "Where's it from?"

"It's sort of a joke – a little self-mockery, as I recall," said Albert. "We've had some great times together over the last few years discussing books or debating any and all subjects and taking long hikes in the woods. Unfortunately, our meetings have dwindled to a halt recently, especially since I got married, and now one of the three of us is leaving town next month. So, it looks like that's the end of our Academy. I hate to admit that I'm sad about it but at the same time a little relieved since I've been spending much more time working out some ideas on my own. Oh, yes - the ones that I've been describing to you."

"It's still good that you could get together with them," said Carl, "Friendships are important."

"Yeah, but as I said, it's not quite the same as when we started out as a rambunctious group of lads," lamented Albert. "We used to rail against the teachers and now one of us is one." He shook his head and walked in silence for a minute. "Say, speaking of friendships" he suddenly continued, "I really enjoyed meeting Paul the other night."

"I'm glad that you two were finally introduced. It's hard to believe that you hadn't crossed paths before this."

"I know." said Albert. "We're the same age, and he says that he uses music to focus his mind, just like I do. He also hates Debussy and Wagner as much as I! I absolutely couldn't understand some of what he was trying to tell me about art, though. He's an excellent fellow, but seems so intense and a little too focused on his recent passion for drawing, if you ask me. He could try and expand his horizons a little, don't you think?"

Carl nodded and hid a smile. Knowing Albert's own current level of obsession, he ventured, "Well, sometimes there's no help in trying to pull a horse up from his oats."

"No, I suppose not," agreed Albert, not catching the irony.

"Say, Albert, I was recently talking with a friend who went skiing for the first time in the new snow this season. I have fond memories of skiing, and after our conversation about trains I tried to imagine what it would be like if I was skiing at the speed of light, but absolutely nothing came to mind. In my mind I was just skiing and couldn't imagine how anything could change, especially the bit about time - which makes absolutely no sense, by the way."

"It's really difficult to visualize what we don't experience on a day-to-day basis, isn't it?" asked Albert falling into a comfortable pace and area of interest. "I'm convinced that what I've described to you is true, but since we can't travel at anything that even comes close to the speed of light, we may need to wait a very long time before any proofs verify what I've predicted. So far, as I've said, all of my experiments have been only in my head."

"If I remember correctly, you said that at those great speeds, distance shrinks and time slows down. That's almost impossible to comprehend, let alone prove, isn't it?" asked Carl.

"Yes, they're difficult concepts and will be hard to verify as a whole, but we do get bits and pieces that can be confirmed." agreed Albert. "The shrinking in direction of travel with increasing speed has actually been observed in experimental trials. Plus, there's an extra dimension to all of this. Experiments with cathode "rays," or quickly moving charged particles, suggest that the charged particles involved actually become heavier the faster their speed."

"What?" asked Carl. "You mean to say that weight changes, too?"

"Yes," nodded Albert.

"Space and time and now weight?"

"I'm afraid to tell you that many things change as one approaches the speed of light. You see, trying to attain that speed requires energy. Usually, the more energy we put into something, the faster we can go. But only up to a point, since it's a case of diminishing returns. Matter can never travel faster than the electromagnetic wave which, I believe, is the speed limit of the universe. So, what becomes of all the energy we expend as we make a futile attempt to get to the speed of light? It transforms into mass, or weight – that's where it goes. Unable to attain the speed of light, matter just gets heavier and heavier as a necessary repository for the energy being expended.

"If you were schussing - it is schussing, isn't it? I've never really skied much," asked Albert as Carl nodded back. "OK, if you were schussing down the slope and somehow could ski near the speed of light, your 200 cm. skis, with you on them totaling, say, 70 kg. would burn down the hill, but never be able to attain the speed of light. If you somehow had a scale that you carried with you – you'd continue to weigh 70 kg. and if you took a meter stick with you and measured your skis, they'd still be 200 cm. Everyone watching you tear down the slopes would be amazed, though. To them, your skis would've shrunk, you'd look like a snowball thrown against a door, your watch would've slowed, and if they could read a weight scale, they'd see hundreds of kilograms registered."

"That just doesn't..." tried Carl.

But Albert continued excitedly, "From your perspective, you'd say that you covered a certain distance in, let's say, one second when zipping down the slope at near the speed of light. The observers on the slope, however, would say that you covered a much shorter distance in the one second they measured and that your clock didn't even reach one second during the same one second interval that they measured."

"But this doesn't make any sense to me at all," Carl finally managed. "In my science classes, we took measurements, made predictions, made more measurements of the results, and everything came out as, well, as the professors said they would. All the experiments were in terms of weight weighed, length measured, and time recorded. Those were the absolutes."

"And they are the absolutes," agreed Albert. "As long as you remain within your frame of reference."

"But we are always in our frame of reference," retorted Carl stubbornly.

"Yes, but," and Albert paused and thought for a moment. "Just to show how important the frame of reference is, imagine that you're in a boat anchored in the middle of the Aare River. You take measurements of your surroundings and find that your boat is a specific length, the banks are a certain distance away, and the bottom is at a constant depth. You can measure the speed of the water flowing by and then calculate when other boats that are floating down the river will pass you. Then someone cuts the rope. You measure the boat and it's the same length, but now the distance to the banks is suddenly changing and the depth is never the same. However, the boats floating on the river are always the same distance from you and the water you are on measures as being still. You are in the same boat, but everything depends on your situation on the river – either flowing with it, or anchored and watching it flow by.

"Here on earth, living our daily lives, we all share the same reference frame. But there's a universe out there, and when we're anywhere else in it, everything becomes relative to our new frame of reference. Out in space, it's impossible to tell if you are moving towards an object or if it's moving towards you. We're stuck on this planet, but once we start moving quickly compared to earth, we enter our own reference frame and like a self-contained ship or train, our laws of physics will move with us," said Albert.

"But even something as constant as time?" asked Carl. "Walking home from that concert I mentioned earlier, I realized that a composer could manipulate time all he liked. I can easily see how time could stray in music – it's a construct of the music, after all, isn't it? But here in Switzerland, we've made a name for ourselves with our clockmakers, and in Bern we live just down the street from that clock tower, and it always keeps the time that we set our watches by. How could something that seems so elemental and essential possibly change?"

"That was the same leap that I had to make," said Albert. "For the speed of light to be constant, as I believe it is, it's time and space that must change to make it possible. And I now know beyond a doubt that that's the actual reality." They'd reached Albert's house, and the two shook hands before Albert went up to his apartment. As Albert headed up his stairs, Carl quipped, "Don't run up too quickly or time will slow, and you'll be late!" not being able to resist. Albert snorted and nearly tripped on a step.

CHAPTER 20

Carl had finalized his drawing of a curving floral pattern for Franz's tailpiece inlay. Within some twisting stems and leaves, he'd incorporated some blossom shapes in both profile and portrait. The mother-of-pearl that he had available was in small, thin squares and was in either of two colors – the pure white common to the shell or some with a golden hue. He decided to make the flowers of the pure white and to use the gold colored mother-of-pearl for the stems that interwove like vines.

Peer had opened the damper of the stove too much so that they were both baking, and the stove was beginning to glow a dull red. Flecken lay stretched out below it, obviously in heaven. After damping the inferno down as much as possible, Carl asked Peer to crack the door open. Peer opened the door and then caught his breath. It wasn't from the cold, but from the girl who had become a more frequent visitor to the area. Carl nodded as Peer shambled up the stairs and after an awkward pause, began talking with his new friend who greeted him with a huge smile. Carl remarked to himself that he hadn't seen Johann around much lately, either.

Under as much light as he could gather in one place, Carl slowly transferred the flower drawings on paper to the surface of the mother-of-pearl squares. Cutting the paper outline of each shape with scissors, he traced each profile with a pencil onto the pearl, and then etched through the pencil markings with a sharp scriber which detailed a fine line into the shell surface. Darkening these fine scratches with pencil lead, he had an outline he could follow with a fine-toothed saw.

He arranged the shell on the work-space so that he could cut it and yet still support it enough to keep it from breaking. With his left hand, he pressed the shell tightly against the support, and with his other hand he worked the ultra-fine sawblade up and down, tracing the outline. The blades were so thin that he would usually break several as he cut out each shape. The hardness of the mother-of-pearl meant that the slightest twist or binding of the sawblade could snap the blade in two. The process was slow, but couldn't be rushed or more blades would break. After an hour, he had three of the flowers cut out. He then had to stop for the remainder of the day to give his fingers and his eyes a rest.

Gathering the mail, he went into the apartment and sorted the letters. Finding one from Maria, he opened it first. Her news ended somewhat cryptically with, "There is soon to be a change in personnel, and I'm waiting to see how my position is affected."

I wonder what's going on with this restructuring, thought Carl. *Maria hasn't mentioned a word about things going badly at the university, so hopefully this is good news.*

◄ ■ ►

Carl had tried to follow the directions provided in the invitation, but was having difficulties since this part of the city was more unfamiliar to him. He was finally able to locate the small art gallery near the university that Paul had referred to by asking students and pedestrians along the way. Paul had been searching for a public venue to display his drawings and had sent a message a few days before that he was having an opening that evening on Seidenweg. The exterior was unassuming, but the interior was elegant and he discovered Paul's drawings on easels interspersed among the numerous paintings for sale displayed on the gallery's walls. Attendees were gathered in small groups around each easel and were moving from one drawing to the next, chatting with wine glasses in hand.

Carl noticed the table with hors d'oeuvres and a sampling of wine situated near the rear of the gallery and joined the short queue. Paul stood in a nearby corner exchanging greetings and banter with well-wishers. After selecting a glass of Eiswein and a small plate of olives, Carl made his way into the cluster of people surrounding Paul to say hello. Breaking politely away from a conversation, Paul stepped over and shook Carl's hand.

"Hello, Carl!" said Paul. "I'm glad that you could make it."

"Me, too," said Carl. "I wanted to see your drawings again and lend my support to your first public showing. So," lifting his wine glass with a little nod toward another small group entering the door, "congratulations; it looks like a nice crowd."

"Thanks," said Paul with a smile. "It's a better turn-out than I expected. Of course, there is the free wine," as he grabbed himself a half-full glass off the table. "I think I showed you many of these prints already, but there are some that you haven't seen yet mixed in with the others. Let me know what you think as you browse around." And as Paul rejoined his previous conversation, Carl walked over towards the entrance and followed the changing groups clockwise around the gallery. There were some sketches that Carl hadn't seen in Paul's portfolio, and he spent more time on these and the few that he remembered being impressed with the first time he'd seen them.

He walked up to one of the sketches near the end of the series, and his eyes suddenly widened. There in front of him was a drawing nearly identical to one of his own sketches – the one he had started of the city that had lacked perspective. This one had the same competing angles and buildings as he'd drawn them, but the edges faded off into a series of geometric patterns. Feeling suddenly embarrassed, he stepped back and unexpectedly Paul was there with an arm on his shoulder.

"I know, I know," whispered Paul, pulling Carl away from the easel. "You can chastise me later, but just watch." Carl turned back to the easel as a trio in the continual flow of patrons paused to examine it. One stepped in closer for a better look, and there was some discussion as they moved on.

"You see?" whispered Paul. "They're treating my take on your idea exactly the same as all of the others. It fits in perfectly."

"But why did you use my sketch as the basis for a drawing?" asked Carl a little indignantly. "Especially given the poor quality?"

"I didn't put this on display to make fun of your work," said Paul. "I displayed it to show you that your work isn't 'bad' - it's quite valid and nothing to be ashamed of!"

Paul was called over by some supporters and made a brief apology as he left. Carl had calmed down from his initial shock and stood eying the viewers as they examined the drawing. Paul was right; they were treating the rendition much the same as they did the others in the series.

Carl had chatted with Paul's mother, Ida, who'd made a late appearance, sipped his way through another glass of wine, and was soon ready to head home. Paul hadn't been alone for the bulk of the evening, so Carl took advantage of a slight opening and went over to him.

"I was really surprised when I saw that sketch like mine thrown in with the others and, of course, was a bit taken aback and curious about why you'd shown it, but now I see that you thought it was for my own good," said Carl. "And you may be right, Paul. Thanks for the encouragement." he said with a smile as he shook Paul's hand and headed for his apartment.

On the way home, Carl pondered Paul's reason for emulating his work, and in a way, he was flattered that Paul apparently had cared enough to even make the effort. He quickly realized that whereas he himself had no aspirations to become an artist, his interest in drawing wasn't something to shy away from, either.

Perhaps something to look forward to in retirement, thought Carl as he made his way home, *if I can ever afford it.*

◄■►

The strings Maria had given him were knotted onto the tail-piece of his new violin and Carl plucked them as he tightened each of the tuning pegs. It took some time for knots and loops to tighten and settle into place and for the steel and gut to stretch, but soon the strings stayed in tune.

He dedicated the evening to his new violin and knew that it was only by playing the instrument that the sound would open up – sometimes within the first hours, sometimes within the first months, and sometimes it took years. It was as if the wood needed to teach itself how to sound and, depending on the instrument, it could take its time about it.

Bowing the strings, he began playing scales and then turned to some favorite pieces. At first harsh and bright sounding, the violin was soon producing deeper resonances, and some of the subtle overtones were developing. Staying up later than intended, he had a difficult time putting the instrument down. He was more than pleased and thought he could hear where the instrument was headed as it matured. He couldn't wait for his friend Süd Hoffman and the guys in the quintet to hear it.

◄■►

The day before, Carl had cut the remainder of the flower shapes out of the shell to be inlaid in Franz's tailpiece and then had begun on the long twisting stems. The sawing of these spindly, thin parts had meant broken shell, as well as broken saw blades, but eventually all the pieces had been cut.

With little dabs of glue, he'd fixed each tiny piece of shell onto the tailpiece in its proper place, but standing proud on top of the wood. He'd then traced around the outline of each piece with a scribe, used steam to remove them all once he had a silhouette, and then had rubbed chalk into the ebony to highlight the outlines he'd traced.

With fine knives, and slightly bigger chisels if space allowed, he'd slowly dug away the wood within the outlines to a constant depth that matched the depth of the mother-of-pearl pieces. This process had required continually checking each shell piece with the channel that had been cut for it until a perfect fit accepted the shell into the wood.

This morning, mixing black ebony dust with glue, he filled each depression with the glue mixture and pressed the shell pieces into their appropriate places. Once dry, the black glue was invisible against the ebony and, after sanding down the wood and shell to a uniform surface, his inlay was complete. Holding it up to the light, he was very pleased with the final product. At certain angles, the iridescent hues of the pearl would shine with the colors of the rainbow.

Glancing up from his workbench, Carl saw Master Ehrlich just outside the entrance struggling with three violin cases and trying to open the door at the same time. Getting up, Carl quickly wiped the shavings and sawdust off his work apron and slipped it off over his head. As he opened the door and let the Master in, he wondered, *Where the hell is Peer?*

"Hi Carl!" said Master Ehrlich as he huffed in with a cold blast of air. "I thought I'd save you some time by dropping these violins off on my way home. They just need a little adjustment and some spit and polish before the big concert – you can fit them in, can't you?"

"Uh, yes, I should be able to. What big concert is this?"

"Why, the one being staged by Mme. Guiveny, of course. The whole school is excited about it, and I've announced the three classes that will be performing. We didn't expect that these violins needed much attention before, but now that they're going to be on display, I thought it would only be prudent to have them look their finest," said Master Ehrlich.

"I'll do my best to have them ready," said Carl. "Although this might mean a delay in some of the others."

"I think these are the only ones left that will be in the performance," said Master Ehrlich. "So, that should be all right. Have you heard about the concert?"

"Oh, yes," said Carl a little nervously. "In fact, I'm going to be in it. You might know Geron's quartet?"

"Yes!" said Master Ehrlich. "The one that Friedrich has played with! You've joined them?" Carl nodded and Master Ehrlich said, "That's great, then we'll definitely see you there." Master Ehrlich was just heading out the door when he turned and said, "Oh, I forgot to tell you something very odd and disturbing that happened just last night."

"What was that?"

"Following our first after-school practice session to make ready for the concert, Jan Rauss was attacked on his way home."

"What? Who would attack Jan?"

"No one has a clue. He said that he was walking on a short-cut that he always uses through a park and three figures jumped out of the bushes and attacked him towards the end of the path. One snuck up behind him and kneeled down so that when one of the others pushed him, he fell over backwards. They didn't expect it, but Jan was up like a shot and ran as fast as he could in the direction from which he'd come. He almost made it out of the park when they caught him and one of them started beating him. All he heard was 'Where is that bow?' and was getting some more beating when a couple walking their dog rounded the corner and his attackers fled."

"God, that *is* disturbing. How is Jan?" asked Carl.

"Oh, Jan's fine, just a little bruised but, without a doubt, shaken up by the incident."

"Does he know who his attackers were?"

"No, no idea at all," said Master Ehrlich. "It was dark, and only one of them uttered a word during the attack. It seems like that bow is of interest to someone. But who'd be aware of it besides you and me and the police?"

"Don't forget," said Carl. "We dragged Jan out of class, and that kind of thing doesn't happen in a school without it becoming a big topic of conversation. So, the entire assembly probably knew about the bow, as did the person who perhaps lost it. This is getting serious – you should mention this assault to the police, if they don't know about it already."

"No, no," said Master Ehrlich adamantly. "The only way I heard about it was through Jan's father, and he doesn't want his name bandied about in a way that would cause him the slightest bit of embarrassment. I'm guessing it won't happen again anyway," and he left cautioning Carl a second time about further publicizing the incident.

Peer showed up a little before noon looking completely exhausted. "What's up Peer?" asked Carl. "Did you have trouble sleeping last night?"

"I'll say!" said Peer. "In fact, I don't think I slept a wink!"

"Why not?" asked Carl.

"Well, I was coming home with some friends last night, and we were joking around when all of a sudden this boy runs out of the park and asks for our help. We knew him sort of – Jan Rauss, the Councilman's son. He said he'd just been attacked, and so we ran into the park to find out who did it but they were gone."

"Incredible!" said Carl. "His music teacher was just here and told me all about it – did you know who did it?"

"No, we never saw them, and Jan said he couldn't tell."

"Couldn't tell or wouldn't tell?" asked Carl.

"I don't think he knew," Peer replied.

"But Jan's all right?"

"Yeah, but he didn't want to go home because he was afraid of what his father would say. I took him back to the *Zum Bären*, and Frieda cleaned up his cuts and scrapes. Trying to be helpful, Max went out to tell Ratsherr Rauss that Jan was safe and I guess they got into a huge shouting match, and Ratsherr Rauss couldn't believe that Jan didn't want to come straight home. Since it was so late, Jan stayed with us, and we were trying to sleep when the police showed up at the door at Ratsherr Rauss's request, and there was a bunch more arguing. Finally, his father agreed that Jan could come home this morning, and we got to sleep just as the sun came up. Of course, he was mad when Jan wasn't home at first light, but it seems like he's mad at everything anyway so who cares?"

"And Max dealt with it OK?" asked Carl.

Peer gave him a funny look. "Carl, Max is used to bar fights. It didn't faze him a bit," he smiled.

CHAPTER 21

The morning sunlight was brilliant and seemed to shine off each snowflake and ice crystal that covered every visible surface. Carl's eyes were tearing from the glare off the snow, and he could only see through the small slits into which he had to force his eyelids. The recent prolonged cold spell that had frozen the surface of the river had dissipated with the cloud cover and heavy snow of the previous day. Yet he'd woken this morning again to clear skies but with much warmer temperatures. Already the smooth snowy surfaces off the foot path were dotted with depressions due to snow clumps falling from the trees, and the streets were just now becoming sloppy with passing cars and carts.

He was heading back home after making an early morning delivery when he blearily noticed Albert walking towards him on his way to the Patent Office. They greeted each other, and Carl changed direction to accompany Albert on the few blocks remaining to his workplace. Both were squinting but enjoying the snowy scene surrounding them. It was still cool enough that they could see their breath, but the air felt comfortable compared to the cold snap they'd just endured.

"It's almost like a spring day, isn't it?" asked Albert. "Except for the snow, of course," he grinned.

"I hope it doesn't warm up so much that we lose all of this snow cover though," said Carl. "It makes everything seem so clean and fresh. It really brightens up the evenings, too, but mornings like this are almost overwhelming."

"I was just thinking when you came up," said Albert, "that our view of the world is like perpetually being in a dazzling morning exactly like this. We're almost blinded by the beauty and captivated by the reflections off each snowflake. And yet, we've no inkling of what lies underneath. Imagine that a day like today is the only one we've ever experienced. We wouldn't be able to comprehend that, for instance, the huge flat expanse we see down there actually conceals a river that's continually flowing with power made up of the combined actions of billions of particles. We wouldn't be aware of the forces in the ground that will bring about an entirely different scene filled with greens and the colors of spring. And," Albert said, "we'd have no idea that the snow is really just one state that the underlying water molecules can form.

"I just know that one day we'll be able to realize the enormity and, at the same time, the incredibly small scale of the patterns and flows of particles and forces of which we're currently ignorant. It'll make our dazzling sunlit morning seem like what it is – a little gem frozen in time. Say, thanks for walking me to work – you're great company," said Albert.

"And you're sometimes more like a poet than a scientist," said Carl. He waved as he headed, tearing and blinking, back to his shop.

◄ ■ ►

Carl finished breakfast, donned his coat, and had to shovel and sweep a new layer of snow off the six steps leading from the raised sidewalk down to the street and then off the angled shutters next to them in order to open the shop. It was by design that almost all the walkways in the old town were raised and set back under the first story of the buildings, keeping them snow free, with hundreds of arches allowing access to the street which lay sometimes a meter below that level. Many shops, like the Rosselli's across the street and the Gelder's above him, were situated along the covered promenade; his shop access, however, was located on the snow-blanketed street. He saw no sign of cat pawprints. The workshop was cold, but the stove warmed it back up quickly. He had both coffee and cocoa heating when Peer opened the door, Flecken scooting in before him, and shook the snow off his coat and boots. Peer removed his galoshes and slipped into shoes he kept in the shop, put on a work apron, and awaited the cocoa.

"How was your breakfast?" asked Carl.

Peer shrugged his shoulders and said, "O.K."

"Would you care for some of this bread and jam to go with your cocoa?" asked Carl. Peer nodded and started wolfing the bread down before the cocoa was hot.

I hope that he's just going through a growth spurt and not having trouble finding enough to eat, thought Carl.

Later that morning, as he was carving the contoured back for another violin, Carl's mind wandered, and he found himself thinking about exactly how it wandered. He realized that in his lifetime he'd only be able to hold or comprehend a finite amount of information and that he had a proclivity to think in a certain manner, so other types of thought would forever elude his grasp. The lens he saw the world through was fairly specific and a little human-centric. He noted that other than his work and music, all the information that he filtered had to do with either himself or how the facts affected people in general.

He couldn't help it or break out of the mold.

Someone like Albert fascinated him. Albert seemed to be able to span many viewpoints and see things in a very comprehensive manner. He was an original thinker – both a mathematician and a musician - and his thoughts went far beyond anything Carl would ever be able to comprehend, let alone arrive at on his own. How minds could differ so much was an amazement to Carl. Everyone had their own type of intelligence and world-view, each deep in themselves and often unfathomable to others, but Albert's seemed to surpass any he had ever known.

"Hey, Carl, is it getting close to lunch time?" asked Peer suddenly. Carl broke out of his reverie with a start.

"A few more minutes, Peer," he replied as he watched the fine shavings of maple curl off the forming back with each consecutive pass of his plane. *Then*, he thought, *there is the intelligence of my hands.*

◄ ■ ►

Carl arrived at Geron's lavish home for a practice of the musical arrangement that they'd play for the upcoming benefit concert and found that Albert wouldn't be joining them. "He's so busy that he sometimes asks to beg off," said Geron. "Friedrich, the talented student who played with us that evening you arrived late is going to join us and take Albert's part for the evening. He seems to be running a little late though, too," Geron added, looking at his watch.

They'd already started working on Mendelssohn's quintet No. 2 when Friedrich finally arrived. The ensemble found that they had to slow down the pace for practice and perhaps maintain it at that *tempo* for the concert, and they worked at finding the right equilibrium for all the players. Friedrich quickly unpacked and apologized, and as he had their attention, also told them that he'd need to leave as soon as the practice was finished. The piece went nicely, and though he was concentrating on his own part, Carl noticed that Friedrich sounded very good although with a different playing style than Albert. Friedrich's youth faintly showed when he vacillated between flamboyance and timidity in his attack which was not always in line with the mood of the piece, so his substitution subtly changed the dynamics and sound of the music. They also played through a piece by Bach, and true to his word, Friedrich packed up as soon as they were finished, saying that his father was waiting for him outside.

Again, Geron's den was warm and inviting, and it was evident that he cherished this time to fence himself in, if only briefly, from the rest of the family. They talked about the upcoming concert, and Carl filled them in on the mystery of the violin bow without mentioning the student's name. They were intrigued and all wanted to see this bow, but Carl said that Sub-Commander Mortensen was keeping it under lock and key.

Carl had a pleasant walk home through a lightly falling snow. His walk was made even more enjoyable when he rounded the corner and saw that the lights to the apartment were on – Maria was home for the holidays!

◄■►

Maria was positively aglow with excitement for the upcoming weeks at home over Christmas break. She dragged out the small gifts she'd already purchased for her parents while in Zurich, and simultaneously filled him in on the end-of-semester dramas that had played out among staff and students. They languidly enjoyed some cocoa next to the fire, Maria preferring to forgo the schnapps he put in his, and then, with some ardor, they were off to bed.

The next morning was a Sunday, and Carl and Maria bundled up and went out to a café near the Munster cathedral for breakfast. They stayed under the covered walkways as much as possible, but at times had to follow the tracks that others had made in the snow. In the café, they chose one of the tables furthest from the door that emitted cold drafts when opened by each arriving customer.

"So, you forgot to tell me about the personnel issue that you said might affect you," said Carl as they sat on the wrought iron seats.

"Oh, did I?" asked Maria and paused. "It must have slipped my mind."

"Uh oh," said Carl, noticing the pause. "What is it, honey? Are you being let go?"

"Possibly," said Maria picking up her cup of coffee. "I won't know for a while."

"Won't know?" asked Carl. "Well, that's not very fair of them, is it?"

"I think it's more me than them," said Maria with a slight smile over her cup.

"What do you mean?" asked Carl. "Are you thinking of quitting?"

Maria shrugged her shoulders.

"Why?" asked Carl.

"Because, I think I'm about to become a mother," said Maria with an even bigger smile.

"What!" whooped Carl, and the entire café turned to see what the commotion was all about.

By then the two were up, and Carl had Maria tight in his arms.

That evening, Carl made an excuse to go down and check on the shop. He lit a candle and huddled next to the still-warm stove, staring off into the darkened edges of the room. The flickering candle made the shadows jump toward and away from the light. Memories flipped through his mind: Günther holding a toddler, exhausted after a birthday party; his father bundling him up to go fishing; his father's watchful scowl whenever he was in the shop; Albert asking if he thought he was a good husband or not. He'd been unquestioning in his answer to Albert's query, but now wondered how he would be as a father. This was the most exciting and yet most terrifying news he'd ever received. How would he fare in parenthood?

Carl was twenty-four when his dad had died from lung congestion, and Carl felt that he was only just beginning to know him at the time. In his recollection of their scant time together, his father had either been at work or off drinking with his friends. The shop situation with his father had been much different than the relationship he had with Peer - his father had forbidden children setting foot on the premises. Then there had been the uncomfortable stage in his very late teens when he was actively encouraged to join his father in luthiery, and was old enough to participate in the drinking, but was still somehow always the child - left off to the side in the conversations and excluded from the main tasks in the shop.

Carl checked that the stove was damped down, and then stood holding his hands over the still-warm surface for a moment. *But I'm not doing this alone,* thought Carl. *I know Maria will help me be the best father that I can be, and I'm going to help her the most I can, too.*

Walking up the steps to the apartment, opening the door and stepping in, his eyes met Maria's, and the two just stared at each other for a long moment. Then after a much-needed embrace, they excitedly launched into the topic of what would be the central focus of their lives for years to come, the new family member who was arriving. After some discussion, they agreed to keep the news to themselves until Maria was further along in her pregnancy.

CHAPTER 22.

It was a week to the day before the concert at Mme. Guiveny's mansion, and a person in black tailored clothes entered Carl's shop. The man introduced himself as Mme. Guiveny's head servant.

"Mme. Guiveny would like her violin put into tip-top condition and 'shined up like it has never been shined before' to quote her exactly. If you could please get it back to us within at most three days, that would be wonderful," said the head servant. He handed Carl a case that looked like it had been covered in patent leather and polished like a fine shoe. Carl took the violin and then the bow case and set them both on the workbench as the servant headed toward the door.

"I'll just take a quick look at them and let you know if that timeframe is possible," said Carl.

"Well, the timeframe must be possible," said the head servant turning his head to look back at Carl. Carl unlatched the violin case, opened it up, and reached for the violin. Taking it in with his eyes as he lifted it from the case, he stood with it at arm's length. He held it like that for quite some time, twisting it a little this way and that.

"I know, she's a beauty, isn't she?" asked the head servant from the doorway. "The missus' father was very proud of that violin."

But to Carl, it appeared as if he was looking at just another of the student violins. It even had some scratches on the finish and fingermarks covered it. Twisting it for the proper lighting showed that there was no label inside. He then gave it a more careful examination. There was no doubt in his mind that this was just a student-grade instrument. Before saying anything, he gently set the violin down and then took the bow out of its case. It was the same – as if it had just arrived from the primary or higher-grade school.

"There must be some mistake," said Carl. "If I hadn't seen you bring in the case, and if I hadn't then removed the violin from that same case myself, I would have said that you'd just given me a student's violin straight out of school or right out of one of these cases lying about here."

"Oh, no, no," said the head servant as if words alone could change the situation. "This is a fine violin made especially for M. Guiveny, probably 50 years ago since he has passed on. It's going to be auctioned and just needs to be cleaned up."

It needs a lot more than cleaning, thought Carl.

◄ ■ ►

Mortensen was at his desk, and he and Carl were awaiting the arrival of Mme. Guiveny. A patrolman brought them in a cup of coffee each and had included a pot of tea in case the others arriving would care for some.

With some fanfare consisting of a slight bow by the desk sergeant as he opened the door, Mme. Guiveny entered followed by her head servant carrying the violin and bow cases.

He'd insisted on maintaining possession of the violin almost as if he suspected Carl of making some kind of underhanded trade in the first place. After they were seated and did indeed desire some tea, Sub-Commander Mortensen opened the violin case and carefully removed the contents. He had Mme. Guiveny describe what she had expected to be in the case, and then had Carl describe what was actually before them. When Carl was finished, Mme. Guiveny spent some time agitatedly going through her handbag and eventually pulled out some documents which she held supported on the edge of the desk while she read the contents slowly, holding a pair of reading glasses to her eyes with the other hand.

"This is a bill of sale dated August 14th,1854. It shows that Georg Voigt made the violin specifically for my father who lived in Vienna at the time. The bow I'm not sure about, but there is a bill of sale that is from England, and it seems to be the name Allen."

"Well, well, Mr. Allen," said Carl almost to himself, and then continued aloud. "I don't know what happened to the violin described on that receipt, Mme. Guiveny, but as I've said, this one is of low quality and of the type churned out by apprentices. It's fine for students and is exactly the same sort of violin I've been working on for months from the schools. I've examined it and can find no identifying labels showing that it was made by Voigt, but there are no marks like those placed on many of the violins for school inventory purposes either. Then again, there are plenty in the schools that have no markings at all. The music teacher there and I have just confirmed that.

"Sub-Commander, do you still have that mystery bow in the office?" asked Carl. Mortensen nodded and unlocked a cabinet next to his desk and retrieved the case. He opened it up and presented the bow to Mme. Guiveny.

"Is this by any chance your bow?" asked Mortensen. Mme. Guiveny held the bow, turning it this way and that in the light and continually adjusting her glasses as she bent in closer and then leaned further away.

"Well, I have to be perfectly honest, and say that I can't remember enough to be absolutely certain. It surely could be," she said a little sadly. Carl thought the sadness might be more for her memory than for the bow.

"It does have an 'A' on the end of the turn screw," Carl explained. "But I never heard back from the Allen's in England to find out how they identify their bows. The small inlay of a flower on the frog could help, but as I say, I haven't heard from them."

"Well, what does that leave us with?" asked Mortensen.

"It hadn't occurred to me until now," said Carl, "but a few months ago a friend of mine had trouble with his violin. I took it into the shop and found that the bridge had been changed, without his knowledge, to a much nicer one that was made in Vienna. This seemed strange, but we had no explanation for the sudden appearance of the bridge. Now it seems possible that we have both the bridge and the bow from Mme. Guiveny's father's violin. Unfortunately, we're missing the violin itself."

"Where can it be?" asked Mme. Guiveny becoming more agitated.

"We have no idea," said Mortensen shaking his head.

"Oh, and remember that assault on Jan Rauss," Carl continued with a start. With suddenly raised eyebrows on the policeman's forehead he said, "Oh, right, Sub-Commander Mortenson – you might not have heard of this. Jan Rauss was attacked the other night by three people he didn't recognize. It appears they were after that bow," and he pointed to the case lying on the desk between them. "The attackers seemed to know that he had possession of the bow at some point, and I haven't heard that they've sought him out again since. The bow seemed to be important to the perpetrators for some reason, and now it's apparent that this is probably in connection with the missing violin. I think that, obviously, we must wonder where the violin itself is, and concentrate our efforts on finding it."

"Would that that were easy to do," said Mortensen. "It seems the school is connected to all of this since the bow first appeared there, but classes are out for the holidays, and we have neither the resources nor the means of tracking down all of the students and their instruments."

"But I must have that violin back for the concert!" wailed Mme. Guiveny. "Its auction was to be one of the highlights of the evening!"

"We'll do our best with what we have, but unfortunately that might not be possible," said Mortensen.

"But it must be," said the matron with rapidly fading hope. They all sat in silence giving her time to process the information. Finally, accepting the futility of the situation,

Mme. Guiveny said with a sigh, "Well, I suppose the piano will have to do."

◀ ■ ▶

What with the excitement of Maria's news and the discovery of the theft of Mme. Guiveny's violin, he'd neglected to show Maria his completed instrument. He polished it once more and set it in a new case before climbing the stairs to the apartment and opening the door to the smell of baking bread. As he set the case on the small dining table Maria turned and said "Oh! So the project I've heard so much about is finally done?"

"Yes, honey," said Carl. "Would you like to hear how it sounds?"

"Very much so," she nodded and sat next to the cooling loaves while he gathered some of the music the quintet was performing in the upcoming concert. "Can I see it first?" He nodded and handed her the instrument while he went to fetch the music stand from the sitting room. "Darling, it's beautiful, and I don't see all of the blemishes and inferior wood you were talking about."

"Yes, I was also surprised at how nice the wood looked after it was carved. But I like the tone even more," said Carl as he accepted the violin, took up the bow, and played.

Maria shut her eyes and swayed to the music as he swept easily through his part of the score. She smiled as she opened her eyes again when he'd finished and said, "You know that I'm no expert but to me, it sounds divine."

"I love it, too, and can't wait to hear what it sounds like after it's been played for some time and the tones open up even more."

"You absolutely must play it at the Christmas concert!" said Maria.

Carl gave a little grimace. "No, to me the sound is still a little closed, and besides, I'm so used to playing my old fiddle that I might make some mistakes if I tried to play this beauty."

"But you played wonderfully just now," said Maria encouragingly.

"Yes, but you know how I get," said Carl.

"Not always," said Maria. "Remember when you used to play with Herman and Kyle?"

Carl nodded and persisted, "Yes, hon – and always in front of friends. Not an entire concert hall." He gave an exaggerated shiver, and they both laughed.

◄■►

"Carl, this is exactly what I had in mind," said Franz as he admired the inlay on his tailpiece. "What great work you've done here!"

"Thanks Franz," said Carl. "It's difficult for me to charge for this – I enjoy inlaying so much that I'd almost pay to do it."

"And it's a pleasure for me to pay for such craftsmanship," said Franz handing over the agreed upon amount. "I can't wait to see it on the violin." He wrapped the tailpiece in some cloth he'd brought and slid it into an interior overcoat pocket. "Say Carl, whatever happened to the violin that you were making for yourself?" asked Franz. "It had such beautiful and unusual color. How did it turn out?"

"Better than I expected," said Carl. "I chose the wood wisely."

"Do you mind if I see it?" asked Franz.

"I don't mind at all," said Carl. "Follow me upstairs and you can have a look." Once in the apartment, Carl introduced Franz to Maria. "Franz, this is my wife Maria, and Maria this is Franz, the gentleman who wanted me to inlay his violin's tailpiece."

"A pleasure to meet you, Franz," and turning to Carl she asked, "What brings you two up to the apartment? And would you care for something to drink? Tea? Coffee?"

"Franz is interested in seeing the violin I've just finished," said Carl.

"No, nothing to drink for me," said Franz as he took a seat on a straight-backed chair, waited for Carl to return, and then accepted the instrument from Carl's hands.

"Nice weight," said Franz appreciatively. "And very nice balance." He plucked the strings and then took the bow from the music stand. Franz played the violin for fifteen minutes without stopping, and Carl and Maria were both enthralled with his technique and the sounds he produced. When Franz finished, he took out a handkerchief and wiped first the instrument and then his forehead. "Carl, I don't know if I've ever played an instrument that sounded better for how young it is," said Franz appreciatively. "Do you make instruments of this caliber routinely?"

"I've built instruments in the past, but mine's a repair shop so I haven't made my own violin in many years," said Carl.

"But this is so impressive," said Franz. Maria and Carl snuck an expression of pride between one another. "You should only build, especially if you turn out instruments like this. How did you achieve the sounds this produces?"

"I guess I finally started using my ears more than my eyes for a change when selecting the wood," said Carl.

"I think I mentioned before that I had the inlay done just to make my current violin look better while I've been search-ing for the right one?" asked Franz. Carl nodded. "Well, I think I've found it."

To Carl's utter amazement, he let Franz walk out of the apartment with his prize violin in a case tucked under his arm. Franz had simply not been able to part with it after playing. He said that it seemed to have been made specially to form to his hand and was exactly the combination of sound and playability he'd been seeking. Explaining that his future as a musician depended upon the right tool, Franz had insisted on an amount that was far above anything Carl would have considered asking. Although they couldn't discuss things with Franz present in the room, Maria had nodded her agreement of the sale especially after Franz's impassioned argument.

After Franz left, Carl sank back in his chair feeling simul-taneously elated and somehow defeated. "I can always build another," murmured Carl a little sadly.

"Yes, you can," said Maria with a smile and tousle of his hair, "and you should!"

CHAPTER 23.

The day of the benefit concert had arrived, and Carl hadn't slept a wink the night before. Except for the news about the baby, having Maria back home had calmed him considerably, and he'd practiced in front of her and sometimes in front of both her and Peer to help with stage fright, but it didn't cure his sleeplessness. The morning passed in a blur. He knew that he didn't trust himself with sharp tools, and so had tidied up the shop as best he could and left Peer to the French polishing. In the late afternoon, he let Peer off early - clutching a bundle of pastries Maria had made for him and his foster parents - and, closing up the shop, went upstairs to change. He fumbled at the buttons as he put on his nicest white shirt and then could hardly buckle his belt as he struggled with his pants and then donned the jacket to the only suit he owned. He found himself shivering, but a long hug from Maria and a small snifter of brandy before they left helped warm him. At the door he repeatedly checked that he hadn't forgotten anything – keys, suit, violin, Maria. Just as he was locking up he remembered his sheet music. Then they walked to the corner cab stand to get a hansom.

Somehow, he became less nervous as they approached the mansion, and by the time he'd paid the hansom cab and they'd joined the others entering the halls, he was much calmer. Master Ehrlich was in the entrance foyer herding students about and chatting animatedly with Hans Klee. Carl brought Maria over and greeted Hans and the Master, and managed, through the Master's distractions, to introduce him to Maria. He saw Geron herding his family and waved, and he and Maria followed the crowd towards the reception area off the small concert hall. At the entrance to the room was Mme. Guiveny, greeting each person individually as they arrived. This caused a small bottleneck, and a line began to form at the portal. She spent quite some time speaking to the mayor and two of the businessmen and their families further ahead in the queue, and then the line began to move again as she greeted people she hardly knew, Carl and Maria being among them.

Inside the reception hall there was a spread of crackers, buns, cheeses, patés, and sausages, as well as fruit punch, wine, champagne, and beer. Carl chose a red wine since he knew this was the type that he drank the slowest and brought Maria a glass of the punch. The cabernet went very well with his small plate of sharp cheese and salty crackers. He chatted with Maria and several people he knew, and saw Thierry and Herr Besson speaking to friends, as well.

"Why do I get like this?" Carl asked Maria when they had a moment alone. "I'm a nervous wreck but I'm only a minor player in a minor role."

"You're not my minor player – and I'll be listening to each and every one of the notes you play," said Maria with an impish smile.

"Ah, thanks!" said Carl in exasperation. And then after looking at her for a protracted moment, "Thank you," he whispered, giving Maria a long kiss. He saw Albert come in and, after some hesitation, head for the champagne. Carl led Maria over as he was served a glass.

"Just one for luck," grinned Albert and took a lick at the foam that stuck to his moustache. "Oh, Maria! I'm delighted to meet you at last!" he said as he was introduced to Maria.

"I've heard so much about you, Albert, and it's nice to finally meet you, too," she said, taking his hand in both of hers.

"You absolutely must meet Mileva sometime," said Albert. "She wanted to be here, but our son is fussy today, and we couldn't find a sitter."

"Well, we must meet over the holidays," said Maria, "I… oh, excuse me," as Ida Klee came up beside her and the two entered into a side conversation.

Carl took a moment to whisper to Albert about the disappearance of the expensive violin made exclusively for Mme. Guiveny's father but of the reuniting of her with the bow and, more than likely, the bridge they'd discovered on Albert's Lina. As he and Maria had agreed, Carl kept the news of the Veblen's expected new arrival quiet for the time being.

Maria helped Ida wheel to a nearby couch so they could sit and visit over a plate of hors d'oeuvres just as Paul was bringing her a glass of champagne. Paul recognized Albert and went over to chat with him, while Carl stood momentarily alone mentally rehearsing his parts, for the umpteenth time.

Once the reception area filled and most of the guests had arrived, there was a clinking of a spoon against a champagne glass. The room quieted and all heads swiveled to the source which turned out to be Mme. Guiveny's butler. Mme. Guiveny, standing statuesquely beside him, cleared her throat and started off at a whisper that slowly increased in volume enough so that all could hear. After making introductions of the Master of Ceremonies and some of the most important attendees and patrons of the arts, she thanked all for joining her in promoting music education.

"I'm afraid that there has been a slight change in the benefit proceedings tonight. I will only be auctioning off the fine baby-grand piano, but not the violin." Various sounds of disappointment arose from the crowd. "Something seems to have happened to my father's fine instrument, and we are making enquiries; however, at this time, it is not available for auction." More whispers sprouted among the listeners. "My regrets to anyone who may have been interested in the violin, although I hope that is not the only reason that you came tonight," and she ended to some laughter.

The attendees were invited to move into the small concert hall and take seats at their leisure. So, like the Brownian motion that Albert had described, people were soon spread out randomly into both spaces. Herr Besson's quintet was scheduled to play in the middle of the concert series and so all of its members chose places nearer the rear of the hall allowing them to move to the staging room without disrupting the finale of the group performing before them. Just as the last concert-goers were drifting into the main hall with their wine and champagne glasses, there came a sudden, deafening crash from the reception hall. The main room suddenly fell silent, and all heads immediately swung in that direction. Many, including Carl, began rushing back to the space they'd all just vacated.

As Carl squeezed through the crowded entryway and turned - there stood young Jan Rauss on the opposite side of the table that had held glasses, bottles, and two punch bowls. The table was now on its side with the previous contents broken and strewn in glittering pieces across the marble floor.

"He made me," Jan muttered softly as he stared wide-eyed at the havoc he had just created. He was about to continue uttering something with quivering lips as more patrons and students flooded into the reception hall, but stopped himself, staring at a knot of his fellow students. Within moments he was yelping under his father's outstretched arm as the man yanked on his ear and kept pulling.

"What's wrong with you? Have you lost your fucking mind?" bellowed his father. "There will be hell to pay!" The Ratsherr raised his hand and was about to start an inquisition on the spot, but noticing the astonished faces around them, thought better of it, and dragged Jan out towards the entrance, his mortified wife trailing behind throwing out apologies as they left. The head butler and several dignitaries followed close on their heels, loudly demanding an explanation.

It took fifteen minutes for the crowd to calm down and for people to make their way back to their respective seats. Meanwhile the doors were closed, and staff began cleaning up the mess. The beginning of the concert was delayed further until the noise from the cleanup and distant shouts from outside subsided.

◀■▶

The house lights were dimmed, and Mme. Guiveny slowly walked to the center of the stage. She began to speak, but projecting to a room of that size was beyond her vocal abilities and after a few sentences she returned in frustration to the side of the stage. After some pleading hand gestures, the mayor was soon in a hushed conversation with her and then helped her back to the center. There were several groans from the audience as they saw he was about to speak.

"Ladies and gentlemen," his baritone voice boomed to all corners of the hall. "This will be very brief," to a smattering of applause. "Mme. Guiveny, our wonderful hostess of this evening's opulent affair, wishes me to inform you that the reason for the extremely unseemly disturbance perpetrated by the son of our Councilman is as yet unknown. I am privy to the fact that there have been some personal issues plaguing the family, and…" Mme. Guiveny tugged at his sleeve, and he momentarily stopped. The two whispered and then he resumed. "Ah, yes," he cleared his throat. "Our hostess wishes me to tell you that the reason for the disturbance is unknown, but she sincerely hopes that the disruption will not affect your enjoyment of the wonderful entertainment she has in store for you tonight. May the concert begin." The applause was heavy after this announcement.

The first quartet had chosen adaptations of various Christmas carols which slowly added a lightness to what had been a tense beginning to the evening. To Carl's surprise, they were followed by Ida and Paul Klee performing two mother-

and-son duets for voice and violin, one by Bach and another by Schubert. Somehow the quality of the music added a measure of calmness back into the room.

Hans Klee next directed his small student orchestra through a rousing piece by Beethoven, altering the room's mood yet again. Toward the end of the set, Carl and his group made their way out of the hall and into the staging area. Carl's hands were cold and clammy, and his shoulders shook slightly as he drew his violin, bow, and music out of their cases. The applause for Hans' group suddenly made his stomach flutter nervously, and he felt light-headed.

The orchestra found its way off stage and then through the maze of coats and violin cases, while Carl, Albert with Lina, Herr Besson, Thierry, and Geron wove their way through them and up to the stage. Carl felt as if he'd been drugged by a combination of a strong sedative and an equally strong jolt of caffeine. Albert glanced at him and gave him a warm pat on the shoulder before they sat and quickly tuned up. As soon as the first piece began, surprisingly, all thoughts for anything but the music disappeared, and Carl ended up quite enjoying playing and interacting with the other quintet members. It was as if they were creating their own little universe. They made a fine performance of it and were happy with the applause that followed.

The next group was made up of the older students, and there was much 'dancing' as his quintet met, side-stepped, and tried to get through the students eager to be on stage. Carl shook Master Ehrlich's hand and wished him luck. He also noticed that Friedrich was among the group and said hello and good luck to him. Friedrich seemed somehow distant and muttered a thank-you as he went by. *Nerves,* thought Carl sympathetically and now feeling much relieved himself.

Carl and the others settled into their seats as the students spent a moment tuning up and then began the first piece. Maria gave Carl's hand a tremendous squeeze as she pecked him on the cheek. All in all, Master Ehrlich's orchestra did a very nice job, but at the beginning one of the violins seemed to drop out of tune, and Carl noticed Friedrich struggling with his instrument and continually adjusting the tuning pegs. He hoped that this wasn't one of the instruments under his care, and he'd need to remember to ask Master Ehrlich and Friedrich if he should take a look at the instrument over the remainder of the student vacation.

By the second piece the nervous students had found their rhythm, and the music flowed very smoothly. Carl couldn't be sure, but to him it seemed that Friedrich was much more hesitant in his playing than he had witnessed previously; however, he knew from talking to him that Friedrich was a fellow-sufferer of stage fright.

With a tap on his shoulder from the row behind, he found Albert leaning forward and whispering into his ear. "I have to go and get back to the family," apologized Albert, and then after a few seconds - "There's a law in physics that two objects can't be in the same place at the same time." Carl turned further around, expecting more, but Albert was already making his way toward the main aisle.

He had no idea what the second utterance had meant. As Albert walked out of the hall, Carl thought, *Well, of course, he must mean that the students couldn't get up onto the concert stage until we left it to make room for them. Still, that was an odd thing to say.* As the piece progressed, his mind wandered, and he was again caught up in the music, but there was still something not quite right with the execution. He looked up and it was evident to him that Friedrich, who was an excellent violinist, was still struggling. His fingerings did not seem to be as intuitive and fluid as they had been in the past.

Then it struck him what Albert meant. Carl whispered something to Maria, got up from his seat, crouched low, and moved as gracefully as possible in front of the other gentlemen and ladies in his row as he made his way out of the hall and into the reception area. Clean-up was still on-going after the mess that Jan had made, but almost all was back into shape for the drinks, presentations, and auction to follow the concerts.

He went across the hall and pulled open the double doors revealing the small sitting room that held the piano to be auctioned. To the side on an ornate highboy sat the shiny violin case holding what they had discovered to be the student violin. A case with a student bow lay next to it. They'd agreed to keep these on display hoping that someone could shed light on the mystery of the missing violin. The disappearance was not to be emphasized, but neither was it to be hidden.

The ever-observant head servant had joined Carl as he walked over to the instrument. Carl unlatched the hasps on the case and slowly raised the lid. The violin inside was not the same one that had visited his shop the week before. As he leaned over, he immediately noticed the white glint of a label visible through the f-hole. The finish in places was beautiful, but most of the top surface was dull and full of small fibers. Looking around to the head servant who gave a nod, Carl lifted the violin from the case. It was light, and as he tapped the top and back, he found it to be very responsive. He moved his fingers lightly along the top surface and then examined the finish closely. It appeared that the deeply transparent shellac had been wiped with something, probably alcohol, to partially dissolve the varnish and it had then been wiped again with a low-quality cloth so that bits of fabric stuck to the surface. Looking into the f-hole, he saw the label of a maker from Austria-Hungary – Georg Voigt.

"Austria-Hungary," thought Carl. Remembering the switch on Albert's violin to a well-made Viennese bridge, Carl examined the manufacturer's markings on this one. It was exactly the same as a student model with no maker's label, and didn't sit well on the surface of the violin. He flipped the instrument over. There had been no attempt to hide the quality of the workmanship and finish here. It radiated beautiful craftsmanship and an expertly applied and polished varnish.

The bow case revealed the same student-grade bow as he had encountered before.

Carl stood for a time and stared at the violin. He nestled it into the case, still thinking. Then he turned to the head servant and began to speak, but stopped. Gradually all the pieces fell into place.

"I think you should summon Mme. Guiveny," stated Carl. The head servant nodded and hastily retreated to call the lady.

Mme. Guiveny walked erectly into the room following the head servant. "Markus tells me that you have some news about my father's violin. Have you found it?"

"As a matter of fact, it's right here," said Carl as Mme. Guiveny gaped.

"I'm sure better minds would have worked it out sooner, but you'll have to make do with mine," said Carl. For some reason, he thought he was sounding like Albert. "I think I now know most of what's transpired concerning your father's violin," realizing that now he seemed to sound like Sherlock Holmes whom he loved to follow in the newspaper. "For reasons I hope we'll soon uncover, one of the students taking part in your summer music program stole this instrument. He knew that he'd be discovered if the violin's appearance was as pristine as it had been when taken, so he altered it to fit in with the battered ones common in the student environment."

"It looks dreadful!" sighed Mme. Guiveny as Carl held out the violin.

"Somehow," nodded Carl, "he switched bridges with the one on Albert's instrument. I assume this wasn't because of the provenance of the bridge, but to make the stolen violin sound less like the high-quality piece of craftsmanship that it was. This instrument had to fit in amongst its lowly brethren both visually and sonically. Next, to cover his deed, the student abandoned the bow, and somehow obtained a bow that would blend in and wouldn't enhance the wonderful voice this beauty must have. The real travesty comes when he degraded the finish of the top so that at first glance it would appear as many of the other violins in the school's collection – well used and dull."

"Is it totally ruined?" asked a dismayed Mme. Guiveny.

"No, it can be repaired," Carl said and paused. "It seems to me that Friedrich at this moment is performing below his usual standards. At first, I'd thought that it was nerves, but now I think it's because he's struggling with an inferior instrument that he's not accustomed to playing. I'm certain that the violin he's using now is the instrument that was just recently in this case."

The three took a moment to absorb this. After a brief discussion, a messenger was dispatched to summon Sub-Commander Mortensen. Mme. Guiveny was staring forlornly at the state of the violin when Carl said, "You could still auction off the violin."

"What?" she asked, surprised.

"We know where the bow is – Sub-Commander Mortensen has had it in his possession since soon after it appeared in the school. I have the original bridge that was on Albert's violin, and we now have the instrument it came from. It's in sorry shape, but I can see that the damage is only superficial. If you explain to the crowd that the violin will be repaired and not in the same condition it's being displayed in tonight, you may still be able to auction this off in memory of your father, if you wish. I'd be happy to restore it to its original condition at no cost."

"Oh, cost is no object, but the ability to auction it is a very fine outcome indeed! I think the exciting story behind it might raise some interest, as well," said Mme. Guiveny with a very slight upturn to the edges of her lips.

◄ ■ ►

Immediately at the conclusion of the performance, Markus stepped up to Master Ehrlich and whispered in his ear. At one point Master Ehrlich's head shot up, but he continued to nod and lean into the speaker's voice. The applause had died down, and Master Ehrlich followed the students off the stage and into the crowded anteroom. He stalled until Friedrich had packed up his violin and made ready to leave and then walked up beside him and led the confused student through another door, down a hall, and into the room where the piano and violin lay on display. Already present were Carl, Maria, Mme. Guiveny, Friedrich's father whom Carl had fetched, and Markus. Friedrich knew that he'd been discovered, but started his defense by playing dumb and then lashing out with denials and excuses. Carl was just pointing out that this was the same as confessing a guilt when Mortensen arrived with the violin bow.

"Now that we're all here, I think I have a good handle on what's occurred if I can just ask Friedrich one question," began Carl. Both Mortensen and Friedrich's father nodded, and so Carl asked, "Did you beat up Jan a few weeks back?" Friedrich's already flushed cheeks turned crimson, and he stood looking down at the floor with his fists tightly clenched. After a long wait, he nodded and slowly relaxed his hands. "Then this is what I think happened, and hopefully someone can help fill in some of the blanks," he said, looking pointedly at Friedrich.

"Friedrich attended the music camp here this last summer. I understand it's a fun and easy-going affair, and the children pretty much have full access to the house since Mme. Guiveny has mentioned that most rooms are opened for private or group practices. Friedrich must have discovered Mme. Guiveny's father's violin and then took a liking to it. The case was dusty, and it was obvious to him that no one had played it since her father passed away."

"That's why I had decided to clean it up and auction it off – it just was of no use to me other than the sentimental value," added Mme. Guiveny helpfully.

Carl nodded and continued, "Either waiting for an opportunity when he knew that he wouldn't be disturbed, or grabbing it on a sudden whim, he took Mme. Guiveny's father's violin and left his own in its place. When he was back home and taking the violin out of its case, he realized that it would stand out in an instant, and that his theft was a folly. There must have been no other chance to switch the instruments back, because I know that's what I would have done."

Once again Friedrich nodded, a more rueful look on his face.

"He realized that it was now imperative to disguise the violin or be caught, so he applied alcohol to the surface and roughed it up to dull the shine. Then it must have been at one of the quartet's get-togethers or performances that he traded bridges with the one on Albert's violin. I still have that bridge in my shop. The violin now neither stood out visually nor sounded as good as was its true potential. Somehow the bow ended up in Jan Rauss's possession – that's one of the gaps that needs to be filled in." He again looked directly at Friedrich. "When the auction for the violin was announced, Friedrich immediately realized that he could be in serious trouble. The substituted student violin was now going to be on display for all to see. In a panic, he attacked Jan in an effort to find out the bow's location. This failed, but even without the bow, he thought he still had a chance to make the switch of violins here at this gathering and return the original to its case before the auction. He threatened Jan again and made him overturn the table to distract everyone's attention while he made the swap."

Friedrich reluctantly nodded. His father had at first appeared to be flabbergasted by the revelations, but then became incensed. "Out with it, Friedrich!" he growled in a low, emotional voice, and then a more tender, "You must confess, son."

With some difficulty at first, Friedrich began to speak. "I don't know why I took the bow along with the violin. As I was leaving the room, I saw another student's bow lying nearby and stuck it in the case. Then I thought I'd been so clever with the bows." whispered Friedrich. After another urging from his father, he continued, "The bow number assigned to me was 19, but I panicked when I realized that I could be caught with two bows, so I scratched out the number and chucked it in the river. Somehow, I couldn't do that to Mme. Guiveny's fine bow, and held onto it. It finally dawned on me that the new bow could implicate me if anyone noticed it and that the number 19 would look the same as 61 upside down, so I stole Frank Meyer's bow with that number. Then I took Jan Rauss's bow and put it in Frank Meyer's bow case, and left Jan holding the fine stolen bow. With the accounting that Master Ehrlich kept, I doubted that my trades would even be noticed." Master Ehrlich looked down and shook his head while Friedrich took a deep breath. "When the auction was announced, I knew I was in for it. I talked two friends from another school into helping me jump Jan in an effort to retrieve the bow without arousing his suspicions that it was me behind it."

Friedrich was not led away by his father grabbing his ear, as Jan had been. He was led away with Mortensen holding onto his collar.

◀■▶

The auction had been delayed by the private meeting with Friedrich, and Mme. Guiveny offered her apologies to the gathering. After a brief explanation of the provenance of the violin along with the recent mystery of its disappearance, and with the promise that the violin would be restored to its original condition, both the violin and piano were auctioned for very generous amounts. It was later Mme. Guiveny's guess that the delay had allowed for more consumption of wine and whiskey, which might have led to the excellent sums that were generated for the children's music benefit. She was all smiles regardless and said that she would need to test this theory at a future fund-raiser.

Carl and Maria left with both the auctioned violin and his own, and Carl promised the delighted winner that he would deliver a flawless instrument within the week.

CHAPTER 24

Despite the cold temperatures, the holidays were warmer and more enjoyable than Carl had experienced in many years. The concert was over, the demand for performance-quality violins was waning, snow had blanketed the city, and he and Maria were busy nearly every minute with friends, concerts, and quietly planning for the new baby. In the days leading up to Christmas, they made a point of walking through the snow-bedecked streets and taking in the candles and decorations that the store and house windows had on display. Maria dragged him to several shops that had infant's clothes and baby carriages to get an idea of what they might need as the time approached.

Herr Besson invited the quintet members and their spouses to his house on Christmas Eve. It began as a somewhat formal affair, mainly because Herr Besson was so reserved, but after a few eggnogs, the atmosphere relaxed considerably. Herr Besson even played piano while his wife sang some Christmas carols, and soon the entire room was joining in. Rather than a sit-down affair, there were two tables covered with ham, turkey, cheeses, breads, pickled vegetables, and small ornate desserts for the choosing.

Albert had arrived with Mileva and Hans Albert, and the baby was of course the center of attention, especially among the ladies. Mileva was more than excited to be out and among people, and soon she, Maria, and Geron's wife were in a corner happily engrossed in conversation. Hans Albert had made the rounds with Mileva, but it was Albert who saw to him for most of the evening, and Hans Albert was soon asleep cradled in one of his father's arms while a pipe was held in the hand of the other.

"Well, that was quite the spectacle at the concert the other evening," said Albert. "What did I miss?"

"Wasn't that a mess?" asked Thierry, as the others of the quintet gathered around.

"And all to try and cover up a theft," Herr Besson said to him.

"Well, you were right, Albert, Friedrich had switched violins to cover up his theft," said Carl as he joined the group.

"Albert knew who did it?" asked Thierry.

Carl nodded, "He prodded me to realize what was going on. I knew that something wasn't right with how Friedrich was playing but couldn't quite put my finger on what it was."

Albert grinned and pointed his pipe stem at the sleeping baby in his arm. "You see, Little Hans? I told you that would end up being what happened!"

"But how could Friedrich do such a thing?" asked Geron. "He's probably the best violinist that Master Ehrlich has had in a long time - and he steals Mme. Guiveny's violin? Why?"

"Who knows?" answered Carl. "It looks like he acted totally on impulse, or at least I hope that's all it was."

"And so, what happened with the violin?" asked Albert.

"I reunited it with the bridge and restored it for the auction winner," said Carl. "So, everyone is happy, except for Friedrich."

"What happened to him?" asked Geron. "I haven't heard."

"Nor have I," said Carl, shaking his head. "Just that the police hauled him away and were going to question him."

"What a shame," said Geron, now also shaking his head. Suddenly his daughters appeared insisting that it was time to pull the Christmas crackers that Thierry had brought back from a recent trip to London.

It was an enjoyable and festive gathering for all, and Maria and Carl walked with Mileva, Hans Albert in a baby buggy, and Albert most of the way home. Maria insisted on pushing the buggy and kept up a running patter with Mileva.

"Have a Merry Christmas," said Carl when they reached Kramgasse, and then paused. "Oh, I forgot that you're Jewish and don't celebrate…"

"No, but we enjoy the season none the less," broke in Albert. "At home, Mileva thought we might light the Menorah in Hans Albert's first Hanukkah, just for a little tradition. He does love the lights at his age!" reaching into the pram and giving his son a nuzzle. "Have a wonderful Christmas, you two!" And both couples waved to each other as they headed off in opposite directions.

"That baby is so darling and it's so difficult to not talk about our pending arrival," said Maria as they walked down Kramgasse to the apartment. "But I know so many women who've lost their babies early. If that happened to us, it would be so painful; I wouldn't want to discuss it with anyone."

"I want to do whatever makes you the most comfortable," said Carl. "I'm realizing now that this baby thing doesn't happen all at once, and we have plenty of time to plan and let others know when the time is right."

◄■►

The students were still out on holiday, but Carl had four violins to deliver to the school where Master Ehrlich would then see that they made it to their proper owners. The four cases were too much for one person to carry, so Carl enlisted Peer to tote two of them. Peer had been enjoying the holidays and treasured the Christmas ornament that the tall girl with intense eyes had given him. He had let slip that her name was Sophie, but so far that was all that Carl knew about her. Carl had said that he could go on home after they made their delivery, and so Peer was walking with an even lighter step.

"That was quite the concert event, wasn't it?" asked Master Ehrlich after Carl and Peer had dropped off the violins. "I never would have thought that one of our students would be capable of such a thing."

"Well, it certainly seemed to me to be a bad decision made on the spur of the moment," said Carl. "It was all of the efforts at a cover-up that showed any malicious intent. And then of course, there was the attack on Jan."

"Yes, I think that was the worst," agreed Master Ehrlich. "Sadly, Friedrich has been expelled from the school, and the police are very serious about pressing charges against him. He's young, but getting little sympathy from his parents, the school, or the police. Confidentially, I think it's partly due to Jan's father who's wielding his influence at all levels. He's furious and embarrassed, both by Friedrich's treatment and manipulation of Jan, as well as his own reaction to the catastrophe at the concert. Apparently, he whipped Jan severely and now feels his own guilt about it." Carl shook his head as Master Ehrlich said this. "By the way, I want to pass on the school's gratitude for your help in tracking down the bow and discovering the exchange of the violins," he continued. "That was a nice piece of detection."

"I really did nothing more than recognize the type of violin that I've been working on day in and day out this semester," Carl joked.

"Well, the school trustees were very appreciative. As soon as word of the switch was heard, they had an emergency meeting in order to begin mitigation of any damage that may come to the school's reputation. One of the outcomes was that they want you to know that you've been given the contract to work on our violins for as long as you like," said Master Ehrlich.

Oh, great, thought Carl a little glumly; "Great, thanks," he said at his next thought of the greater financial security this would bring.

◀■▶

Carl and Maria were both becoming worried that they hadn't seen Flecken since a little after Christmas. "Where do you suppose he could be?" asked Maria. "It's winter, after all, and he usually likes the nice warm shop."

"I have no idea," said Carl. "Maybe he found a warmer place with a better menu?"

"I hope so," said Maria. "Still, I miss seeing him around."

"I know, me too," said Carl. "I wouldn't worry since he's done this once or twice before. He's getting on in years, but he can still take care of himself."

Coincidentally, Flecken limped up the next morning after Carl had pulled open the shutter doors and was starting downstairs. The cat's hair was matted, and the white blotches were nearly as dark as the black ones. There was a tear on his left ear, and he approached skittishly.

"There you are, old boy!" said Carl, scooping up the cat who to him felt several pounds lighter. "What's happened to you?" Instead of heading down to the shop, Carl wrestled the shutter doors shut again and climbed back up to the apartment where they were met at the door by Maria and a small cry of anguish.

"Flecken! You poor guy!" she reached out and gently touched his damaged ear away from the tear.

"And, he was limping when he came up to me," said Carl.

"Well, let's get him cleaned up and see how he is," said Maria.

Flecken accepted the warm bath with little protestation, and while cleaning and wiping him down, they found several scabs on his shoulders. As he was being dried, Carl noticed that he'd always seen Flecken as a white cat with black splotches, but now thought he may be a black cat with white markings. His left front paw was tender, and he was not happy about having it examined, but did no more than let out a low growl as it was gently bent and twisted.

"I think he's all right," said Maria, "but it could be that his roving days are over." He was ravenous and rasped in his strange voice to let them know about it. They found him some left-overs and cream that he soon devoured.

Carl carried him back down to the shop, but had to lift Flecken up to his perch where the cat slept the remainder of the day. Late that afternoon he had to help him down from the shelf and didn't have the heart to set him out onto the street for the night as was usual.

From that evening on, Flecken was accepted up in the apartment as a member of the household.

◄■►

Maria boarded the train for Zurich at the end of the first week of the New Year – 1905. She and Mileva had enjoyed becoming acquainted at Herr Besson's Christmas Eve party, and a few days after the holiday, Maria had stopped over to visit Mileva and to dote on Hans Albert. Mileva was grateful for the company, and Maria told Carl later that they had some very lively discussions and that it was both fun and revealing to interact with the baby. Maria spent another day during her last week in Bern over at Mileva's while Carl worked.

"Mileva's such a natural mother," said Maria as she and Carl had tea the morning of her departure. "I only hope it comes as easily to me. It was such an eyeopener to watch her interactions with Hans Albert. She's an absolute jewel."

"It's so great that you've made a new friend in Mileva," said Carl sipping at the tea.

"Yes!" said Maria. "She's so intelligent and opinionated – which is good, by the way," as she turned a smile towards Carl. "And she and I have somehow felt like we've discovered true friends in each other."

"Well, now we have another reason to stay in Bern," Carl said hopefully.

"Oh, I don't know – people do move around you know," said a grinning Maria. "But with a baby on the way, it might be nice to have someone like Mileva with some experience on the subject nearby." They had had some conversations during this break about the best home base for the two of them and, so far, Bern had been winning out, and it was making more and more sense financially.

"Mileva had been a student in physics. Did you know?" asked Maria. "She actually understands most of what Albert talks about – which is quite a lot as I understand, and at first she was even able to help him out with his ideas and equations. Then she had trouble passing her exams and now she has her hands full with Hans Albert. But that hasn't stopped her curiosity and wish for better circumstance for both herself and Albert."

"Yes, I've gathered that, professionally, Albert's feeling somewhat passed over and neglected here in the Bern Patent Office," said Carl.

"It's the same with Mileva at home," said Maria.

Carl walked Maria to the station and then helped her get situated in the rail car. This time it was even more difficult to say goodbye; he started to miss her as soon as the train pulled out of the station. He could see how time would run more slowly for both of them as the train picked up speed on its way to Zurich.

CHAPTER 25

"You've certainly heard that Mileva and Hans Albert are going to Zurich for a week and are going to stay with Maria for a night or two? Isn't that great?" asked Albert, unconsciously moving his hands as he asked the questions. They stood on a street corner curb between the flow of pedestrians near the building and the lane busy with carts and cars behind them.

"Yes, I gather those two have grown quite close," said Carl who was delivering a violin to the train station for shipment to a client in France. "Maria's written me that she's busy with school, but is looking forward to seeing Mileva over the weekend. They're both excited about a visit that consists of more than just an afternoon over tea."

"Oh, Mileva certainly is," said Albert above the noise of a passing tram. "And I, like any husband I'm sure, have mixed feelings about her trip. On the one hand, I'm happy she has relatives and a friend in Zurich and can get out of the house, and yet on the other I realize that I've become dependent on them being around – and on her cooking."

"Well, we can remedy that by having dinner sometime while she's away," said Carl.

"The perfect solution," said Albert. "And, I hate to be selfish, but I've been trying to find the time to write up some of the ideas that we've talked about for journal submissions. I have one paper done, but just can't seem to get the time to write any more. I'm looking forward to using that week to finalize another, or maybe two more articles."

"So many?" asked Carl. "I can't imagine even writing one. Will dinner get in the way of your writing?"

"Oh no, that will only mean that I don't have to try and cook," said Albert thankfully as they parted.

Carl walked away feeling oddly depressed as he made his way back to his shop. *Am I not looking forward to that dinner with Albert?* he wondered vaguely. Then he realized that it was Albert himself who'd caused the odd reaction, and Carl thought about why.

Here was a man caught up in thinking about space, light, and such, but he was only twenty-five years old – he had the luxury of philosophizing about time, but Carl himself was beginning to feel the true effects of it. And he was beginning to see that no one knew how much of it they had left. Albert hopefully had a long life ahead of him and was already coming up with these amazing ideas, while Carl was facing middle age. *And what have I done with my life?* he wondered. *What have I contributed or what am I leaving behind? Hopefully a child, at least?* Albert had said that time slowed down the faster one went, and yet to Carl, the years were zipping by while he was standing still. He realized that what he'd initially taken as depression was probably some form of jealousy at what Albert had already accomplished and what he had ahead of him. It was difficult not to feel a little inadequate by comparison. *But we're very different people,* thought Carl suddenly, feeling grateful for their friendship that had developed in spite of this.

◄ ■ ►

In harmony, the shop door swung open and the bell at the top tinkled. Carl looked up to find Paul entering and shaking his coat from the light but warm rain. Behind him stood a bedraggled figure whose mood, it seemed to Carl, was more hang-dogged than his appearance.

"Hi Carl," said Paul ruffling his wet hair. "Finally, some spring rain!"

"Yes, we needed it - how are you?"

"Great," said Paul. "However, the pair of us come to you for reassurance."

"About what?" asked Carl.

"Well," began Paul. "Last night we were playing in a quartet as a benefit for the Russian Students' Association to provide funds for those who fell in St. Petersburg. The performance went well with pieces by Beethoven, Schubert, and Hayden and I understand that we helped raise quite a bit of money, by the way. Unfortunately, just before we went on stage, Fritz," and he nodded at his sullen companion, "accidently hit a chair and popped the bridge out of his violin. We set it back and, crossing our fingers, hoped that the intonation would be correct, or at least acceptable. As I said, the performance went well, but we noticed some scratches and wanted to make sure that the violin has survived the mishap."

Fritz solemnly placed the violin case on the workbench and began to open it.

"You see," said Paul. "It's a Guarneri del Gesu lent to Fritz by Frau von Sinner, and God forbid that we've ruined such an august instrument."

Carl was in awe. He'd previously only seen and been able to play one other violin by Guarneri, reputed to be either a rival of, or even better than, the great Stradivarius, depending on taste. He took the offered violin and sat down on his work stool carefully going over every detail of the instrument. He could see the light scratches where the bridge had been rudely dislodged, but other than that all appeared to be well.

"There's no real harm done," said Carl. "And I can easily fix the finish so that it'll be just as you received it, if that's alright." Two heads nodded furiously. Carl de-tensioned the strings and removed the bridge, checking again that it hadn't been damaged. Holding a rough cloth, he buffed up the area where the bridge had marred the finish and then took a finer cloth with some light buffing compound and worked the fine scratches out. He then lovingly and lightly buffed the entire instrument, set the bridge, and retuned the violin.

"There," he proclaimed. "As good as new. Do you mind?" Seeing no objection, he took up the bow and played a simple *adagio* that he had memorized. The moment for him became one of his most cherished.

Packing up the violin, Fritz asked, "How much will it be to pay for the repair, Carl?"

"You've already paid me by letting me play it for a bit," Carl smiled.

"Well, thank you so much for saving us," and they both shook Carl's hand. He patted Fritz on the back as the relieved violinist seemed to bounce up the stairs while cradling the valuable instrument.

Paul wandered over and petted Flecken, eliciting audible purrs. "Since I'm here, I must ask how your drawing is progressing," said Paul, turning back to Carl.

"Well," stammered Carl. "Progress would mean that I was actually moving forward, but that doesn't stop me from trying. Since your gallery show, I find myself thinking too much about what I'm doing when I draw, but I sort of understand now that it's going to take a combination of practice plus some intuition for me to make any progress. I never had the chance to thank you for drawing a sketch like mine. I don't know yet if art is something I'll seriously devote any time to, but if I do, at least I have an inkling that I'm headed in the right direction. And," he continued, "since that showing, I keep hearing more and more about your paintings, and all the reviews are good, by the way. Oh, and speaking of reviews, I've also read some of the music reviews that you've written and I think they're very insightful. You're a very busy man."

"Well, thanks," said Paul. "Although I've found an error in your statement – I regret to say that I'm not now, and may never be, a painter."

"But all that you've shown me . . ." began Carl.

"Etchings especially, yes, drawings, designs, sketches, most certainly - but not paintings. You see, my problem is that I'm incapable of incorporating color – in fact I'd say that I've absolutely no sense of color whatsoever and so shy away from paints. When I do try, I struggle with them - unfortunately the only palette in my brain is black and white. I'm afraid that I may forever be constrained to monotone drawings, which is just fine with me since every sketch is both a challenge and a new dimension – more than enough to work with. But I have to admit that I stand flabbergasted by a paint brush."

"You have such talent that I'm sure this is just a temporary setback and that it's not insurmountable. It'll come with time," said Carl. Paul smiled, trying to hold back, and then suddenly burst into laughter.

Gaining control, he said, "I'm sorry! I suddenly saw myself telling you the same thing!" Carl nodded and then chuckled himself.

"OK, let's both agree to try harder." They shook on it.

"I've been keeping in touch with a group of artists in Munich, and I'm hoping to perhaps move back there next year. I shouldn't be saying anything, but Lily and I have plans, as well," beamed Paul.

"That's fantastic!" said Carl. "You said next year, right? We should plan to have you and your mother and father over for dinner this summer after Maria gets resettled. Would that be good? We'll get in touch with the date."

That would be wonderful," said Paul. "Maybe we could arrange the timing to be during one of Lily's visits – would that be OK?"

"The more, the merrier," grinned Carl.

◄ ■ ►

Carl met Albert at *Der Sturm* in early spring. The walk there had been pleasant, warm, and filled with the subtle scent of cherry and apple blossoms. The grip of winter seemed to be finally loosened for good, and the house and shop could be aired out during the warmest part of the day.

"I've never eaten here before," said Albert. "What a perfectly decent and quiet restaurant."

"Isn't it?" agreed Carl as they sat, "And the food is actually quite good. Maria and I discovered it – quite easily as it happens because we live just around the corner – and we've become regulars." At that, a waiter brought a bottle of red wine to meet with Carl's approval. Somewhat sheepishly Carl nodded, and Albert agreed that some wine would be an excellent idea. "I hope it's not a bad sign when a waiter automatically brings you over a bottle of wine," winced Carl.

"I think it's a compliment," said Albert taking an exploratory sip. "Say, this is a great wine. What are the grapes?"

"A *Blaufränkisch* from Austria-Hungary, and at a very decent price, too," commented Carl raising his glass.

Albert raised his in reply. After another taste, they both got up and navigated their way to the menu posted near the entrance.

"If you don't have anything in mind, I'd really recommend the game hen with an herbed rice," said Carl after they'd spent some time examining the menu. Albert noticed the price and balked. "No, my treat," insisted Carl. "You really should try it. It's Maria's favorite when it's in season."

"Well, thank you very much, Carl," Albert happily accepted as they made their way back to the table.

The waiter stopped and took their order as the two talked about Maria and Mileva and their fortunate meeting, and of the need for the music group to begin practices again in earnest since they'd only met for a few times following the holidays. Then the topic turned, as it would with Albert at the table, to physics.

"Do you remember our discussion previously about how things change with increasing speeds?" asked Albert clearing some room at his place as the dinner plates were set before them.

"Yes, I've been thinking about it a lot, in my own way," said Carl.

"Then I should tell you about my epiphany," started Albert. "I spoke about it with my friend Michele only this morning, but you're the first other than him to hear of it. I don't know why I'm so excited, but I just know it's going to shake some things up in the physics departments."

"What is it?" asked Carl, now even more interested.

"In another one of those strange mental leaps – this one as I was falling asleep the other evening - I've fit another piece into the puzzle that I make of the universe. So many things are making sense to me now." He took a sip of wine. "It's tied to the conversation we had last time - and I vividly remember it because of the skis. Do you recall me saying that with increasing speed, that mass, or weight, increases?"

"Of course I remember," said Carl. "Because I still can't understand how that could be possible."

"The faster something goes, the heavier and heavier it becomes, as the cathode ray experiment showed. The reason is, light speed is the sole province of pure energy. Nothing else is allowed in. The energy being poured into any system trying to achieve that speed must go somewhere – and that's into mass. My epiphany was this simple equation..." He dug in his pocket and pulled out a crumpled piece of paper filled on one side with what to Carl were complex computations.

Carl looked at the figures with wide eyes and said, "Um, Albert. Do you really think that I could understand..."

"No, no, it really *is* simple," said Albert. Not finding what he wanted on the front, he took a pencil from his breast pocket and turning over the sheet, somewhat excitedly wrote: $m = E/c^2$. "You see, 'c' represents the speed of light which is a very big number, and I've squared it so now it's a huge number. We physicists typically think of energy in units that are a square, and that's why I've squared the speed of light. Anyway, chugging away at slow speeds requires a small amount of energy. Dividing that small amount of energy, or 'E', by a huge number means that mass, or 'm', stays pretty much the same. But with the gigantic amount of energy required to approach the speed of light, as energy gets bigger, mass gets larger and can increase immensely. Now, your mass can never be less than it is right now because we're sitting still, and the increase I'm talking about disappears when you stop moving again – but it does increase when you're in motion."

"So, even on a fast train, I might actually weigh a little more?" asked Carl.

Albert looked down at the equation and nodded, "Yes, a minute hair more." He cut a piece of game hen and, chewing, obviously enjoyed the choice. Pointing the fork towards Carl he continued, "Now, combining this idea with some observations of radium by others, has implications that I'm still grappling with, but of which I'm somehow quite confident." Albert poised his fork momentarily above the plate and then took another bite.

"Do you know what radium is?" asked Albert, after he chewed another morsel. Carl, with a mouthful of rice, shook his head. The conversation stalled as Albert took a sip of water and eventually continued, "Radium's an element that releases units of high energy which are now being called radiation. Rocks containing radium can even feel warm to the touch. However, for all of the energy they're emitting, the rocks lose miniscule amounts of mass, or weight – hardly even measurable, and they've been radiating energy for thousands of years. We're not accustomed to seeing such high amounts of energy with negligible depletion in the source and no evident change in the weight or mass.

"There's an axiom that energy cannot be created nor destroyed. Energy simply changes forms – it can be potential, kinetic, radiant, and so forth, switching from one form to the other, but it doesn't come from nothing, and it doesn't disappear. Thinking about the changes in forms of energy along with the gain in mass at increasing speeds led me to conclude that mass, sort of what you are used to thinking of as matter, and energy are really the same thing - only different outward appearances of what is really a continuum. Mass is at one end of the spectrum largely as stored energy, and pure energy, like light, is at the other end of the spectrum. That is essentially what my equation is saying – they are equivalent."

"Do you mean to say that we are related to light?" asked Carl incredulously.

Albert beamed and nodded. "Yes, in a way, you and light are the same. We've always been looking at these as two separate things, but I think that they're actually very tightly bound to one another. Mass is nothing but stored energy, and energy is nothing but potential mass. You, sitting across from me, are an example of mass; and light is the visible expression of pure energy. I think that most of the energy in matter just functions to hold it all together and stable. Radium's the result of the partial breaking of the bonds at some elemental level. A large amount of energy with no change in mass means, to me, that there's a huge potential of energy remaining in the mass."

"Is that sort of like all of the electricity that a battery can store?" asked Carl.

"In a way," said Albert, "but even more so. That electricity is dwarfed by the energy stored in the matter that makes up the battery itself. Even a dead battery has more energy comprised in its structure than we could ever store within it to produce electricity."

Carl shook his head. "That seems impossible to me," he said.

"No, really. For a small amount of mass there's an incredible amount of energy available."

"So, the 70 kilograms in me?" asked Carl.

"Well, let's see. We would just need to rewrite my equation to solve for energy," said Albert scribbling with the pencil again. "It would look like this." And he turned the paper around to show Carl the equation: $E = mc^2$. "The energy available is the same as multiplying the mass in you times the square of the speed of light – again, a very, very big number." Carl stared at him questioningly as Albert paused. "It would be enough to power the lights and trams on the earth for years," quipped Albert.

"No!" said Carl, flabbergasted.

"Really!" said Albert seriously. He then tilted his wine glass towards Carl who smiled and reciprocated.

◄■►

After dinner back in his apartment, Carl had lit a candle and begun to read, but now sat reclined in his chair with Flecken asleep on his lap. Next to him on the chair lay the newspaper, and he'd just read an article on the growing industry focused around the new motion-picture camera. He and Maria had gone to a picture-show in Zurich recently as a lark, and he'd had a strange feeling afterwards. He'd enjoyed the show but had somehow latched onto the fact that these frames had captured something that no longer existed – they had frozen these people in time so that the same events were shown over and over. It made him feel that the pictures were dead and the figures on them were ghosts dancing around on the screen. Thinking about his conversation with Albert tonight, however, he'd now suddenly seen that the light shining through the frames brought them to life – the very light that was necessary to capture the images in the first place. And now Albert had said that he was energy itself, that they all were essentially light, and he couldn't help but feel that incredible energy surge through him.

Carl was now nearing sleep along with Flecken, and his thoughts seemed to jump. *Atoms and light,* and his body felt again like it was abuzz with the new electric currents recently put into the apartment. *Has this cat put my limbs to sleep?* he vaguely wondered from the tingling sensation that he'd become aware of. Once again, Albert had put him into a thoughtful mood. *We are light,* came to him as he began to doze off.

Just as he fell asleep, he wondered, *What if this feeling, these currents run through everything?* And he had a strong intuition that perhaps they did. Now picturing a glowing form growing within Maria, he was enveloped in a sensation of utter warmth.

CHAPTER 26

Sooner than expected, Maria was back in Bern. They'd learned that the cellist Pablo Casals was going to perform with the Bern Symphony Orchestra, and Maria had jumped at the chance to see him. The bonus was that Paul would be playing violin in the same concert. Carl had secured tickets, and Maria had managed to find a substitute lecturer for her classes. She arrived mid-day on a Friday, and they went out for dinner at *Der Sturm*, almost a home away from home. The game hen was still on the menu, so Maria ordered that, as well as some *pomme frites* as an appetizer.

"I'm starving all the time," she said as the potatoes arrived. "I know exactly why I should be hungry, but I'm still surprised every time I eat more than is normal for me." Maria was now showing noticeably and had begun wearing an outer smock over her loosening waistline. Carl couldn't help but picture a bundle of light growing within her and smiled.

"The midwife visited me last week, and she said that I'm very healthy and that the baby appears to be developing normally," said Maria as she nibbled on a *pomme frite*.

"Well, that's a relief!" sighed Carl.

"It certainly is!" replied Maria. "She said that my having a child somewhat later in life might be a cause for concern in some cases, but that everything looks fine. She did remark that it was surprising that I hadn't been pregnant before now, and I said that it wasn't for a lack of trying." Carl blushed and looked around to make sure that no one was listening in on their conversation.

"We always assumed that there was something wrong with one of us, but that we were fine not having kids," whispered Carl. "Did she have any reason why we should be having one now?"

"She had not a clue," replied Maria. "A miracle, she said. She also asked if she should put me on her schedule for delivery sometime in June or July, and I told her I'd let her know when I returned to Zurich. So, what do you think, Carl? Will the child's home be here or in Zurich?"

"Some of it depends on your teaching position," said Carl. "Do you know for certain if the University will keep you on if we move to Zurich?"

"I think so," said Maria. "They've been very liberal about allowing me to continue teaching as I'm starting to show. They said that as long as I'm healthy and continue to wear covering smocks, that I can at least finish out the term. Further than that, they offered very little commitment."

"So, we should be thinking – 'What would be best for our family?'" said Carl. "Zurich has excellent medical facilities, your teaching position, and I'm sure I could easily establish my business there."

"Yes, but Bern has our friends, your shop, and also decent hospitals," retorted Maria. "You know what?"

"What?" asked Carl.

"It makes most sense to stay in Bern," said Maria decisively. "You have a good location for business here and there's no point in moving your entire shop to Zurich. I can easily move, and I'm pretty sure I could secure some kind of position in the University of Bern, especially with my credentials from the University of Zurich. I'm going to write to the University here and see what my possibilities are, and talk to the local midwife tomorrow morning to see if I can be on her schedule for this summer. If those two work out, I think Bern is our best bet."

"And we can always visit Zurich," offered Carl, inwardly pleased that Maria was happy with the idea of settling in Bern. "I also think," he continued. "especially since it's becoming increasingly obvious, that we let others know you're pregnant."

"Me, too!" replied Maria.

◄■►

The next day, Maria had arranged an intimate gathering with Ida and Mileva which began mid-morning and lasted well into the afternoon. Paul and Carl helped Ida in the slow and deliberate process of climbing the steps into the apartment, and Mileva arrived with Hans Albert in her arms soon after. There were happy shouts of surprise as Maria revealed her news. Paul gave his congratulations and went off to practice for the concert, and Carl descended into his shop for the afternoon.

On Sunday, Carl and Maria walked arm-in-arm up the bricked streets to the concert hall on a warm spring evening. The circular fountains along Kramgasse were freely flowing now that winter had passed, and several apartments were already drying laundry outside in the more agreeable weather. They arrived early and chose aisle seats far to the right and near the front with Maria on the aisle. Soon Hans and Paul helped wheel Ida down the carpeted access and secured her wheelchair next to Maria. They all wished Paul good luck as he headed to the backstage with his violin. While they talked, the concert hall filled, and they could hear the tunings and quick rehearsals of the orchestra backstage.

The heavy burgundy curtains opened to a roar of applause. After the orchestra was seated, the by-now world-celebrated cellist entered from the left and took his chair set in a prominent position, nodding his appreciation as the room quieted. When the music began, it seemed to Carl that the prelude was rocky and a glance at Maria, who nodded back, confirmed that she agreed. The conductor had begun at one tempo, but then suddenly deferred to Casals who bowed some notes and then tapped on the back of his cello to establish the rhythm. From then on, however, the performance was incredible. The orchestra played two Mozart pieces and an overture by Spontini, and Carl, Maria, and Ida all noted the exquisite executions not only by Casals, but also by Paul. Casals graced the audience with two solo renditions of Boccherini and Bach at the end. The conclusion resulted in a thunderous and immediate standing ovation.

Remaining behind with Ida until Paul emerged from backstage, they excitedly reviewed the performance as the hall emptied. Ida and Hans were both swelling with pride that Paul had been able to perform with such a renowned musician.

"Oh, the performance was excellent!" exclaimed Ida as Paul approached.

Paul broke into a grin. "Thanks, Ma," he said. "You'd have wondered about that if you'd seen us last night, however. Casals arrived late, there was a miscommunication, and things went downhill from there. The conductor and he could not agree on the tempo, and the conductor wasn't deft enough to pick up on the pace that Casals preferred. Casals ended up storming out of the practice! Luckily, it all came together tonight. Did you notice the prompts he gave the conductor?" All of them immediately nodded. Paul shrugged. "At least it was memorable?" he asked.

"In so many ways," said Carl, and they all smiled in agreement.

As he and Maria walked back to their apartment, Carl said, "Paul's climbed so high in the music world – can you imagine - he just played with Pablo Casals! He's so successful and yet wants to devote himself to art. I know he's young, but what I don't understand is how could he possibly have the courage to make such a huge change. Like jumping off a cliff into the unknown."

"I don't know, Carl," said Maria. "I've talked with Ida about it, and she said that, while she doesn't understand it herself, she can actually see the flame going out in his eyes when he practices or is preparing for a concert. And yet, he can spend hours working on a single drawing and comes out even more energized than when he started. She said that she has almost no choice other than to support him. She doesn't think even a Swiss national award in music could get him to turn away from becoming an artist at this point."

"I suppose not," said Carl. "And what you've said is exactly the impression I get when I talk to him, too. But still, it takes a courage that I don't think I'd have."

◀ ■ ▶

Carl was crossing the street at a busy intersection and glanced up at the traffic guard as he passed. He continued on for a few paces, stopped for a moment, and then went back to the tall cadet in a dark blue uniform. "Friedrich?" he asked.

Recognizing Carl, Friedrich at first made a sheepish expression, but then straightened his shoulders, standing even taller, and offered Carl his white gloved hand. "Hello, Herr Veblen, how are you this afternoon?"

"I'm fine, thanks," said Carl. "How are you? I almost didn't recognize you in this official garb."

Friedrich stood proudly and brushed at his uniform sleeve. "Yes, I am now a police cadet," he said in somewhat clipped tones.

"I can see, but I'm also surprised," said Carl. "How did this come about?"

Friedrich surveyed the street to make sure that there was no traffic to concern him for the moment, walked with Carl to the curb, and said, "Most unexpectedly, for me, Herr Veblen. After the hearing, I was forced into community service by Jan's father, and he had me cleaning streets for weeks." He paused and walked into traffic to stop the main flow of cars and carts so that a fully laden horse-cart could make it across at the side-street. He waved to another cadet to come take over for the moment. Returning to where Carl stood, he continued, "I was so angry then at what I'd thought was a huge injustice. In a fury one day, I kicked over the collection can I was filling and was about to run off when by chance a policeman stopped me and sat me down right there on the curb. We talked for half an hour. He asked me about my situation, and I explained what had happened at school and afterwards. He told me that I obviously had problems with compulsion and anger and that if I didn't bring those under control, I'd likely end up a criminal. Then he said that the best thing for me would be the discipline of the army or the police force." Carl nodded thoughtfully and he continued. "Well, I reflected on what he said and decided to try the police, and I've just finished my cadet training."

"That's an amazing story," said Carl. "I was so sad that things went the way they did for you after the violin incident – especially given the temper of Ratsherr Rauss."

"Well, I'm not sure what punishment I really deserved for what I did, but I'm so glad that policeman sat me down and talked to me."

"He must have been very persuasive," said Carl.

"Yes, he was," said Friedrich. "It was the thing he said as he left me at the curb that made up my mind."

"What was that?" asked Carl.

"He said, 'Remember, if you're in the police, you'll always be highly respected, even by someone like Ratsherr Rauss.'"

Carl thought about this and then nodded and said, "It looks like you've chosen wisely, Friedrich. Good luck."

"Thank you, sir," said Friedrich with a small salute as he went off to join his companion cadet in the melee of traffic.

◄ ■ ►

Following the Casals performance in Bern, Maria had developed an even greater passion for attending all the concerts she possibly could while she was still living in Zurich and before the arrival of their baby. She was writing a book on the relationship between music and landscape poetry, especially from the 18th and 19th centuries, and was gathering all the information and inspiration that Zurich could provide, either in the library or in the concert hall. Since musical performances were something that they both enjoyed hearing together and given that most concerts were held on weekends, Carl was happy to make trips to Zurich to attend them with her. They'd come to realize that it was only a two-hour ride each way after all, and he was free on his weekends when most of the concerts were performed. This was his third visit in a month and, as they took their seats in the Tonhalle auditorium, Carl shook his head. He was beginning to enjoy Zurich and thought he might miss coming here regularly once Maria was with him again in Bern.

They'd chosen a concert by the Zurich Symphony that included Dvorak's Serenade for Strings; they'd both enjoyed a performance of it previously in Bern and were excited to hear it again. Maria had convinced herself that the piece represented a harvest celebration that still spoke of a deep appreciation of nature, and this performance ended up cementing that notion in her mind. To her, this interpretation of the music fit in perfectly with a selection of farming poems for a section in the book on rural influences. Watching the musicians file in and take their seats, Carl was surprised to see that Franz, who had purchased the violin he'd so lovingly crafted, was the first chair and pointed him out to Maria.

As the music began, Carl was taken by the overall sweetness of the piece. And he realized that it was both the musical key and the choice of instruments responsible for that impression. It was, after all, the instruments that made the music. He sank back in his seat with that thought and realized how often he forgot it really was the instruments that were the creators of what he was hearing. At concerts such as this one, he was focused on the composition itself, and yet here he worked on instruments daily, and the fact that there would be no music without them should be glaringly obvious. Centuries had molded the violin, viola, cello, bass, and all the wind and brass instruments not represented in this string performance, into the unique producers of sound that they were. Each had been adjusted, elongated, shortened, widened, and fattened until just the right tone resulted.

He marveled at how integral nature was in what he was hearing in a very real way. The fingerboards and tailpieces of ebony in these stringed instruments came from hot continents far away, and harvesters locally sought out the prime figured and flamed maple and the select spruce that comprised the necks and bodies. Each species or quality of wood was chosen for its ability to portray beauty and project the precise tone that was required. Craftsmen had taken these raw materials and transformed them into works of art, the best of which stood out in both sound and appearance. He reflected that these instruments, these carefully machined and fabricated bodies - so concrete - had no other purpose in existence but to lead the listener into a state of ethereal pleasure. "Is it not strange that sheep's guts should hale souls out of men's bodies?" That line from 'Much Ado About Nothing,' perhaps the only line he remembered from Shakespeare's play, resonated with him.

Form and materials had been crafted to produce the rich basses, full middle tones, and penetrating but not piercing high notes that he was hearing at this instant. Viewing the orchestra, he was unexpectedly awed at the thought of all the precise care in construction that had come together to create the exact sound that he and Maria were enjoying at this very moment. The earth had provided, and man had created, in both the wood shop and the music room. He took some pride in being part of the process with Franz playing an instrument he himself had crafted.

Thinking the concert was finished, he was surprised when Franz stood up and played Bach's Chaconne for solo violin as a finale. He played flawlessly, and the instrument's tone was superb. As he finished and took the instrument from his chin, the hall erupted into a standing ovation. There were several bows, by the orchestra and then by Franz again. Just as the applause was abating, Franz held the violin up and then pointed his bow straight at Carl and gave a low bow towards him. None of the crowd took in the meaning of this, but Carl gave a big smile and a nod back. He knew then that he had to make others like it.

◄ ■ ►

Back from Zurich a few days later, Carl had taken a break from work and sought out his favorite square to have a coffee and enjoy some of the early May sunshine. He was caught up on his backlog of violins for the moment and had been working on restoring a cello that had been found in the basement of a local physician. He was feeling relaxed and knew that he had all summer to work through the student violins that would inevitably show up at the end of the school year. Albert noticed him as he was heading home from the Patent Office and joined Carl at the outdoor table he'd chosen fully in the sun.

"Carl!" Albert shouted as he approached. "I hear congratulations are in order!" And he grabbed Carl's hand and shook it vigorously. "Mileva told me awhile back that you two are expecting!"

"Yes, thanks very much!" replied Carl. "I'm nervous about this, so you know that I'm going to rely on you for some parenting tips."

"Ach," replied Albert with a misshapen grin. "You might be able to find some better sources than me, but I'll do what I can." He took a seat and blinked up at the sun. "By the way, Mileva really enjoyed her trip to Zurich, and I understand that Maria is coming down for a few weeks at the end of her spring semester?"

"Yes," said Carl. "And with the baby due, that might be her last teaching session for a while. We're investigating her future possibilities at the university here in Bern. By the way, she's looking forward to seeing Mileva again."

"And like-wise," said Albert, as he waved down a waiter and ordered a coffee. "It turns out that the week Mileva was in Zurich helped me immensely. I was able to get a critical section of my writing completed – and now I don't even need to rob as much time from patent reviews, which helps a lot with job security as well," said Albert with a wink. Again he faced into the welcome rays. "Ahh," he let out a huge sigh, emphasizing his feeling of contentment by throwing wide his arms and legs into the sunshine and letting his head fall back for a moment. Sitting back up he said, "You know, I feel that I've arrived at an elegant solution that to me is a beauty to behold. It's so simple and yet contains so much. It doesn't ne-gate what had been derived before, but allows for expansion in the future, especially along the trajectory of my theories. For me, it's like sitting in the sunshine on a peaceful day, as we are now, where you can really feel in touch with the planet – and the universe. Or, come to think of it, it reminds me of listening to – no, playing - Bach's Aria in Suite Number 3, the Air on the G String – achingly beautiful and at the same time incredibly simple." Albert relaxed in his chair and positively beamed.

"You remind me of a shipwreck survivor," laughed Carl and Albert immediately joined in.

"Ha!" yelped Albert, "and I feel like one!"

"Seriously, though," Carl continued, "you've put so much time and effort into your theories that I'm glad to see them finally come to fruition. I still wish that I was smart enough to understand them, but you'd be surprised at how much they've affected me."

"Oh, how so?" asked Albert.

"Well for one thing, they gave me an awareness of the energy that we're all made of, and it's somehow added a needed spark to my outlook on life, so thank you for that. Also, I keep thinking about your physics in human terms, somehow even more so now that I'm about to become a father. I know that there can be a universe of interpretations, but I've decided on something that makes sense to me from what you've described." Albert peered at him good-naturedly over his coffee and nodded. Carl assumed this meant for him to continue. "You're investigating the physical side of things, but you're also creating something else in the process. My thinking is still admittedly muddled on this, but it has to do with our ability to create ideas that develop a permanence, even after the original thinker has passed away. Every day we have thoughts and emotions that seem fleeting, and to me these mercurial notions are like energy – your light particles flitting about. But these thoughts can sometimes gel into a lasting concept – like your theories probably are.

"So I wondered – what is the matter?" He looked at Albert and then quickly added, "Oh, no, I don't mean what's wrong – I mean what is the human or mental equivalent of matter?"

Albert grinned with a twinkle in his eyes. "That's what I thought you were getting at."

Carl continued, "I was reading a book the other day, and it struck me that here is something seemingly permanent that can be given to anyone who can read and the same basic ideas can be extracted by every reader. When we formalize our fully developed ideas and put them down on stone or paper or even palm leaves, they're stored so that they become actualized when others read them. Once recorded, depending on the ideas, they can have incredible power that lasts for centuries. Written concepts become concrete – like matter with some mass or weight – and they hold the potential for releasing that energy for further thoughts and more ideas. We humans have, then, stored up our essence in recorded ideas – both oral and written."-

"Interesting," said Albert, "you've become very philosophical, Carl." And he sipped his coffee and stared across the square in silence for a time. "This is a novel way of making an analogy from my theories that includes the human condition, and I have nothing but admiration for someone who can break out of the norm and form a concept like this," said Albert. He leaned across the table and looked Carl in the eyes while shaking his hand. "I'm sure you'll take your ideas further, or even if you don't, you've contributed to what makes us essentially human, in my opinion, just through your expression," said Albert releasing his hand and taking another sip of coffee. "I'm thinking of the power of ideas at the same time, however. Some could potentially be so dangerous or explosive that they might destroy social orders, or religions, or countries, couldn't they? Considering the inherent power to which you've alluded, perhaps we need to be mindful with some of our ideas and keep them protected – under lock and key as it were. Now that I think about it, even my idea about the latent power that exists in the matter we find around us could result in uses both beneficial and harmful to us. So, I can see there may be some we might even wish to bury away forever."

"I hadn't considered that," said Carl hesitating, "the notion that we also create ideas that are actually threatening to us. Unfortunately, I don't think destroying the book or paper eliminates the concept, does it? What if those ideas have a way to reappear on their own? What can we do to be vigilant about that?"

Albert shook his head and said, "In the end, I guess we must rely on man's inherent compassion and intelligence to recognize what is safe for us all and what isn't. God, I hope that's enough."

CHAPTER 27

On a new workbench which Carl had constructed at the back of the cramped shop were the parts of a cradle, a crib, and a high chair – all in various stages of assembly. And, very unexpectedly, this had somehow become Peer's domain. Perhaps it was the end of adolescence, or the news that Maria was pregnant and was moving home, but a change had come over Peer that spring of 1905. He was not only more serious, but also very industrious, and began spending late hours fashioning and assembling the furniture.

By late May, Maria was back in Bern. It surprised both of them that it took two trips, even with Peer's help, to accomplish the move due to the amount of furniture and books that she'd accumulated in the years she'd kept the small apartment there.

Peer was sanding the spindles that would make up the crib when he suddenly dropped what he was doing and rushed to the door. Carl hadn't noticed, but Maria was making her way bow-leggedly down the steps. Peer had the door open by the time she reached the bottom and led her over to a nearby stool. Carl noticed that Maria no longer tousled Peer's hair, but spoke to him like an equal.

"Thank you, Peer," said Maria. "That was very gentlemanly of you."

"You're very welcome, ma'am," replied Peer with a grin and a slight bow.

"I just wanted to let you two know that lunch is ready," said Maria with a smile, "but I thought it best not to carry it down here unless you wanted it all over the steps. Oh! I see the crib is taking shape nicely." Peer was about to reply when a tall shape was at the door and gently tapping. He hurried over to greet the visitor, and in walked the young lady whom had caught his eye the previous fall.

"Hello, Sophie," said Maria warmly, taking her hand. "How nice to see you again."

"Hello, Frau Veblen," said Sophie with a big smile. "You didn't need to get up for me."

"Oh, yes I did," said Maria. "And for the absolutely last time – I don't care how you were raised – please call me Maria."

"OK, Maria," said Sophie with an effort. "I curse my parents, and will try to remember, I promise. I just came to get Peer for some lunch."

"Oh, please join us instead," said Maria. "I've made more than enough, and it's waiting - piping hot up in the apartment." After some mild protestations by Sophie and Peer, all four of them made their way upstairs with Peer holding Maria gently by the elbow all the way to the top.

◄ ■ ►

As the season moved fully into summer, Carl seemed to meet Albert only at quintet practices, and not always then. However, he happened to run into him just outside the entrance to Albert's apartment building early one evening. They stood on the stoop at the base of the stairs and exchanged greetings as Albert lit a pipe.

"How have you been, Carl?" asked Albert. "And how is Maria doing?"

"I was just going to ask the same of you," replied Carl. "It seems rare that I run into you except at the quintet practices lately. We've been a little overwhelmed preparing for the baby, and it's up to me to run all of the errands now. But Maria is due any day, and it should be easy after that." After a pause, they both broke out into a laugh.

"If not easier, at least more gratifying," Albert commiserated. "I've been very busy as well, so I haven't gotten out lately, nor taken enough walks," sighed Albert.

"Busy with work or with your physics?"

"Well, physics," said Albert. "I've been submitting my papers to *Annalen der Physik*, and they've accepted them. One was submitted in March, another in May, and both were published last month. At that same time, I submitted a third, and I think by early fall the fourth paper will be ready to send off. Oh! And at the end of April, I finally submitted my doctoral thesis."

"My god!" exclaimed Carl. "Maria said that you were working furiously on the days she was visiting Mileva, but perhaps that was an understatement."

"Yes, actually Maria was a life-saver and kept Mileva, and thus me, sane," said Albert.

"What were the papers about?" asked Carl.

"They were on the very topics we've spoken about in the conversations we had over this winter," said Albert. "The first was on the photoelectric effect where packets of light can free a charged particle from metal, and on the calculations to predict the number of charged particles based on the frequency and amount of light. The second was on Brownian motion that proved that we could calculate the molecules in a solution based on the travel of a particle of known size. The third is on the idea that space and time have to be relative to the observer and that they change to maintain the speed of light as a constant, and the fourth proposes the equivalence of matter and energy. All wrapped up in a neat bow and presented or nearly finished! It'll be interesting to see the reaction to these papers."

"To me, it was all novel, and I'm sure that the scientific world will be astounded," complimented Carl. The pipe smoke drifted away on a light breeze, and Albert looked more relaxed than Carl had seen him lately at the practices.

"I still have a huge problem that I'm thinking about more and more," Albert added. "I might have mentioned that I can't figure out how gravity fits into the picture? Ah well, I'm sure it will come. At least I can give it my best effort." Mileva called down that dinner was ready. "Do you want to come join us, Carl?" asked Albert. "Mileva's a great cook."

"Yes, come join us, Carl!" Mileva shouted from the window, apparently intuiting what Albert had just said.

"Thanks, but I'd better get back to Maria!" Carl yelled back up to her and waved. Then to Albert, "I left some stew on top of the stove all day to slow-cook, and I'm worried that

Maria might not notice if it starts to burn. But thanks anyway, and tell Mileva I'll join you next time."

CHAPTER 28

Carl watched her breathe. It was amazing to him that the tiny movement in her chest would be enough to keep anyone alive, but she was. Very much so. He marveled at the blood vessels in her nearly translucent eyelids and the incredible delicacy of her minute hands. Helene lay tucked up against Maria's armpit and both were dozing after a busy night. She had arrived early in the morning of July 14th and they were now all exhausted but content. The midwife had not only delivered the baby, but had helped restore the bedroom afterwards, so now there was little that needed Carl's immediate attention.

They'd had a difficult time choosing a name, and for a while Elise, Maria's grandmother's name, had been a top contender. Then in pouring through some books, Carl had discovered that Helene meant 'ray of light' and somehow that had seemed appropriate and fitting, both to him and Maria.

He crept out into the kitchen and quietly stoked the fire to make some coffee. Flecken heard him and circled Carl's legs a few times before taking up his favorite spot under the firebox. Sitting near the stove, Carl gazed through the open damper into the flames while waiting for the water to boil. He thought back to the afternoon Maria had announced she was pregnant and his time in the shop afterwards contemplating their future with a headful of questions and worries. In his mind, he'd seen everything happening at once – getting the room ready, her birth, what sex she would be, her health, what she would become, his parenting skills.

Now there were no more questions, and no real worries. Helene was here and everything after would unfold with the same pace as the rest of their lives. Things would come as they would come. Carl poured a cup of coffee and savoring the bitter flavor, relaxed as he hadn't in months.

◄■►

The late afternoon sun was streaming through the window, and Maria sat in a chair gently rocking the sleeping baby in the new cradle. A blanket draped over one end protected Helene from the light, but Maria sat facing the glare with her eyes closed. They slowly opened as she heard Carl climbing the steps and quietly entering the room. Seeing her awake, he tiptoed over, gave her a kiss, and plopped down in the chair next to her with a heavy sigh.

"How's our little one doing?" whispered Carl sitting back up and bending over to peer into the cradle.

"She certainly is full," said Maria. "I just put her down; it was the third feeding since lunch." Putting her hand on his knee, she looked him over appraisingly and asked, "Why the heavy sigh, Carl? Haven't you been getting enough sleep?"

"It's not that - I'm not the exhausted kind of tired," said Carl. "I'm only weary of the endless pile of violins. I fix them up merely to have them come back a year later. I just finished a violin, 'Heinrich', that I've repaired three times now." He gazed down at his hands. "I don't usually think much about what I'm doing," he sighed again. "But having this violin show up again made me realize how futile my job can be."

"I'm sorry, darling," said Maria. "I know you love your work, but it can be discouraging when something like that happens."

"Yeah," said Carl. "The only thing is, this afternoon I suddenly realized that I don't love my work so much anymore." They sat in silence as the sun began to dip behind the building opposite.

"Well, let's do something about that!" said Maria suddenly.

Carl stared at her for a moment and said, "Well, I can hardly quit my job ... especially now."

"No," said Maria. "But we can change it. Just think of the adjustments we've already made this summer, Carl. I've quit my job in Zurich and moved back here, and we have a brand-new member of the family suddenly transforming us magically into parents. Why shouldn't you change, too?"

"We have to survive is why, Maria," said Carl. "Especially with Helene to care for now."

"Do you remember how incredibly fulfilled you were when you built the violin that Franz purchased?" asked Maria. "Why not give up on repairs and start building your own instruments?"

"Because we would need the income that I'm bringing in now," said Carl.

"Easy, just charge enough that the income doesn't change."

"What if no one will pay what I would need to charge?" asked Carl.

"Oh, they will," said Maria nodding to herself. "They will. Franz was more than happy to pay much more than we expected. Plus, I'm going to start teaching part-time at the University of Bern in the fall and wouldn't be surprised if I'm not full-time within a year or two. This is the perfect opportunity for us to make a new start on everything," she said encouragingly. "I just didn't realize until now that this included your situation, too." Carl nodded and said he would think about it.

CHAPTER 29

"I guess it's become normal," said Albert, "that we see each other almost weekly, yet we've not had a chance to really talk in the last year or so, except for some brief words after quintet practices."

"I know," said Carl. "But you realize what it's like with small children. My time after work has had its own demands. That's why I thought we should come to the tavern when practice was finished and have a beer. I think that Helene is old enough now that I don't have to always rush off afterwards." He held up his mug and Albert clinked his against it.

"A very good idea, too," said Albert. "So how have you been, Carl?" asked Albert as he took a long pull on his beer.

"Busy, as I say, but in a very good way," said Carl. "Now that I'm only building my own instruments, my shop is much less cluttered, and I'm not struggling under someone else's deadlines. I'm enjoying it immensely."

"I wish I could afford one of your instruments," said Albert. "The one you built for Geron sounds like a dream when he plays it. Really a marvelous piece of work."

"Thanks, Albert, I'm sorry I have to charge so much, but that's what the market – and Maria – dictate," Carl said with a wry smile. "And what's going on in your life?" he asked.

"The same as always, but I'm even more busy if you can believe it," said Albert. "At least I got a raise at work when

I finished my PhD. I've applied for some teaching positions based on the degree, but still no one is interested. It turns out that not only do I need a degree, but experience lecturing as well – which I can only get in a teaching position!" Albert shook his head and took another sip of beer. "I'm writing more papers too, and I'm also reviewing several at the same time, so any social life is becoming a rarity."

"Oh!" Albert then exclaimed, "I have to tell you about the most fortuitous thought I had after work the other day. I was playing Lina, lost in the music, when suddenly something I'd been struggling with crystalized." Albert beamed as Carl smiled, took a sip of beer, leaned back in his chair, and nodded for him to go on. "Now, that's a friend!" said Albert as he continued. "Do you remember my analogy about being in a train and not being able to tell if you were stopped or were moving at a constant speed? That everything seemed and acted the same relative to where you were, like when we bounced the rubber balls in the rail car?"

"Of course, I do," said Carl. "That little trip was so unexpected."

Albert smiled. "Well, I might have mentioned – or maybe I didn't - that in space a little gravity would be necessary to make the train seem normal. But gravity isn't really part of the physics I was using in moving at a constant speed. I've been struggling with the idea of gravity, but I've been unsure how to tackle the problem, and my sudden insight has now shown me the way forward."

"How so?" asked Carl.

"There's a peculiarity that hadn't made sense to me, and this might take a little imagination," started Albert.

"What that you've ever told me hasn't required imagination?" asked Carl, leaning forward.

"Ah," smiled Albert. "Now imagine you're in your shop and that it's a box floating in space. It would be an absolute mess."

"That goes without saying," said Carl. "You mean more so than normal?"

"Yes, because there would be no gravity. Everything would be floating around – the entire space would be filled with wood, tools, and sawdust. And since there was no gravity holding you in place, if you wanted to touch the ceiling, you'd just kick off from the floor and you'd be there. Now, the curious thing is that if something pushed against the underside of the shop at a constant rate, everything would fall towards the floor. In fact, at the proper rate of motion, it would be absolutely impossible for you to tell if you were in the shop being pushed along, or if you were planted safe and sound on earth. Everything would be just the same."

"So, why is there no difference between gravity and a constant force pushing you?" Albert probed. "I'm now seeing a way to look at gravity that fits into the idea of relativity – that everything is relative to your frame of reference. I'm not there yet, but I'm sure that this is the key to heading in the right direction."

"Very good," said Carl as they ordered another beer when Frieda came by to check on them.

"We both have our work cut out for us," said Albert raising his mug and nodding to Frieda after she handed them their steins. "But I believe it's worth it." The foam sloshed over the edges of both mugs as Carl and he clinked in another toast.

◀■▶

A week later Carl found himself back in *Zum Bären* on an evening when Maria and Helene had retired early and he wasn't yet ready for bed. "Hi Carl," said Max in greeting, "you just missed Hans and Paul. I gather Paul is back in town for a short visit and is catching up with his dad. He says that he loves Munich."

"Oh, too bad I didn't come in sooner," said Carl. "I haven't seen Paul in quite some time."

"And he said that marriage suits him!" said Max. "A beer?"

"Please," said Carl, "Good for Paul!" He looked around, "It doesn't seem too busy tonight," and then he moved to a nearby table as a large party of university students came in through the door. Strains of violin music out on the street entered with their lively chatter. He'd noticed the street performer as he'd neared the tavern and the now barely audible tune from the player's instrument caused the image of the Yenish gypsy to jump into his mind. *I wonder how he and his violin are doing anyway?* he thought since he hadn't seen him around lately.

Carl suddenly became aware of the contrast between that gypsy who relied so heavily on his instrument, but couldn't afford to replace it when something happened to it, and Mme. Guiveny who owned a beautiful violin but had auctioned it off because it wasn't being used. Then there was the cello he'd repaired that had been discovered languishing in a basement earlier. On the one hand were people who needed instruments, many young students included, and on the other were those who had violins gathering dust. It just didn't seem right to have the instruments not being played.

An idea began to form, and after another beer, Carl had a plan. He was going to approach Mme. Guiveny whom he knew was an avid patron of the arts and who made a point of nurturing young musicians, and see if she would be interested in organizing a violin donation project that would hunt up unused instruments and have them either be sold for proceeds for the poor or given to those who couldn't afford to buy one. Thierry and Süd came to mind as the sort of people who might be able to help in a project like this. He knew that he didn't have the influence or standing to spearhead a project like this on his own, but perhaps he could take advantage of those who could. Maybe an insignificant moon could nudge the orbit of a substantial planet. He made up his mind that he'd soon see if that would be possible.

◄ ■ ►

Carl took a break from the shop and went upstairs to check on Maria and the kids. Since it was a Saturday, she had no classes and was watching Hans Albert while Mileva ran some errands. Helene was now three and Hans Albert four, and the two were beginning to play well together – today it was drawings and letters with chalk on slate boards. Flecken was spending less time in the shop and more time up in the apartment and occupied the wooden box that the art supplies had been stored in.

"Hi, Dear," said Maria as he came in and poured himself a cup of coffee.

"Hi, hon," he said as he raised the coffee pot. "Do you want some?" Shaking her head, she raised her cup of tea in reply.

"Mileva had some good news when she dropped off Hans," said Maria. "Albert has been offered a lectureship at the University of Bern."

"That is good news!" said Carl as he sat at the table and listened to the children playing school. "He's been waiting for as long as we've known him to teach in a university. I always knew that he'd become a professor someday."

"Yes," said Maria. "Mileva said that the university had required him to submit a new thesis to them, and he finally relented and wrote one. They almost immediately accepted him into a position."

"You mean all of this time he only had to write something, and they would take him in?"

"Well, it *was* an entire thesis, but yes, and apparently he knew that was the requirement the whole time. He just thought it was a needless hoop to have to jump through."

"He really can be stubborn at times, can't he?" asked Carl with a chuckle. "Mileva must have been thrilled at the news."

Maria craned her neck to check that the children were engaged and then turned back to Carl and whispered, "She rarely seems thrilled anymore."

"Why's that?" whispered Carl.

"I'm not sure, but I don't think things are going well between them," she said in a low voice. "She's becoming a little resentful and, I'd say, bitter towards Albert." Carl raised his eyebrows. "Albert's always busy," her voice was even lower, "and is being invited to give talks around Europe, and - she's suspicious that this has made him attractive to other women. She said he always has had an eye for the ladies."

"Well, I doubt that anything is really going on," said Carl. "She's probably just jealous – more so about his growing recognition than about the women."

"For their sake, I hope so," whispered Maria, "but now that I think about it, you're probably right." They raised their voices and talked of other things, and the kids became tired of playing school. As Carl got up to return to the shop, Hans Albert came over and tugged at his pants leg.

"Can I go downstairs too, Uncle Carl?" he asked in his high voice. "Please?" Carl rubbed the boy's hair and looked over at Maria. She nodded and he said, "OK, but not for too long – I'm a little busy. And you promise to work only on your special stack of wood?" Hans Albert nodded and raised his hand to take Carl's.

Helene noticed what was happening and piped up, "Me too, Daddy? Me too?"

"Not today, Helene, Daddy's very busy."

Helene was about to protest but Maria deflected her by suggesting that they make cookies instead. Happy with this, the two headed to the kitchen while Carl left with Hans Albert, swinging the boy to clear every other step.

◄ ■ ►

"What do you think, Carl?" asked Albert as they passed a tree just beginning to show new leaves. A songbird had called loudly from one of the lower branches. "When these birds pair up and start building nests, do they spend the time and find the best spot for one first? Or do they build the best nest they can wherever they were when they met? And which bird decides?"

"I have no idea," answered Carl. "Why do you ask?"

"Oh, just wondering," said Albert, which made Carl ask himself what that meant and whether Albert was really talking about birds.

It was a beautiful spring day, and they walked across the bare gravel bed to the narrow channel the Aare had become. Albert had said that he'd never really fished much and that he'd like to give it a try. Carl had said that they might not catch anything, but this was a good time to fish for the elusive trout before the thaws at higher elevations turned the Aare into a milky torrent. They stood near a big pool in the river channel, and Carl tied a fly on each of their lines.

"Carl, I have some happy and sad news," said Albert as he gazed at the clear water in the pool. "And they're both the same thing."

"What is it?" asked Carl. "Is everything alright with you and the family?"

"Yes, everything is ... OK," replied Albert somewhat cryptically. "The news is that I've been offered a professorship in Zurich, and we'll be moving there in a month. I'm delighted to receive the position, but sad to be leaving friends like you and Michele."

"Oh..." said Carl with some hesitation. "But that's great news! I know how long you've sought an academic career and now you finally have one - how incredible is that?"

"Yes," agreed Albert. "Finally."

"We'll miss you, of course," said Carl. "In fact, I don't know if Mileva and Maria will be able to survive it; they've become so close. But staying in Bern would make absolutely no sense at all for you. Except for our decision to stay in Bern, we could have been in Zurich all this time as well. And, given the way the world works, I doubt that Zurich will be your final landing place. Say, weren't we just talking about nesting birds? Who knows where your ultimate home will be?"

Carl handed Albert his pole and showed him how to swing the bait out into the pool. After a few tries, Albert had his line well out over a deep section of the stream. Suddenly, there was a splash of water and Albert's line went taut.

"Now give a firm but not wrenching tug on the line," whispered Carl. Albert set the hook as though an expert. "Got him!" shouted Carl as Albert played the trout and then worked him in to the shore.

This was the only fish they caught the rest of the morning, but it was a beautiful trout.

CHAPTER 30

The windows were open to let the heat escape, and laughter and conversations drifted out of them onto the street below. Carl and Maria had invited several mutual friends over for a farewell celebration for Albert and Mileva. Maria, Mileva, Geron's wife, and Sophie were busy in the kitchen, chatting as much as cooking. Michele and Thierry were in a conversation with Albert. Herr Besson was smoking a cigar with Geron near the window, and Frau Besson and Geron's daughters formed a circle in the center of the room. Carl and Peer made their way between the kitchen and the living area ferrying trays and drinks. And Hans Albert and Helene played with blocks in a corner, occasionally jumping up to touch base with a mother or Geron's daughters. As the evening progressed, the groups morphed and intermingled.

After the main meal, Herr Besson brought out bottles of champagne and insisted on a toast to Albert, which he followed with a very touching but formal speech. Thierry spoke next with some funny anecdotes, Geron with praise for Albert's violin skills, and Michele with some heartfelt but obtuse references that no one but Albert caught. Then it was Carl's turn.

He ducked into a backroom where an older and thinner Flecken lay curled up on the bed to escape the excitement. He quickly scratched the cat's head as he lifted the violin case lying next to him and carried it back to the living room. Setting it on the table, he opened the case and carefully withdrew the instrument.

"Albert, this is for you," was all he could manage, but it was enough. Albert was astounded and stepped up to take the instrument. He looked at the violin and back at Carl several times and then took the bow that Carl offered. Albert played up and down the scale and then launched into a Mozart sonata that soon changed into a well-known folk melody. The refrains drifted out into the street, and as he finished, the entire room erupted in applause. Albert first hugged Carl and then the violin.

"I just don't know what to say," Albert muttered, obviously overwhelmed. "I'm not usually at a loss for words, as some of you might know." They all burst into laughter as Albert reached for a glass of champagne, and he could barely be heard as he said, "To you all." They toasted again, and then the room broke into smaller conversations.

"I hope that Lina won't be offended that she now has some competition," said Carl while Albert was putting the new violin in its case.

"Oh, no, she won't mind at all," smiled Albert.

"What are you going to name this one?" asked Carl.

"Why 'Lina' of course!" said Albert. As Carl looked at him questioningly, Albert winked and said, "The current Lina is not the first, you know. It's always Lina." They both laughed as Albert clicked the hasps on the case shut. "I can't thank you enough, Carl," he said sincerely and then suddenly grabbed his glass and clinked a spoon against it, quieting the crowd.

"I almost forgot!" he said looking at his wife. "We also wanted to let you know that Mileva is expecting another baby!" There was a cheer, and then everyone surged over to hug Mileva and offer their congratulations. Albert hung back as several of the men came over to shake his hand.

As the party wound down, Mileva and Maria spent time with Hans Albert and Helene, trying to explain that Hans Albert was going on a great adventure, and Helene would not be able to see him again for some while. They had a difficult time accepting this themselves. Albert had brought a pad of paper and had everyone write down their addresses so that he could stay in touch. Mileva for some reason had done the same.

Maria was downcast after the others had all departed and they were cleaning up. "I don't know what I'll do without Mileva," sighed Maria. "And the kids spent so much time together, how will they cope?" Carl picked up Helene, who was playing with a doll, and took Maria's hand.

"Bern won't be the same without them, and I'll miss Albert, too," agreed Carl, giving Helene a hug. "We can't help that they're drifting away as they must, but hopefully we three are held together by something more lasting."

Carl was just setting Helene down when she looked up at him and asked, "Can I go inna shop now, Daddy?" to his surprise. "Hans said I could have his wood."

"Well, maybe the parting pangs won't last that long after all," said a now grinning Maria under her breath.

EPILOGUE

May 5, 1939

My dear Carl,

Greetings to you and Maria and dear Helene who must be a fine young woman by now. You may have heard that I have moved to America and, unfortunately, have no plans to return to Europe anytime soon. The situation for me now is far too dangerous, and I am paying the price for my background and my notoriety. I also regret to say that my second wife Elsa passed away three years ago now, and I miss her terribly.

Japan is now at war with China, and I fear for Europe as Hitler is massing troops and becoming increasingly belligerent. I'm sure you have heard that my fellow Jews are being persecuted, but I understand that half have already fled Austria-Hungary and many are fleeing Germany at this moment, but it is becoming increasingly difficult for them to do so. I weep for them and for all of the citizens of Europe as I see no means of stopping this menace. I pray that Switzerland remains neutral through the coming conflict, and that you and your family remain safe.

I cannot go into details but have heard that some of the very things we feared should be kept hidden away are being contemplated by Germany as I write this while the world does nothing to stop it. I feel compelled to do what I can and know that I am not alone.

May the world and your family weather this storm,

Warmly,
Albert.

December 3, 1939
My Dearest Albert,
As you have predicted, war has broken out and Poland has already fallen. I, too, fear for Europe, but it is some consolation that Norway and our Switzerland have both declared neutrality.

Around the time that you left Bern, Mme. Guiveny began an instrument donation program to provide those less fortunate with instruments and also contribute needed funds to the poor. Unfortunately, Mme. Guiveny passed away some years ago now, and many, including Maria and I, offered our assistance to keep the program going. With the rapid influx of refugees over the past few years, that program has grown into a major relief effort. Much to my surprise, Maria has jumped in to head the program, and it is a major focus lately for the both of us. Hopefully it will make a difference, but I too despair with every passing day, especially as I hear of the arrests of hundreds of Jews and others across our borders.

We were sorry to hear of the loss of your wife, but we are glad that you are in the relative safety of America. May you stay that way as things progress. Our best wishes also to Hans Albert and Eduard, and we hope that they are safe with you.

Always,
Carl

August 15, 1946

My dear Carl,

I hope this letter reaches you amid such trying times as we have endured. I'm sorry I haven't written much since the outbreak of the war.

During the last years I've remained very busy in my research, my teaching, and, of course, in peaceful efforts to stop the fighting. As it was perhaps fated to happen, others have built on my ideas and unleashed the horrible bomb that stopped the Japanese, but I take some solace that this too is already part of history. As a surprise to me, I still think often of your ideas about the attractive principles in humans and the effects on those around them. This is surely something I would never have considered myself, and after watching the incredible rise of the demon Hitler (and thankfully, his ultimate fall), I found myself thinking often about the dynamics of human interactions and the incredible charisma that can drive an empire. I'm not sure if you pursued your thoughts on the subject, but I find myself, as always, engrossed more in the physical world.

I still have fond memories of our walks together and your patience with my blithering, and I still cherish and play the Lina that you were so kind to craft and gift to me.

I hope that you, Maria, and Helene are all well and have come out of/on the other side of our world-wide calamity in safety and health.

Warmly,

Albert.

October 3, 1946

My Dearest Albert,

It was so good to receive your letter and be remembered by you. I also think fondly of our talks and your incredible efforts to speak to me in a language I could vaguely understand.

I have followed you in the news and was amazed, but now that I think of it not so surprised, that your ideas helped harness the energy required to save us from the tyranny of the Axis. I am forever grateful to you for that. I know from your nature that this is one of those ideas we discussed that you might rather have kept locked up safe and sound, but that there was no help for it.

We in Switzerland, and you in America, fared much better than most of the rest of the world. Thank our lucky stars for that. Helene is happily married and living in Zurich with a wonderful husband. Maria is much more frail, but finally able to retire from the relief agency now that her efforts are no longer as necessary. I am also lucky that Peer, who started off cleaning up my shop and then became my apprentice soon after you left Bern, became a competent luthier and has stayed with me in the business. He still lets me putter in the shop, but has taken up the main work load, so I guess I am more than semi-retired. His wife Sophie is now like a second daughter to us.

Gravity is slowly claiming me. It has taken my back, my hips, my humor, and my mind.

I hope this finds you well, and I remain amazed at your accomplishments,
Always,
Carl

ACKNOWLEDGEMENTS

I'd like to thank my friend Eric Peter for reading the raw first-draft and providing comments, beta-readers at Entrada Publishing for great feedback, my wife Lynn Ate for her excellent edits, Jessica Hatch for her insightful editorial assessment and suggestions, and Kyle Elsasser at WSU for ground-truthing and making suggestions in the portions on physics.

AUTHOR'S NOTES

After Albert and a pregnant Mileva moved to Zurich, Albert's second son, Eduard Einstein, was born in 1910. Albert and Mileva were divorced in 1919. Albert married his cousin Elsa in 1919. Albert played violin throughout his entire life, and named every one of them Lina.

Paul Klee in fact had his first public exhibition in 1910. He found his color sense in Tunisia in 1914, and his work has been noted to contain a certain musicality. He really did play in a concert with Pablo Casals.

I realize that the word 'gypsy' is less than acceptable today, and that Roma or Romani might be more appropriate, but in 1905, the 'Travelers' were believed to come from Egypt and thus the term. I have used it to help with the historical placement of the novel and not in a pejorative sense.

It is likely that Albert's discoveries took place over a much shorter time-frame in the spring and summer of 1905, but I have stretched this back into the fall and winter of 1904 to build the story.

Much of what we now take for granted about the universe was unknown to science in 1905 when Albert Einstein developed his ideas. In Bern, he worked in relative isolation, cut off from the mainstream of the physics community, its resources, laboratories, and thinkers. He tackled some of the enigmas of physics at the time, and in rapid succession produced the results presented in this book in what was known as his "Miracle Year." Ten years later, he was able to expand his special theory of relativity developed in 1905 and incorporate gravity into his general theory of relativity presented in 1915. He was awarded the Nobel Prize in Physics in 1921 and, in 1930, received his own patent for refrigeration in partnership with Leo Szilard.

We are now aware of the Big Bang, the general nature of gravity, the expansion of the universe, the existence of other galaxies, and nuclear fission or fusion, among many other advances. Due to Einstein's theories and subsequent progress by others, we have the following picture pertinent to Albert's and Carl's musings:

Before the expansion of the universe, all energy and matter, particles, and anti-particles were condensed into an infinitely small space with pressures enough that energy and matter passed freely between each other – matter into energy and energy into matter and back again; the particles and anti-particles, including light, canceled each other out and then reappeared. With the Big Bang, the immediate expansion, reduction in pressure, and cooling, left energy that had turned into matter largely trapped in that material state without the necessary pressure and heat to switch back. Similarly, the particles and anti-particles gradually annihilated each other and disappeared from the universe. By chance a larger percentage of particles than antiparticles was in existence at the moment of the Big Bang, and so the makings of the physical universe were present.

All of the matter and particles spread out in the expansion, and more massive bits of matter began to attract less massive bits. As these collections became more substantial themselves, they became more attractive and gradually accumulated enough mass to create planets and stars. It was not the size that counted, it was the mass, or accumulated weight, in this process that was significant. As matter coalesces and possibly burns and explodes to be scattered and recombined, the less massive aggregates are fated to be attracted to the more massive aggregates – either to be incorporated into them or to be trapped in an orbit around them, continually falling and unable to escape.

As massive objects form, the spin that inevitably develops causes friction and a heated core. Eventually the object can become so massive and the core so hot that nuclear fusion can begin. In a star, the core produces so much pressure and heat that two small hydrogen molecules with one proton each can fuse and become a molecule of helium which then has two protons and has a slightly lower energy state than did the two separate hydrogen molecules. So, as the fusion occurs, a high-energy photon is released as helium drops to a lower energy state. Eventually two helium molecules can fuse to become a molecule of beryllium with four protons, releasing yet more photons in the process, and so on. These high-energy photons originating at the center of a star collide with and excite other atoms which in turn release other photons and after 40,000 to 100,000 years, atoms near the surface of the sun or star are finally excited and emit photons of visible light – and these photons begin their journey to the earth or across the universe.

It takes eight minutes and twenty seconds for a photon, or the light from the sun, to reach the earth. The nearest star to the earth is 4.22 light years away, or the distance that light would travel during 4.22 years at roughly 300,000 kilometers per second. Since we are not in the center of the Milky Way, the majority of the stars in the galaxy are between ten and one hundred thousand light years distant from us, and the galaxy contains more than one hundred billon stars. The oldest star in our galaxy is approximately 13 billion years old. It is estimated that there are at least one hundred billion galaxies in the portion of the universe that we can see. There is a large portion of the universe that will never be visible to us because the expansion of the universe makes it impossible for the light from those galaxies to overcome the rate of expansion from our perspective. The light leaving our sun that misses earth and other objects will go on forever. The light from the sun or other stars that just misses our planet may be distinguishable as having undergone the earth's lensing effect, and this subtle shift could be detectable to a discerning viewer at some distant place and time.

READING SUGGESTIONS

In addition to the written works by Albert Einstein, the reader might find the following books interesting reading:

Bodanis, David. *E=MC² A Biography of the World's Most Famous Equation*, London: Pan Books, 2000.

Clark, Ronald W. *Einstein (the life and times)*, New York: HarperCollins, 1971.

Isaacson, Walter. *Einstein: his life and universe*, New York: Simon and Schuster, 2007.

Klee, Paul. *The Diaries of Paul Klee 1898-1918*. Berkeley: University of California Press, 1964.

Piccioni, Robert L. *Einstein for Everyone*, Mumbai: Jaico Publishing House, 2010.

ABOUT THE AUTHOR

David Ackley grew up in Fairbanks, Alaska and raised a family in Juneau. His professional career in Alaska included both fisheries biometrics and management positions with the state and federal governments. David is now retired and living in northern Idaho, where he began a small business in lutherie – building guitars, Irish bouzoukis, and ukuleles (www. dastringedinstruments.com). While his wife was conducting research during a recent stint in India, he devoted time to trying to improve his Tamil and writing fiction to escape the heat of mid-day. Finding himself unable to multi-task easily, the lutherie business has flagged somewhat while he gets some stories onto paper. Please visit the Rain and Breeze Books website, www.rainandbreeze.com, for more information about David and his books.